UNBROKEN

A *RUINED* NOVEL

ALSO BY PAULA MORRIS

Ruined: A Novel

Dark Souls

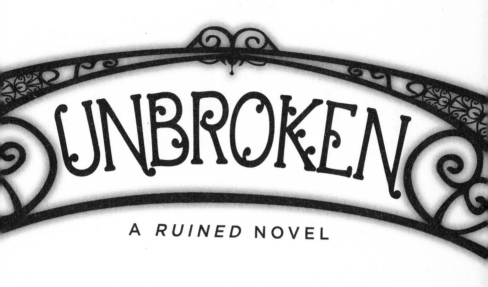

UNBROKEN

A *RUINED* NOVEL

PAULA MORRIS

Point

Library of Congress Cataloging-in-Publication Data

Morris, Paula.

Unbroken : a Ruined novel / Paula Morris. — 1st ed.

p. cm.

Summary: Returning to New Orleans for spring break, sixteen-year-old Rebecca finds
herself embroiled in another murder mystery from more than a century ago, when she
meets the ghost of a troubled boy.

ISBN 978-0-545-41641-2

[1. New Orleans (La.) — Fiction. 2. Ghosts — Fiction. 3. Haunted places — Fiction.
4. Mystery and detective stories.] I. Title.

PZ7.M82845Un 2013

[Fic] — dc23

2012013461

12 11 10 9 8 7 6 5 4 3 2 1   13 14 15 16 17/0

Printed in the U.S.A. 23 · First edition, February 2013 · Book design by Elizabeth Parisi

FOR ANISE AIELLO

"The position of New Orleans certainly destines it to be the greatest city the world has ever seen."
THOMAS JEFFERSON, 1804

"Louisiana to-day is Paradise Lost."
EDWARD KING, 1873

PROLOGUE

New Orleans, March 1873. The Civil War is over, but the spirit of the city has been broken. New Orleans is dirty and disease-ridden, a place of political and racial violence, looting, and unsolved murders. The city is on edge, ready to explode.

The docks are still busy, loading and unloading heavy cargoes of cotton, sugar, and coffee every day. The river is crowded with steamers, its levee piled high with cotton bales. When the wind blows, pinches of cotton drift through the air like snow.

New arrivals flock to the city, hoping to make their fortune. Many end up starving and poverty-stricken. Many succumb to yellow fever, the mysterious and feared disease ravaging the city. Some are robbed — or worse — in one of the many dark alleys or hidden courtyards of the old town.

One damp spring day, as a misty evening begins to settle on the city, a teenage boy hurries away from the dock. He wends his way through the streets of the Quarter, speaking to nobody. His face is pale and sunken; his trousers — ragged at the hems — are flecked with cotton dust. More than one of the city's legions of pickpockets notice the way he pats his jacket every few steps.

1

With every nervous pat, he gives himself away: They can tell that he's carrying something precious, something unfamiliar in his pocket. Perhaps it's money; perhaps it's something valuable he can sell or trade. Perhaps it's something he's stolen himself.

He crosses the broad, muddy expanse of Rampart Street, dodging carts and carriages, soldiers on horseback, washerwomen balancing bundles of laundry on their heads. A dark-haired, burly man follows him, taking care to keep up.

On the far side of Rampart, they both disappear into Tremé, the old neighborhood built decades earlier for New Orleans's free people of color. They'll both end up in a small house on St. Philip Street, fighting over the tiny piece of hidden treasure in the boy's pocket.

Neither will make it out alive.

CHAPTER ONE

THE FIRST TIME SHE SAW THE BOY WITH BLUE EYES staring at her, Rebecca didn't think much of it. This was New York. The city was full of boys with big attitudes and no manners.

Rebecca was waiting for her best friend, Ling, at the Fulton Street Fish Market. She'd just plodded through thirty endless minutes of a piano lesson. Rebecca hadn't practiced enough this week, she knew, and her fingers had felt cold and leaden.

"Uninspiring," her teacher had said, handing Rebecca the sheets of music at the end of the lesson. "I hope to see some improvement next week. Otherwise you're just wasting my time and yours."

Now Rebecca was wasting even more time, standing around like a lost tourist just so she and Ling could go eat what Ling called "yummy chowder in a bowl made of bread" at some nearby restaurant. Rebecca lingered near a big sign that described the fish market and docks back in the nineteenth century. She wished the wind weren't so icy and willed Ling to hurry up.

Rebecca wasn't sure how long the boy with blue eyes had been standing there — just a few feet away, leaning against a cast-iron lamppost. But once she realized he was staring, Rebecca felt incredibly self-conscious. His eyes seemed to bore into her in the most brazen way.

She tried staring back at him, to shame him into looking away, but that didn't work. When she caught his eye, the boy just smiled. He was good-looking, she thought, in a gaunt, emo-ish way, and his eyes were as intensely blue as the East River on a sunny day. But Rebecca had no intention of getting into a conversation with some random stranger.

He'd probably come there trying to scam tourists, or maybe he was planning on asking her for money. He didn't look any older than seventeen or eighteen. In his scruffy dark jacket and trousers, he looked much more ragged and unwashed than the stockbroker types marching by en route to their waterfront lofts, ties flapping in the wind. There was something desperate about him, something pathetic, even as he continued to smile at her.

She was relieved to spot Ling clattering toward her across the cobblestones.

When she glanced back to look at the boy again, he'd disappeared.

"Did you see that guy who was standing over there?" she asked Ling. "He was staring his eyes out at me."

"Was he cute?" Ling wanted to know. "If he's cute, you can take it as a compliment."

"And if he isn't cute?" Rebecca linked her arm through Ling's, shivering as the wind from the river cut through her thin jacket.

"Then he's a freak or a pervert, of course!" Ling laughed.

Ling was short and athletic, her glossy black hair cut into a sharp bob, and her explosive laugh was infectious. Rebecca had been friends with her since elementary school, when Ling was the smallest girl in their second-grade class and Rebecca was tall and awkward, all sticking-out knees and elbows. These days they weren't so freakishly different in height, but Rebecca's long brown hair was as wayward and wavy as Ling's was smooth and straight.

Ling wanted to be an architect, and Rebecca wasn't sure at all about what she was going to do with her life — though clearly, becoming a concert pianist was not an option. She'd been thinking about studying art history in college, even though she was only taking the subject for the first time in school this year. Rebecca had always loved going to the Impressionist rooms at the Met, and listening to her father's stories about the lives of the artists: wild Van Gogh in the sunflower-filled fields of Provence; Gauguin in barefoot exile in the South Pacific;

Degas, with his fading eyesight, sketching ballerinas in dusty Parisian rehearsal rooms. Ling didn't share this fascination; she said Rebecca was just way too nosy about other people's lives.

"This chowder in a bread bowl better be good," Rebecca warned her friend now as they scuttled off together, buffeted by gusts of wind. "I'm freezing."

"OK, OK — it's just over there! We've walked past it a hundred times."

They both went to Stuyvesant High School, way downtown. They knew this part of the city pretty well, though Rebecca had lived all her life in the same apartment on the Upper West Side, overlooking the trees of Central Park.

Well, she'd lived *practically* all her life in New York. This time last year Rebecca had been living in New Orleans with her aunt Claudia and cousin Aurelia, in their falling-down little house across the street from Lafayette Cemetery in the Garden District. She'd even attended school at the snooty Temple Mead Academy, where a girl named Helena Bowman and her clique ruled the roost. Rebecca hadn't really made any friends at that school. But she had befriended someone she'd met at the cemetery: a girl named Lisette.

Who happened to be a ghost.

There was no way Rebecca could explain Lisette to her friends in New York, not even Ling. Who would believe her?

Who would believe the story about a terrible curse on girls in the Bowman family, because one of the Bowmans had murdered Lisette back in 1853? Who would believe that the curse could only come to an end when a seventh Bowman girl died on the eve of her seventeenth birthday?

And how could Rebecca ever begin to explain the shocking secret she'd learned in New Orleans: that *her* real name was Bowman, not Brown. That she and the awful Helena were actually cousins, and that either she or Helena would have to die for the curse to end?

Now that Rebecca was back in New York, she sometimes wondered if the whole thing had been a dream — or a nightmare. She tried not to think too much about the night the curse ended, when she had almost died on the steps of the Bowman tomb. But it was impossible to forget. Lisette had helped her run away, and a boy named Anton Grey — the other person Rebecca had connected with in New Orleans — had helped her escape from the cemetery. But there'd been no escape for Helena. The stone angel that loomed over the Bowman tomb had crashed to the ground, killing Helena instantly.

That meant the curse was over, and Lisette could finally rest in peace. But Rebecca still felt guilty and sad and confused about everything that had happened in New Orleans. She was still in touch with Anton, and really wanted to see him again. But Rebecca wasn't sure she wanted to return to that haunted city any time soon. And she was a hundred percent positive she didn't want to deal with anything involving ghosts and curses ever again.

Rebecca's dad was waiting for them in the tiny restaurant, at the end of a row of brick houses in the shadow of the Brooklyn Bridge. He'd been in the area anyway for work, so Ling had suggested Rebecca invite him along. Rebecca appreciated how well her dad got along with her friends — he never seemed stuffy or unapproachable like some other parents she knew.

The three of them sat by the window, at a scrubbed wooden table, and they each ordered chowder as an appetizer. But later, whenever Rebecca thought about this particular evening, she could barely remember what else they ate. One minute she was unfolding her napkin, and the next she was looking straight into the piercing blue eyes of that strange boy.

Through the steamed-up window she could see his pale face, out there in the cold street, gazing in at her. Rebecca let out an involuntary squeak and almost knocked her water glass to the floor.

"Are you OK, honey?" her father asked. All Rebecca could do was shake her head and stare at the window. One moment the boy was there, his angular face bright as the moon, and then he was gone.

"What is it?" Ling peered at the steamy window, following Rebecca's gaze.

"I thought . . . I thought I saw someone," she stammered. There was no point in trying to explain it all now. Her father would just get worried if he thought some creepy guy was stalking her. "It's nothing. Just my imagination."

Throughout dinner Rebecca kept glancing up at the window in case the boy came back. She was so preoccupied wondering who he was, and why he seemed to be following her, Rebecca didn't realize that her father was asking her a question.

"Rebecca?" Ling looked excited. "What do you think?"

"About what?"

"About us renting a place in the Quarter during your spring break," said her father, pushing his plate away. "Ling could come with us."

"The Quarter?" Rebecca's brain was struggling to catch up. "You mean, the French Quarter? In New Orleans?"

Her father gave her a concerned look. "Too soon?" he asked quietly.

Ling frowned at her. "But it's, like, almost a year since you left," she said. "Don't you think it would be fun?"

Rebecca nodded. She didn't trust herself to speak. *Fun* wasn't quite the word that sprang to mind.

"My company has just signed a tech contract with the city council," her father was saying, "so I need to go down there soon anyway for meetings. And I thought maybe you might want to meet up with your friends."

"I don't really have so many friends there," Rebecca mumbled. Ling looked at her as though she was crazy.

"Hello? What about Anton? Tall, cute, rich, texts you all the time? The one who helped you with that house-rebuilding project in — where was it again?"

"Tremé," Rebecca's father told Ling. Rebecca was glad he was doing the talking, because just the mention of Anton's name suddenly rendered her tongue-tied.

"Why the Quarter?" Rebecca asked. Her father was looking at her so expectantly, she had to say something, even though her head was reeling — New Orleans, Anton, the boy outside the window . . .

"Your Aunt Claudia knows a place we can rent there. Tremé is just a short walk away, Ling, if you want to see the house Rebecca and Anton helped fix up. Maybe there are some other projects you girls could help with. There's still plenty of rebuilding work to do."

"It would be my absolute *dream* spring break," Ling enthused.

"I think it would be good for us as well." Her father shot Rebecca one of his trademark Meaningful Looks. "Starting over again with the city, in a way. A fresh start. Able to come and go without . . . without fear of anything."

"I guess," said Rebecca, and she tried to smile when he squeezed her arm. However hard she tried to forget, her father was also a member of the Bowman family, born and raised in

New Orleans. He'd lived in self-imposed exile for years, but Rebecca knew that he missed it — the way she would miss New York if someone told her she could never come home again.

"Fear . . . hmm, that's a good point," Ling said, ripping a bread roll apart. "My parents will probably say there's way too much crime down there."

"We'll watch out for you." Rebecca's dad stared down at the tablecloth. Rebecca wondered if he was thinking about the other kinds of dangers she'd had to confront in New Orleans last year, ones Ling could never imagine.

But that was all in the past now. Maybe her father was right. A fresh start, in a different neighborhood, with Ling by her side for support — that might be the best possible thing. And going back to New Orleans meant seeing Anton again. Just thinking of him washed another wave of nerves through Rebecca's body. She'd never met any guy in New York who was anywhere near as smart and interesting and — she had to admit — as handsome as Anton Grey.

When her father stood up to pay the bill, and Ling went to the bathroom, Rebecca tapped a quick text to Anton into her phone: going 2 NOLA 4 spring break with dad + my friend Ling. But the message failed; the reception in the restaurant was terrible. She'd have to go outside.

Rebecca wriggled into her coat and darted out the red front door. It was drizzling, so she huddled under the small awning, shoulders hunched, resending her text. When she looked up, the boy with blue eyes was standing right in front of her, close enough to touch.

"Please," he said. His eyes were the deep blue of the Chagal painting her father liked so much in the Met: They were intense, almost unnatural. The boy was tall, like Anton, but his face was as white as chiseled marble, and he sounded foreign — British or Irish or something.

"What do you want?" Rebecca hissed, edging toward the restaurant door. Just because he was good-looking didn't mean this guy wasn't dangerous.

"You don't know me," he said, still staring at her, "but I . . . I've seen you before."

"Are you following me?"

"No — please!" the boy pleaded, and he stepped forward, one hand outstretched as though he was going to grab her. "I'm not talking about last week. I mean last year, or even longer ago. You were down in New Orleans. I saw you with Lisette."

Lisette. The name hit Rebecca harder than the cold wind. The trees that lined the street, budding their spring leaves, whispered the name over and over: *Lisette, Lisette, Lisette.*

Nobody in New York — apart from Rebecca's dad — knew about Lisette. It had been ages since anyone had said her name out loud. Rebecca's stomach twisted; she felt short of breath.

Something surged through her — a sickening dread, charged with the electric tingle of excitement. This boy knew Lisette.

He knew her name, at any rate, and he was saying that he'd seen Rebecca *with* Lisette. So did this mean he was a ghost, too? No, that was ridiculous. It was impossible.

"I saw you with her on St. Philip Street, in Faubourg Tremé," the boy went on, his eyes huge in his face. "It was November. Not the November just passed. The year before."

"Uh-uh." Rebecca shook her head, averting her own eyes to avoid the boy's intense gaze. She could barely speak. How could he possibly know all this?

Every November, on the anniversary of her mother's death, Lisette had made the long pilgrimage on foot from Lafayette Cemetery in the Garden District to the streets she'd known as a child in Tremé.

"You were with her that day," the boy was telling her, and Rebecca's feet felt frozen to the spot. Every word he said clanged in her ears, loud as cathedral bells. "I saw you with her, holding her hand."

Rebecca bit her lip, still saying nothing. She'd *had* to hang on tight to Lisette's hand that day, because that was the only way she could see the other ghosts of New Orleans. If she'd dropped Lisette's hand, the ghost world around her, thronged with the dead of many centuries, would have disappeared from sight.

"I saw you with her," the boy said again, a desperate edge to his voice. Rebecca's heart thudded. Nobody could have seen her that day on St. Philip Street, because when Rebecca held Lisette's hand, she disappeared from view. She was invisible, just as Lisette was invisible to other people. They could walk through the crowded streets of the city, unseen and undetected by anyone. Anyone, that is, except other ghosts.

As though he understood what she was looking for, the boy inched back his jacket. His white shirt was stained with a huge dark splotch of what might have been ink, or was more likely blood.

Rebecca gasped. The day she had walked through the streets of New Orleans with Lisette, she'd seen dozens of people with similar stains sullying their clothing, or clotted and mashed on their skin. They were wounds, Lisette had explained — from knives, gunshots, chains, blunt instruments. If someone was murdered, they kept walking the earth as a ghost. The signs of violent deaths were visible everywhere in the ghost world. This boy looked as though he'd taken some mortal blow to the stomach.

"You have to help me," he said. "I have to return to New Orleans tomorrow. Please. I need someone who can find something for me. Something very precious. Very valuable. If it isn't found, then I'm doomed to haunt the docks, here and down there, for eternity. Back and forth, back and forth . . ."

He looked so utterly despairing, Rebecca felt sorry for him.

"What's this thing you need to find?" she asked. But before the boy answered, the front door of the restaurant squeaked open.

"There you are!" It was Ling. "Aren't you freezing to death out here?"

In the instant it took for Rebecca to glance at Ling in the restaurant doorway, the boy with blue eyes disappeared.

One speedy cab ride later, Rebecca was back in her bedroom. She was trying to calm down from her encounter with the blue-eyed ghost when her phone began buzzing like an enraged wasp.

"Hey," said a familiar voice. Anton. Her heart skipped, just as it always did when they talked on the phone. "Is it too late to call?"

"Sure — no. I mean, it's OK." Rebecca pushed her door shut. Should she tell him about the ghost boy downtown? She hadn't said a word about it to Ling or her father, but she was aching to share the story with someone.

"So," said Anton. "I got your text."

Right. After the confrontation with the ghost, Rebecca had forgotten all about texting Anton. Now, something in the tone of his voice worried Rebecca. He didn't sound very enthusiastic.

"The thing is . . ." he said, trailing off.

"What?" Rebecca braced herself. He was going to give some excuse for not seeing her, she just knew it. Too much time had passed since they last saw each other.

Too much time since they last kissed.

Rebecca felt herself blushing. He probably had a girlfriend in New Orleans now. This was probably going to be one of those awkward "we have to talk" conversations.

"It's . . . It's Toby," Anton said at last. "Toby Sutton. He's run away from home and from school — his new school, the one in Mississippi."

Rebecca swallowed hard. She felt relieved that the "thing" was about Toby, but no news about Toby Sutton was ever good. Toby had been part of Helena Bowman's gang; his sister, Marianne, was Helena's best friend. He was thuggish at the best of times, and to say that he disliked Rebecca was a major understatement. Wherever Toby went, trouble turned up as well — usually in the form of an arson attack. He'd even tried to burn down his own school.

"So," said Anton, "I think he's hiding out somewhere in New Orleans. He's been sending me all these weird texts, rambling stuff about unfinished business. He's still pretty bitter about what . . . you know, what happened to Helena. If he finds out you're back in New Orleans, I don't know what he'll do."

"Maybe he won't find out that I'm there," Rebecca suggested, though she knew this was unlikely. Some Temple Mead girl would probably spot her at the airport and send alert texts to everyone on the entire Gulf Coast. And then Toby would turn up with a bad attitude and a box of matches. Who knew what would happen?

"Maybe." Anton sounded doubtful. "But I was kind of hoping that . . ."

"What?" Rebecca had to prompt him again. They were always

really awkward with each other on the phone. Texting was so much easier.

"Well, um," Anton mumbled. "I was thinking that maybe you would come to the Spring Dance with me. Your friend could come as well. There's a new guy at school from California. He doesn't know anyone here, and I promised him I'd help him find a date. Spring Dance is stupid, I know, but it's kind of a big deal here."

The Spring Dance. Rebecca knew *exactly* how big a deal it was. It was one of the social highlights of the teen year in the Garden District, when the boys of St. Simeon's escorted the girls of Temple Mead to a dance at the country club. The girls in her old class at Temple Mead were probably working themselves up into a hysterical fever pitch about it right now.

"Sure," she said, without thinking. "Why not? As long as Toby doesn't show up and try to set my dress on fire."

She was trying to make a joke, but neither of them laughed. They said awkward good-byes, and Rebecca flopped back on her bed. She wanted to pull the covers over her head, and hide from the world.

The boy with blue eyes had unfinished business. Toby Sutton had unfinished business. The girls at Temple Mead, who'd be out in force at the Spring Dance, had plenty of unfinished business with her: Rebecca was quite sure of that. So much for a stress-free trip to New Orleans. Why couldn't they all just leave her alone?

CHAPTER TWO

T HE VIEW OF LOUISIANA FROM THE AIR, REBECCA thought, made it seem like no other place in America. Instead of dull brown fields or sprawling towns, the landscape below the plane was green and watery, a swampland that felt mysterious, unfinished, maybe even dangerous.

Ling's face was pressed against the window, and she was fizzing with questions: Was that the lake? Was that a bayou? What was the difference between a bayou and a swamp, anyway?

Rebecca, in the aisle seat, leaned across her friend to peer out. The plane was descending, skimming the western end of Lake Pontchartrain. Sun glinted off the water. The bridge, stretching below them like a gray ribbon, was the longest causeway in the world. The dark dots swooping across the ragged edges of waves were probably brown pelicans.

Rebecca remembered all this from the first time she'd flown into New Orleans. Everything, in fact, about arriving here again felt surprisingly familiar: the tinny piped jazz at the airport as they waited by the baggage carousel, the surprising heat outside the airport doors, the pungent, sweet tang of the air. Even the taxi driver's accent, an odd mix of Southern drawl and Brooklyn swagger, felt like . . . home? Perhaps that was what New Orleans had become in a way, Rebecca mused — a second home. Given what happened to her here, that was a weird thought.

Her dad had kept a protective arm around Rebecca while they were waiting for the cab. But now he was beaming and pointing out the sights as they sped along I-10 toward the city, craning to get his first glimpse of the white-lidded Superdome.

"Nobody here calls the city 'the Big Easy,'" he told Ling. Rebecca resisted the urge to roll her eyes. Her father was always happy to bore people with tidbits of information. "It's called the Crescent City because of the way it's scooped by a giant bend in the Mississippi River."

Rebecca had forgotten all about the river. Although New Orleans was squeezed between bodies of water — the river, the lake, the bayous — Rebecca hadn't seen them at all when she was living here. The lake was too far from the Garden District, where she had stayed with Aunt Claudia and Aurelia. The Mississippi was hidden behind its high green levee. The only water she'd seen was the torrential rain that could drench you in seconds.

"There's no ocean beach, though, right?" Ling was asking. Rebecca's dad started talking about the beaches of the Gulf of

New Mexico, an hour's drive to the east, or the slivers of beach on Lake Pontchartrain. New Orleans wasn't really a beach town, Rebecca knew, but the colors of the place reminded her of being near the sea. It had to do with the washed-out blue of the sky, or maybe the sallow sand-colored concrete of the empty canal near the highway. Maybe it was just the knowledge that you were surrounded by water. The city had been inundated after Hurricane Katrina, filling up like a basin. Water lay in wait here, she decided. It encircled the city like a watery noose.

"Rebecca?" Ling nudged her. "What's up?"

"Nothing," Rebecca replied. Somehow she didn't think the others would be so taken with her "watery noose" idea. "I was just . . . thinking about . . . rain, I guess."

"No rain today or tomorra," the cab driver said over his shoulder. His car smelled of stale cigarette smoke and fried food. "But maybe later in the week. Just in time for Jazz Fest on Friday. You all in town for Jazz Fest?"

Ling arched her eyebrows at Rebecca. Jazz Fest took place over two long weekends, and this weekend was the first. Ling was excited; she'd already downloaded the schedule onto her iPad. But the tickets were really expensive, and Rebecca noticed the way her father changed the subject away from the musical festival. Maybe he didn't want Rebecca wandering around in such big crowds. Last time she was in a big crowd in New Orleans, it had been during Mardi Gras, and she was kidnapped and almost murdered.

20

The cab zoomed off the highway, swinging down the ramp marked "*Vieux Carre*." Old Quarter: That's what it meant, though it was better known as the French Quarter. And that's where they'd be staying this week. Hopefully the house Rebecca's dad had rented wouldn't be as weird as Aunt Claudia's small yellow house on Sixth Street, cluttered with dusty tribal masks and voodoo charms, and practically leaning into the house next door. Aunt Claudia hadn't picked them up from the airport because Saturday was her busiest day of the week: She told fortunes in Jackson Square. But she was going to meet them at the rented house and give them the keys.

"This is, like, the most AMAZING place," Ling said, her voice squeaky with excitement. She'd lowered her window to take pictures, and the breeze that blew into the car was warm. They were driving across Rampart Street, one of the boundaries of the French Quarter, and passing a cluster of tall old buildings with the broad cast-iron porches known here as galleries. Some of the galleries were a vibrant jungle of drooping ferns, but the house on the corner looked almost derelict, its windows boarded up and its brick façade gray with dirt. It looked as though it had been empty and unloved for a long, long time.

Rebecca wondered why it wasn't renovated and occupied like the others next to it, or like the similar old town houses in the Quarter itself. Maybe it was because Rampart Street wasn't such a desirable place to live. Aunt Claudia had always warned her to avoid Rampart Street, though Aunt Claudia had warned her about a lot of things — like staying out of Lafayette Cemetery, for example — and Rebecca hadn't really listened.

It was strange to be back on Rampart Street now. There was nobody in sight but a woman walking out of a tattoo parlor and pausing to light a cigarette, and a guy in ripped jeans hosing down the sidewalk outside a bar. *Real live people*, Rebecca thought with relief, rather than battle-scarred ghosts. While she had to admit she was curious about that good-looking ghost boy with blue eyes, and whatever it was he was trying to find, life was much easier when ghosts weren't popping up all over the place. Instinctively, she wriggled down in her seat, glad she was wearing sunglasses.

Driving through the Quarter was a lot slower than speeding along the highway. The streets were all narrow and one-way, with STOP signs at almost every corner. A broken-down car on the next block forced the taxi driver to take a detour, and then they were crawling along in the wake of a mule-driven carriage. Even when the carriage turned to clip-clop its way down Bourbon Street, a sea of people washed across their path.

Ling didn't care about their zigzag route: She was halfway out the window taking pictures of everything — the Lucky Dog salesman, with his hot-dog-shaped cart; the candy-colored old Creole cottages; teenaged street musicians lugging their trumpets and tubas to another corner. A woman carrying a yapping dog — both wearing purple bandanas round their necks — strolled in front of the car as though it were invisible, and didn't even turn around when the taxi driver honked.

"She got all the time in the world," he complained to Rebecca's father, the cab inching its way along a crowded Royal Street. Here the railings of the galleries spilled over with flowers and dangled long strands of Mardi Gras beads — purple, green, gold, silver, red. The last time Rebecca saw Mardi Gras beads, she was throwing them from a float in the Septimus parade. What did New Orleans have in store for her this time?

"Here it is!" announced her father when they finally screeched to a halt on Orleans Avenue. Rebecca clambered out of the taxi, taking it all in. The one-story building had a steeply pitched roof, and cracks were visible in the yellow-painted brick, with four long windows (or maybe they were doors?) hidden behind pale blue shutters. She'd seen lots of houses like this in the Quarter before, old houses that sat right there on the street without gates or gardens, the kind of house you'd love to peer into as you walked by. But with their shuttered windows they always seemed completely closed off to strangers, with no apparent way of getting in or out. Everything was secretive in this city, she thought, even the houses.

A heavy iron gate to the left of the house creaked open, and Aunt Claudia stepped out, jangling the keys and then dropping them onto the terracotta cobbles of the sidewalk.

"Rebecca, honey!" she called, her voice cracking with emotion. Her kohl-lined eyes — green and intense as the sea — were moist with tears. She pulled Rebecca into a hug, and Rebecca felt her own eyes filling. The minute she saw her aunt — not a real aunt, but whatever — Rebecca remembered how kind a person she was, how welcoming and generous. She also wore the craziest clothes, but this was a Saturday after all, and she had to wear her "work" gear.

"I packed up early so I could let you all in," Aunt Claudia murmured. "I'm so glad you're here. Aurelia's on a school trip today, otherwise she'd be here as well."

"This is my friend, Ling," Rebecca said, guiltily relieved that her aunt wasn't wearing her most extreme gypsy costume, and didn't smell *too* strongly of incense.

Ling dumped her duffel on the sidewalk so she could shake Aunt Claudia's hand. With her headscarf and hoop earrings, Aunt Claudia *must* have seemed a little weird. The frizzy gray hair, the clanking bangles, the purple boots: This was a relatively normal look for Aunt Claudia, thought Rebecca, but Ling wouldn't know that. Ling's mother worked in an office and wore a dark suit and pumps to work every day. She carried a briefcase, not a tatty crocheted bag with a gris-gris pouch and a molting rabbit's foot swinging from the strap.

"You're home," Aunt Claudia said to Rebecca. "We've missed you so much!"

"I missed you, too," Rebecca told her. "It's so good to be back here." That was true, she realized. Despite everything that had happened, she was excited to be in New Orleans again.

"This house looks so cool." Ling stared up at the row of wooden-slatted shutters. "Your dad was just saying it's over one hundred fifty years old, and that there's a courtyard out the back."

Rebecca's father had paid the driver, and was standing over the bags, talking to Aunt Claudia. Though Rebecca was pretending to admire the house, nodding while Ling raved on, she was really thinking about Anton. They hadn't made any firm plans to meet up yet, but Rebecca realized she'd been hoping, secretly, that he would be waiting for her when they arrived. She'd texted him the address of the place in the Quarter — just as a casual FYI — and now it was hard not to feel disappointed. They hadn't seen each other since last May, and all the IMing, texts, and calls in the world couldn't make up for those long months of separation. Anton might have changed. *She* might have changed. And this whole Spring Dance thing was just another layer of pressure. . . .

"So tomorrow morning at eight?" Aunt Claudia was asking them, and Ling was nodding.

"The Big Sweep," she said. "Sounds cool!"

"I'd join you," said Rebecca's father, "but I have to go to a business roundtable. Even though it's a Sunday — I know!"

Rebecca knew what a business roundtable meant — a big fat lunch somewhere fancy — but it took several more minutes of perplexing discussion until she realized that the Big Sweep was a community cleanup on the shores of Lake Pontchartrain.

She and Ling *had* talked about volunteering. They might as well start right away, even if all they were doing was picking up trash. At least — according to the cab driver — it wasn't going to rain.

Her phone was buzzing, and Rebecca fumbled for it in her bag. *Anton!* In her eagerness to read his text, Rebecca almost dropped the phone.

here?

Really, that was the best he could do? One word.

yes, she replied. Two could play at that game.

in MS, sorry, he texted back. MS. Mississippi. His family's fish camp, Rebecca remembered, swallowing back disappointment. So there was no way she'd see him tonight. Her phone buzzed again.

c u at big sweep?

yes, she texted again, relieved. Suddenly the Big Sweep sounded like the best possible way to spend a Sunday.

Everyone else had already stepped through the gate, their voices fading as they walked down the narrow flag-stoned alley. Rebecca stowed her phone and bent down to pick up her bag. And in that instant, that brief moment of bending and straightening, the boy with blue eyes materialized right there on Orleans Avenue.

Rebecca gasped — with surprise rather than fear. He was standing just a few feet away, next to a spindly tree that grew, roots bulging, out of the cobbled sidewalk. In the sunlight his clothes looked even shabbier, if that were possible. His eyes bore into her like lasers, transfixing her.

"You came," he said, and then he smiled — a slow, shy smile. "I knew you were a good person, that day I saw you with Lisette. I knew you'd help me."

"Help you with what?" Rebecca asked, trying to keep her voice low. She wasn't scared of him anymore, the way she had been outside the restaurant in New York. There was something so sweet and gentle about him. His stare wasn't brazen; she'd been wrong about that. His eyes were pleading with her. Maybe he really *did* need her help.

"Rebecca!" Her father was calling her. "Where are you, honey?"

"Just closing the gate!" she called back. She fingered the straps of her bag, wondering how to handle all this. There was nowhere for them to have a private conversation, and anyway, her father would come out looking for her any second. The boy was still gazing at her, his eyes inky, as though he was about to cry.

"Can you wait?" Rebecca whispered to him. "I'll come back out when I can, OK? It may be a while. . . ."

She tried to think of possible excuses for her to wander off alone this afternoon, and not a single one came to mind. Even if she could shake off her father, Ling would want to come out to explore the Quarter.

"I usually haunt the corner," the boy told her, pointing toward Rampart Street. "I'm there most of the time."

"The corner." Rebecca nodded, and the boy smiled at her again.

"My name is Frank O'Connor," he said.

"Rebecca Brown," she said in reply, but before the words were out of her mouth, he was gone — just vanished, in that weird abrupt way ghosts had. Rebecca could have sworn that his smile, broad and sweet, was the last thing to disappear.

CHAPTER THREE

THE HOUSE THEY WERE RENTING WASN'T REALLY just one house. Behind the main house lay a secluded courtyard, which led to yet another building, two stories high, its only staircase outside. This building was the old slave quarters, Rebecca's dad explained. When the main house was built in the 1840s, he said, the kitchen would have taken up much of the ground floor of the slave quarters. Upstairs were rooms for the "help," as Aunt Claudia put it: slaves before the Civil War, and servants afterward.

These days the kitchen was in the main house, along with the master bedroom, where Rebecca's dad was sleeping. The slave quarters were a warren of small rooms, the lower story mainly used for storage, as far as Rebecca could tell. Upstairs, opening onto a narrow gallery shaded by banana trees, there were two small bedrooms and a bathroom for Rebecca and Ling.

Right now this was really, really good news, because it made it much easier for Rebecca to slip away.

It was early in the evening, and they'd all spent the last hour or so strolling the still-busy streets of the Quarter — around Jackson Square and down to the river levee, stopping every few steps so Ling could take more pictures. Soon they'd be heading out again to eat, but in the meantime, Rebecca had a chance to go outside unseen. Ling was taking what she called "a nice long shower," and Rebecca's dad was lolling inside the main house, with its closed shutters, watching golf on TV and checking his e-mail.

Rebecca crept down the wooden steps, across the courtyard, and along the narrow alley that led to the street. She didn't have long, but she really *had* to know what the ghost boy — Frank — was looking for so desperately. Maybe he was like Lisette, trapped in ghostdom by some terrible curse. How did he die — and why did he die so young? Ling was right: She *was* too nosy about other people's business.

It was dusk, but still warm and hazy. Rebecca scampered up to the corner of Rampart Street and paced up and down, trying to make herself as obvious as possible. On the far side of Rampart Street a tour group emerged from Armstrong Park and climbed into a waiting minibus, but otherwise the broad street was pretty deserted. Where was Frank? Wasn't this the place he told her to wait?

"Come on, Frank," she said aloud, tapping the curb with her foot as though the noise might summon him. "Show yourself!"

"I'm right here," said a voice behind her, and an icy breeze shivered through Rebecca, cold as winter in New York.

Frank was standing by the doorway of the boarded-up house, looking like a smudge of dirt. Rebecca retreated into the shadows of the house as well, leaning against one of the rough boards. She had to keep an eye out for anyone walking past: They'd think she was crazy, talking to herself. Standing this close to Frank, shaded by the building's rusted iron galleries, it was all Rebecca could do not to shiver. All the warmth seemed to have been sucked out of the day.

"I can't stay long," Rebecca whispered. "Tell me what this is about."

"A locket," said Frank, his eyes fixed on hers. "A locket that someone tried to steal from me the day I was murdered."

"And . . . when *was* that?" Rebecca asked, trying not to sound too freaked out.

"It was March of 1873," Frank told her.

"In New York?"

"Here, in New Orleans. Not far from here." Frank nodded toward the other side of Rampart Street, where the streets of Tremé began.

"So . . . why did I see you in New York? I don't really understand. Are you *from* New York?"

"I lived there," Frank explained. "But I'm from Liverpool, originally. Liverpool in England."

"Like The Beatles!"

Frank looked mystified.

"I came to New York with my family when I was twelve," he said. "I took whatever work I could on the docks there, and sometimes I'd get work on a ship sailing down here. Spring was high season for cotton."

"So you worked loading ships?"

Frank shook his head. "The colored men, they unloaded cotton from the steamboats. Lads like me, sometimes we'd be paid to guard the bales on the levees. People were always thieving from them, pulling cotton from a bale and running off. Times were hard after the war — that's what everyone said. Too many people of all colors looking for work. So I went back and forth to New York and worked up there as well. That's why he remembered me."

"Your murderer?"

"No, the artist. The artist who gave me the locket. I carried his bags for him and his brother in New York, and then he saw me again down here, a few months later. I was running messages to one of the cotton offices on Carondelet Street, and when he saw me there he remembered me."

"What's a cotton office?" Rebecca didn't want to seem stupid, but she really had no idea.

"Where cotton is bought and sold," Frank said, frowning. She guessed that this *was* a stupid question as far as he was concerned. She must have still looked uncertain, because he explained some more: Men in these cotton offices would buy picked, raw cotton from planters all over Louisiana and Mississippi, and then sell it, so it could be shipped to the big mills in England and woven into material.

"I get it," said Rebecca. She'd never thought once, in her whole life, how her cotton T-shirts made it from fluffy stuff on a plant to an item of clothing sold on Broadway. "So, this man — the artist — he gave you the locket in this cotton office place?"

"No, no. Sometime later — a month, maybe. He was boarding a ship to Havana. I was down on the docks that day, looking for work. I saw him say good-bye to his brother and the old man from the cotton office, and then they left. Not long after, he came walking down the gangplank. That's when he saw me."

"And you said he remembered you?"

"Yes. He handed me the locket and told me to take it straight away to his uncle's house on Esplanade Avenue. He said he wished his cousin to have it. I promised I would do as he asked."

"What was this man's name?"

"I don't know. He never told me."

Rebecca bit her lip, feeling increasingly intrigued and confused at the same time. "And how do you know he was an artist?"

"I remembered his brother joking when I carried their bags in New York. There was one bag I was to be extra careful with, because there were paints and brushes in it, and a sketchbook. His brother said the gentleman was a *Grande Artiste*. They were foreign, you see."

Frank was foreign, as far as Rebecca was concerned, but she didn't point this out.

"And I looked inside," he continued. "Just a little peek, you know."

"Inside what?"

"The locket. There was a little picture, a tiny painting. It was a lady, and I thought it might be his cousin."

"And what was this cousin's name?" she asked.

"Desirée," Frank said.

"Sounds French," said Rebecca, and Frank nodded. "What was her last name?'

"It sounded like *moo-son*," Frank said. "I think her father was one of the partners at the cotton office. The old man I saw at the dock here. I'd heard that name before."

Rebecca thought for a second. "If he was one of the partners, his name would be on the sign outside the office, right?"

"Yes," Frank agreed. "But I never learned my letters."

"Oh." Rebecca felt herself blushing, though Frank didn't seem embarrassed.

"And even if I could read," he went on, "that particular cotton office had closed. Places were always going out of business then. One day you'd carry a message somewhere, the next day the place would be empty."

"How did you know where to deliver things, if you couldn't read names or the numbers on buildings?" Rebecca asked, hoping this wasn't too rude a question. "And how would you know which house on Esplanade you were looking for? How would you even know which street you were on?"

This question seemed to surprise Frank.

"All of us lads who took messages, we had to learn which was Canal Street, and which was Rampart, and so on," he said. "It wouldn't take long if you had half a mind to learn it, and we never had to venture far from the river. To find a house or an office, you would ask people. Servants, porters, laundresses, oyster-sellers. The men sweeping the road. Once you'd run an errand somewhere, you remembered it." He paused a beat, studying her, and Rebecca willed herself not to blush again. "So you can read, then?" Frank asked her.

"Yes." Rebecca tried to imagine what it would be like if she couldn't read, if street signs and house numbers were mysterious marks that made no sense. It would be like living in a foreign country, one with a different alphabet, for your entire life.

"You're lucky," said Frank, and Rebecca realized that this was true.

"So what happened after he gave you the locket?" she asked, and glanced nervously over her shoulder. Time was racing by; Ling might have wandered over to the main house, looking for her. "Someone stole it from you, right?"

"It wasn't stolen," Frank said quickly. "Someone *tried* to steal it. He beat me, and dragged me into a house. Then he robbed me of my money. The artist had given me a dollar as payment for delivering the locket to his cousin."

A dollar in 1873 was probably a lot of money, Rebecca thought, especially for someone who earned money carrying bags and running errands.

"He took the dollar, and he would have taken the locket as well, if he'd managed to find it. He killed me before he could find it."

"So it's in your pocket?" Rebecca didn't understand. Frank shook his head.

"I hid it," he said. "I dropped it between the floorboards of a house — the house where he murdered me. It's still there now. I swear to you, it's still there now."

"But wouldn't it fall right through to the ground?" Rebecca knew that a lot of the old houses in New Orleans sat on piles, so air could flow underneath.

"Not in this house," Frank said. "It's lying on a plank of wood, two inches below the floor."

"You're sure nobody has found it in all these years?" she asked. Frank shook his head.

"It's still there," Frank assured her. "I go over there to check it all the time. The house is empty — half falling over, to tell you the truth of it."

"Why can't you just go and get it?"

"We can't pick things up and carry them around." Frank sounded sad, defeated. "Believe me, if we could, I would have done it a century ago. We need someone from the world of the living to help."

Rebecca thought about how long the locket was hidden in that house. The building might be empty now, but for years it must have been someone's home. "Couldn't someone living there at some point have helped you?"

Frank frowned. "Most people don't want to have anything to do with ghosts. They scream, or call in exorcists, or move out because the house is haunted. That's why, when I first saw you — you know, with Lisette — I thought you might be different. You might not be a person who was terrified of ghosts."

Rebecca thought back to that day a year ago when she'd seen all the ghosts of New Orleans. And Frank had been among them, somewhere. "How did you know I wasn't a ghost myself?" she asked.

Frank smiled, as though this was the silliest question he'd ever heard.

"You were holding Lisette's hand. You never see two ghosts doing that. You only see it when we're escorting someone from the world of the living. And that is very unusual."

"You can say that again," Rebecca muttered. She couldn't help noticing that he had a beautiful smile, though.

"I looked for you the November just gone, but Lisette didn't make her walk then, and the other ghosts were saying she was no longer with us. So when I saw you in New York, down where the docks used to be, I knew it was a sign."

"I'm not sure I believe in signs," Rebecca said. She glanced over her shoulder once more, worried that her dad and Ling were looking for her out the window. "Look, I really have to go back now."

"Back to New York? But you just arrived!"

"Back to my house," she told him. "The place I'm staying. I snuck out, and my Dad'll freak if he realizes I'm not there."

"Freak?" Frank asked.

"Get all upset."

"Rebecca," Frank said. Her name sounded unfamiliar in his soft accent — as entrancing and seductive as his deep blue eyes. "Please. You have to help me. I've been waiting for a hundred and forty years. I may never have this chance again."

"But you haven't told me *why* you need to get this locket," Rebecca whispered. "Or what I'm supposed to do with it."

"Please," said Frank, his gaze practically splitting her in two. "I thought you'd understand. I broke my promise. I should have taken the locket straight to the house on Esplanade Avenue, but I didn't. Lying under those floorboards, the locket is as good as stolen. Until it's given to its rightful owners, I'll be stuck here in the afterlife, condemned to be a ghost for all eternity. Please — you have to help me!"

Rebecca thought of Lisette, desperate to escape the relentless loneliness of the world of ghosts. All Lisette wanted was to see her mother again, to rest in peace. Lisette had been trapped by a complicated curse, but all Frank needed was the rescue of this locket — a locket that lay undisturbed, he said, in an abandoned house just a few streets from here. It seemed like such a small thing to do. How could she say no?

"I'll find you again," Rebecca told him, backing up a few paces. "I don't know when, but I'll come looking for you. Then you can show me the house."

CHAPTER FOUR

T HE NEXT DAY WAS BEAUTIFUL, SUNNY, AND MUCH
warmer than in New York. Not a day to be thinking about
ghosts and buried lockets, but the conversation with Frank was
still on Rebecca's mind. She hadn't been able to shake him from
her thoughts all through dinner last night.

Now, she stood on a grassy bank looking out at Lake
Pontchartrain, its water metallic blue, ruffled with white by the
breeze. In the distance, the long bridge called the Causeway
stretched toward the North Shore. Seagulls cried overhead and
a pelican soared past, plunging into the water to scoop up a
fish. Sailboats lurched by, puffed with wind.

Really, it would have been an idyllic scene if Rebecca weren't
practically knee-deep in garbage, pulling bottles and cans out
of a ditch clogged with mud and sand.

"Hey, look!" Ling shouted from farther down the shore-
front. Like Rebecca, she was wearing shorts, a red T-shirt that
read FRENCH QUARTER TRADERS ASSOCIATION, and a pair of
oversized gardening gloves. "Another one!"

Ling was heaving a rusted shopping cart — her second of the day — out of the water, to the cheers of the workers around her. Rebecca raised an empty soda can as a mock toast to Ling's efforts, and then crammed the can into the trash bag tied to one wrist. She couldn't believe how much garbage people threw into the lake, or hurled into one of the storm drains. In addition to the hundreds of squashed cans and broken bottles, they'd pulled out plastic bags, cell phones, a decomposing baby stroller, assorted shoes, an LSU flag, and a crumpled car bumper.

Almost two thousand people were taking part in the Big Sweep today, they'd been told, working in teams on both sides of the lake. Anton was here, somewhere, with his soccer team, but Rebecca didn't know how he'd ever find her.

Ling clambered up the bank and together she and Rebecca stood watching one of the women in their team pull a barbecue grill out of the water: It was ensnared with weeds, twisted plastic bags, and — unbelievably — a broken string of silver Mardi Gras beads.

"Hang on to that grill, baby!" The overenthusiastic zone captain walked up, his gloves stuffed into one pocket. He was bald, chubby, and any age between forty and maybe sixty. He owned a restaurant on Bourbon Street. This guy had organized the group, handed out the red T-shirts they all wore, and had insisted that everyone call him Z-Cap. "We might need to cook us some lunch on it. Right? Right?"

"Man, we really got to do this in New York when we get back," Ling said, tugging on her gloves again. Fearlessly, she reached into the storm drain and pulled out a dripping, empty cigarette packet. "Maybe we could adopt a stretch of highway, like Bette Midler did."

"Rebecca!"

Rebecca heard a familiar girl's voice and blinked into the sunlight.

Her cousin, Aurelia, was thundering toward them along the bank. "Rebecca!" she called.

Rebecca reached out her arms, which was just as well: Aurelia tripped on an exposed concrete pipe, staggered the last few steps, and almost fell on top of her.

"Oh my god I can't believe I found you," Aurelia said in one breathless rush, turning her fall into a crushing hug. "We're way, way down there, and Miss Shaw is so mean — she wouldn't let me come look for you even though I said you were my cousin and all. But then we fished out a body, and she got sick and had to lie down in the back of her car. So I ran off to look for you."

Rebecca felt a chill. "You fished out *a body*?"

"We thought it was, but it was just a nappy old wig and a tire with a coat hanger sticking out of it."

"*This* is your little cousin?" Ling asked, laughing.

Rebecca could understand Ling's reaction. Aurelia was thirteen now, and she'd grown an implausible amount in the past year. She wasn't the little cousin with a swinging ponytail any-more. Her dark curls were shorter, and she looked taller and skinnier. She was still just as affectionate and exuberant, though, hugging Ling as a greeting, and then hugging Rebecca again even tighter.

"I wanted Mama to bring Marilyn over to your house yester-day, but she said no," Aurelia told them.

"Is Marilyn your friend?" Ling asked.

"She's the cat," said Rebecca. "Fluffy and silly, just like Aurelia!"

Aurelia beamed. She *did* look like a fluffy chick today, in her yellow TEMPLE MEAD JUNIORS T-shirt. She was also wearing the pair of denim shorts that Rebecca had left behind last May. Aurelia had sewn a purple patchwork square over the torn pocket. It looked suspiciously like the fabric of Marilyn's cat blanket.

"Are you on spring break, too, this week?" Ling asked, and Aurelia shook her head, rolling out her bottom lip in mock despair.

"We had it already. But maybe I can come down to the Quarter after school one day to see you?"

"Any day you like," said Rebecca, squeezing Aurelia's bony shoulders.

"And Uncle Michael said I could come with you all to Jazz Fest on Friday."

"We're going to Jazz Fest on Friday?" Ling screeched. Aurelia clapped a hand over her mouth, her eyes wide with horror.

"It was supposed to be a surprise," she whispered. "Don't say that I told!"

"We won't," Rebecca promised her. So that was why her father had changed the subject so quickly in the cab. He'd been planning it all along.

"I better go back," Aurelia said, frowning again. "Claire's covering for me."

"As usual." Aurelia and her friend Claire were longtime coconspirators.

"Whatever! Hey, have you seen Anton Grey yet?"

"Um — no," Rebecca said, trying to sound casual. "I'll probably see him later."

"You *wish* you could see him later." Aurelia giggled. " 'Cause you have mud all over your face! And he's walking over here right now."

"She's right," Ling agreed. "In your hair, too. And on the seat of your pants."

Rebecca cringed. Earlier that morning she had been trying to free the pieces of an upside-down plastic chair from its muddy grave, and had ended up sprawled in the dirt, a broken chair leg in hand. Z-Cap, wandering by, had shouted "Looking good, baby! You show that chair who's boss!"

There wasn't any time — or place — to get cleaned up now.

No sooner had Aurelia scampered away, disappearing into a sun-blurred crowd of workers, then Anton materialized, walking toward her like someone emerging from a mirage.

Rebecca rubbed sweat out of her eyes with the back of a grubby hand — how could hands get *so* dirty when they were inside gloves? — and tried to ignore her flip-flopping heart. Seeing Anton for the first time in all these months was always going to be weird, but it was even harder with thousands of people around, and Ling standing right next to her. Anton also had a friend with him — a blond, stocky guy.

Rebecca felt intensely self-conscious, and not just because she was half covered in mud.

Anton's dark hair was more closely cropped than before, maybe, and he looked almost dorky in his Big Sweep gear: purple soccer shorts, and a black T-shirt that read ST. SIMEON'S SERPENTS. But not so dorky, Rebecca thought, her stomach clenching with nerves, that she could just look at him calmly, like a normal person.

"Hey," they both said at the same time. Anton took another tentative step forward, as though he was going to kiss her, but all he ended up doing was sort of clasping her shoulder and leaning vaguely in her direction.

Not that I'm any smoother, Rebecca realized. She just stood there, her arms like lead weights, her feet glued to the ground. It was hardly a romantic reunion.

"I'm kind of muddy," she said, by way of an apology. Anton flashed her the briefest smile, and she thought that maybe he was as nervous as she was.

"This is Phil," he said, gesturing at the blond guy next to him. Phil had a wide, completely non-nervous smile. He stepped forward to shake Rebecca's hand, and then Ling's. Rebecca was so tongue-tied, Ling had to introduce herself. Anton wasn't doing a much better job with conversation, but luckily, Phil and Ling seemed ready to fill the void.

"It's so cool that you're doing something like this on your spring break," Phil said to Ling. "You just down here for the week? I'm only here for the semester. We're going back to Portland as soon as school's out."

"Portland, Oregon? Hey, my sister went to Reed!"

"No way!"

Phil's father was some kind of medical specialist, and he had a gig, as Phil called it, at Truro Hospital. Phil was attending St. Simeon's this semester, and it seemed as though Anton was his only friend.

"He's good with waifs and strays," Phil joked. "People from foreign lands. Other states, anyway."

Rebecca and Anton grinned at each other. Phil was right: Anton had been really good to *her* when she was a waif and a stray.

"Hey," said Ling, nudging Phil's arm. "Want to see what we just pulled out of the lake?'

·

Rebecca felt a wave of gratitude toward her: Ling clearly realized that Anton and Rebecca were going to keep standing around awkwardly, saying as little as possible, until they were alone. Before Ling and Phil were halfway down the bank, Anton stepped closer to Rebecca.

She caught her breath, and wondered for the second time in the space of a few minutes if he was going to kiss her.

"I wanted to tell you," Anton said in a low voice. "I saw Toby Sutton."

"He's *here*?" Rebecca looked over her shoulder, in case Toby was creeping up at this very moment.

"I'm ninety percent sure I saw him in the parking lot when we got out of the van this morning. Maybe he's sleeping in his uncle's boat in the marina. You know, he's kind of unhinged right now. He's really angry about having to move away and go to another school."

"As opposed to the school he once tried to burn down?"

"Better the devil you know, I guess," said Anton with a wry smile. Rebecca had seen that smile hundreds of times in photos — on Facebook, on her phone — but in person it had a very different effect. No wonder all the Temple Mead girls were so outraged when she'd "nabbed" him last year. They were *not* going to be happy when she turned up by his side at the Spring Dance this Thursday.

"Sometimes it's hard to break with the past," he was saying.

"Old habits. Old friends. I guess we're all loyal to people and places even if . . ."

"Even if they suck?" Rebecca fanned herself with her gloves. Either she'd had too much sun today or she was blushing. Whatever had kindled between them last year was still smoldering; she'd known that all along. But really, she had to get a grip.

"Just don't wander around anywhere alone, OK?" Anton looked her straight in the eyes, and Rebecca felt herself melt a little. So much for getting a grip. For a moment, she considered telling Anton about Frank, but she held her tongue. Not here, not now. Even *she* wasn't sure how to make sense of her conversation with the ghost.

"Be careful," Anton added. "Maybe don't go to the cemetery this time, just in case."

"But I *would* like to go," Rebecca told him. She couldn't come back to New Orleans without seeing Lisette's tomb. "I don't want to spend all this week in hiding. It's just crazy."

"If you want to see the grave, I'll take you, OK? Let's go tomorrow after school. No wandering around by yourself."

"You sound like my dad."

"Well." Anton laughed. "As long as I don't look like him. Because that would be weird."

"You know what's weird?" said a guy's voice, and Rebecca nearly jumped out of her skin. But it was only Phil. He and

Ling had walked up without Rebecca noticing. She wondered how much they'd heard.

"People throwing shopping carts into the lake?" Anton didn't seem at all fazed, and Rebecca admired his cool. He'd always seemed more grown-up than other boys his age. That was one thing she really liked about him. It wasn't just that he was tall, dark, and handsome. Really.

"I mean, why don't we do this kind of cleanup thing *everywhere*?" Phil was exploding with enthusiasm. "There has to be something like this going on in Portland. As soon as I get back, I'm going to find out and, like, mobilize every single person I know."

"I know, right?" Ling nodded. She was standing with her hands on her hips, and Phil was beaming at her. Rebecca wondered if he'd met many girls since he arrived in New Orleans, or if the Temple Mead seniors were giving him the cold shoulder because he wasn't from the right kind of local family.

Anton caught Rebecca's eye, and smiled. Everything was OK. Rebecca felt herself relax. They hadn't kissed, or hugged, or had a dramatic emotional reunion, but everything was going to be fine.

"So we should get back to our . . ." Anton nodded in what must have been the general direction of the St. Simeon's group. "But tomorrow, yeah?"

"Tomorrow?" asked Phil, and Ling shot Rebecca a searching look.

"Rebecca and I are giving you out-of-towners a tour of Lafayette Cemetery," Anton explained. "After school."

"Great!" Ling looked thrilled. She must like Phil, Rebecca decided. It was just as well, given that he'd be her date for the Spring Dance on Thursday. Something Rebecca had completely forgotten to mention to Ling. . . .

"But doesn't the cemetery close at, like, lunchtime?" asked Phil. He turned to Ling. "Whenever I think about going in there, it's all locked up."

"That's no problem," said Rebecca quickly. "Anton has a key. You still have it, don't you?"

Anton nodded. "So it's a date then," he said, smiling right at Rebecca, and she felt herself melt a little bit more.

CHAPTER FIVE

REBECCA THOUGHT SHE COULD HEAR THUNDER, which didn't make sense on a blue-sky afternoon like this one. Then she realized what she could hear were drums, pounding out a beat. Drums and snatches of music — the swoop of a trombone, the peal of a trumpet. It sounded as though someone was having a party in the street.

They were in Tremé, driving back from the Big Sweep with one of the volunteers: a woman named Miss Viola, who owned a vintage boutique on Chartres Street. They'd taken what Miss Viola called "a divergence" to drop off a bartender named Sandy, and Rebecca was eagerly peering out the window, wondering which of these houses might be Frank's "locket" house. This was a neighborhood of small old houses, mostly shabbier versions of the places Rebecca saw in the Quarter, but she hadn't spotted anything yet that looked abandoned or boarded up.

The drums distracted her: They were more insistent now, and the music louder, and soon she could hear crowd noise, too, whooping and shouting.

"Where's the music coming from?" Ling, riding shotgun, wanted to know.

"It's coming right at you, baby," Miss Viola told her, laughing. She slowed down the car by the intersection. "It's a second line. The Lady High-Kickers, I think. Look!"

A huge mass of people were making their way toward them, led by a group of black ladies all wearing vivid purple pantsuits and broad-brimmed hats. They were waving giant fans made from purple and white feathers. Behind them trailed a brass band — mainly young guys in baggy T-shirts, blasting away on horns while the ladies twirled and danced down the street. Along the route, people were out on their porches or followed the parade along the sidewalk, dancing and clapping and calling out.

"Can we get out to watch?" Rebecca asked, intrigued by the sight. This was sort of like a Mardi Gras parade, but without the floats. The ladies were too old to be marching girls, and anyway, they weren't really marching. They were half walking, half dancing, flapping the fans in the air.

"You can join in if you want," Miss Viola said. She stopped the car there in the middle of the road and turned off the engine. "Anyone can second-line. Just follow the band."

Ling was already out of the car, fumbling with her phone so she could take pictures. Rebecca climbed out as well. She shaded her eyes with one hand, in awe of the approaching parade.

"What are they celebrating?" Ling asked, shouting over the raucous noise of the band.

"Just bein' alive," Miss Viola told her.

A sweating teenaged boy carried a banner with the words THE LADY HIGH-KICKERS S & P CLUB, ESTABLISHED 1992 in silver letters. Rebecca had only the haziest recollection of social aid clubs. They were just another of New Orleans's secret worlds, with their own schedules and rules and members.

"One club or another is second-lining every weekend," explained Miss Viola. "You never heard of a second line?" she said to Rebecca. "I thought you used to live here."

"In the Garden District," Rebecca told her. The only parades that Amy and Jessica, her sort-of friends at school, had ever talked about were carnival parades. The weeks leading up to Mardi Gras were just when people took part in parades — or so she'd thought.

"People from Uptown like a second line, too," Miss Viola insisted. "Doesn't matter if you're black or white, from Uptown, downtown, back o' town. My cousin who lives Uptown, he's in the Young Men Olympians — they even have their own tomb in Lafayette Cemetery. When you die, you can be buried in there and it won't cost your family a penny. You never saw them when you lived on Sixth Street? They parade right by the cemetery, end of September."

"I didn't get here until November," Rebecca told her. She

wished she'd seen these other parades last time, and was glad to get a glimpse of this one.

"I love the band," said Ling, retying her hair with a red bandana. "What's a second line?"

Miss Viola nodded toward the parade. "See the club members and the band? They're the first line, making all the noise. Everyone who follows along behind is the second line."

Rebecca had never seen so many people dancing in the street before — not following any choreographed routine, but just *dancing*. After the front-line ladies whirled by, swooning and dipping, dancing with each other or just by themselves, the band trudged past, blasting out a song Rebecca didn't know.

And then there were dozens and dozens of people, maybe more than a hundred, of all ages. Most of the people were black — Tremé was mainly a black neighborhood, Rebecca knew — but not all. Some banged tambourines or blew on whistles, some carried umbrellas to fend off the afternoon sun. Some people had their dogs with them, or were pushing baby buggies along the street. Some had just dashed down from their front steps or porches to join in the dancing. Two little boys, no more than seven years old, were putting on an expert show on the sidewalk, practically leaping in time to the music, cheered on by everyone around them.

Even though she was tired and dirty after her day's exertions, and even though she was still thinking about Frank's dilemma —

not to mention the threat of Toby Sutton — Rebecca felt her spirits lift. There was something about the stomp of the band and the energy of the dancing that was exhilarating; it was impossible to keep still. Ling was feeling it, too, Rebecca could tell; she stood swaying in time to the music.

The whole time she lived here, Rebecca thought, she felt like an outsider. Maybe she'd approached it the wrong way — waiting to be invited in. Sometimes you just had to make the leap.

But now Miss Viola was hustling them back into the car, shaking her head when Rebecca suggested they could walk home.

"Isn't it safe here?" Ling asked, fastening her seat belt.

"Well . . ." Miss Viola exhaled. "It's safe and it's not safe, like everywhere in this town. Don't go strolling around at night, looking like you don't know where you at. Don't speak to the boys hollering at you over on Bayou Road. And don't go wandering over to Lafitte looking for an ice cup. That's my advice to you."

"So Tremé is OK?" asked a baffled Ling.

"Well, there are some *elements* we don't need hanging around the neighborhood," said Miss Viola cryptically. "We don't need those elements anywhere in the city, making everybody afraid. But you know, this is one of the most historic neighborhoods in this city, and very few tourists bother to cross Rampart Street. The only second line they ever get to see is in Harrah's Casino."

"I worked on a rebuilding project on St. Philip Street last May," Rebecca told her.

"Why, I grew up right there on St. Philip!" Miss Viola swung the car in a violent U-turn onto the other side of Rampart. "Most of my family still lives there — like my nephew here. Look at him, just sashaying on by without even saying hello! Raphael! Raphael!"

Miss Viola honked her horn, swerving to a very abrupt stop. Two teenage African-American boys looked startled, then annoyed, and then — after they peered into the car — they started laughing. Miss Viola lowered her window.

"We thought you were trying to run us over," one of the boys said, leaning in. He was lean and long-limbed, his hair cut short, a tiny scar like a frown line above one eyebrow. "You driving without your glasses on again?"

"This is my nephew, Raphael," said Miss Viola, ignoring the question. "These young ladies are from New York. They've been helping with the Big Sweep today, just like you and Junior could have been doing if you weren't so money-hungry."

"We been busking," Raphael told Rebecca and Ling. He was carrying a trumpet, Rebecca realized. His friend, Junior, jingled whatever 'it was he was carrying — a hat, maybe — to demonstrate how much money they'd earned. "Sundays we can make a lot, unless it's raining. Usually four or five of us come down, but the others had a parade."

"I don't know how you made a penny today with just one trumpet," Miss Viola sniffed. "What are *you* playing, Junior? Aside from the fool."

"I sing and dance, Miss Viola." Junior did another demonstration, this time a few steps, though it was a struggle for him to balance the hat of money, hold up his jeans, and dance at the same time.

"We'll be volunteering this week," Raphael reassured his aunt. "After school, clearing the weeds."

"That's right." Miss Viola tapped the wheel, then turned to look at Rebecca. "You should tell your daddy about that. Maybe it's something you girls might want to help with? Raphael's school is clearing land and putting in a garden." She gestured out the window, rolling her eyes. "And with workers like these two, they need all the help they can get."

Rebecca agreed right away; the more time she got to spend in Tremé, the more chance she'd have to see the house Frank had talked about, and work out a plan to find the locket.

They were near Orleans Avenue, so Ling and Rebecca climbed out of Miss Viola's car, calling out their good-byes.

The old town house on the corner of Orleans looked forlorn and scruffy. Rebecca couldn't see Frank anywhere, even though this was the exact spot they'd stood talking yesterday. But there was someone else standing there, leaning against the boarded-up door, his face half obscured by shadows. A scowling middle-aged man with dark hair, who looked at them for way too long as they rounded the corner.

"Perv alert," Rebecca muttered to Ling, gesturing toward him. But by the bemused look on her friend's face she could tell that Ling had no idea what she was talking about. Rebecca might be able to see the dark-haired man — he lurked just a few feet away — but Ling couldn't see him at all. And that could only mean one thing.

He was another ghost.

Safely inside "the compound," as they'd started calling it, Rebecca scrubbed off all the lakeside mud in the shower. She was still dwelling on Frank and then the dark-haired ghost she'd seen as she drifted into the main house thirty minutes later, looking for her father.

"Is that you, honey?" her dad called.

"Yeah." Rebecca stood in the doorway, blinking into the gloom of the living room. With the front shutters always closed, it was quite dark in there. The exposed brick walls, dark wooden ceiling, and black sofa didn't help, and the TV — golf on, sound off — was the only glimmer of color in the room.

Her father sat with his laptop perched on his knees, the sofa and coffee table a mess of scattered papers and files.

"You're working?" Rebecca perched on the arm of the sofa, the only available place to sit.

"Way too much to do this week," her father said, squinting at the screen. Rebecca leaned over to flick on a standing lamp so he had more light. "Sorry to be so boring. Good day?"

"Tiring day," she admitted. "But good."

"Miss Viola called," said her father. "Your Aunt Claudia gave her my number. She said you girls were real troopers. And something about a gardening project at a school in Tremé. You and Ling are interested?"

"Definitely." Rebecca picked at a loose tuft on the sofa. "Dad, do you . . . I mean, have you . . ."

"Have I what?" He was clicking from one document to the next, frowning at the screen.

"Have you ever heard of a New Orleans family called *Moo-son*?" She tried to echo the way Frank had pronounced it.

"Mousson? Sounds like the kind of name you'd hear around here. French Creole."

"How would you spell it?"

"M-O-U-S-S-O-N, I guess. Why?"

"Oh — no reason. It was just a name I heard. Something to do with a local artist. I wondered if it was famous."

"Maybe." Her dad was clearly distracted. "So, Tuesday lunchtime. We can go check out the house."

Rebecca's heart jumped. "Which house?" she almost shouted. Was her father some kind of psychic? How could he know about the house where the locket was hidden?

"The house you and Anton worked on last May. Lisette's house. What is *wrong* with you?"

"Sorry — nothing. I guess I'm just kind of tired."

"Of course you are. Anyway, I thought we could see Lisette's house and then check out this school garden project. I don't want to send you girls off there without seeing it first myself. We could go tomorrow, but I have meetings all day, and then we're having dinner at Claudia's."

"Oh, yeah." Rebecca was impatient to see the locket house, but another day wouldn't hurt, she decided. More time to think up a brilliant plan. "We'll just meet you at Aunt Claudia's tomorrow, OK? Ling and I can take the streetcar uptown. We're going to meet up with Anton in the afternoon, and show Ling the neighborhood."

This wasn't the whole truth, exactly, but Rebecca didn't want to say "Lafayette Cemetery." She and her father hardly ever mentioned that place anymore, and she didn't want him to freak out — as she'd said to Frank — at the thought of her going back there.

"Wish I could ride the streetcar with you," her dad lamented, squinting at the screen again. "I haven't done that for years. But I'll probably just get a cab to save time. You probably don't want me around anyway."

"Don't be silly!" she protested, though he was right: She didn't want him there, telling her to keep out of the cemetery.

"Whatever," he said, laughing. "Anton will make sure you girls keep out of trouble."

"Sure," Rebecca said, slithering off her perch. "I'm just going to go get ready for dinner."

"Rebecca," said her father, before she had a chance to disappear. "Have you ever mentioned anything about . . . you know, what happened last year? To Ling, I mean. Does she know anything about Lisette?" He'd lowered his voice to a concerned whisper.

"Nope." Rebecca shook her head.

"That's good," her father said, pushing his glasses higher up the bridge of his nose. "She probably wouldn't believe it, anyway. It's all in the past now. No more ghosts, right?"

"Right," said Rebecca, trying to smile. There wasn't any point bringing up Frank with her father right now. He'd probably tell her to steer clear, to keep out of someone else's unfinished business. Lisette had been a Bowman; she was a Bowman family ghost. Rebecca's fate had been inextricably linked to hers. But Frank O'Connor was just a sweet boy from Liverpool who'd come to New Orleans to make his fortune — and ended up murdered in a house in Tremé. His history had nothing to do with Rebecca or any of her ancestors. Rebecca had no reason to take on his troubles. That was exactly what her father would tell her.

She walked back into the dappled light of the verdant

courtyard and slowly climbed the wooden staircase to the upper gallery. Ling was getting ready in the bathroom, singing some approximation of the song they'd heard in the parade today.

Her father was wrong, Rebecca thought. *Nothing* was in the past — or, at least, things that were meant to be in the past didn't always stay there. They came back to haunt the present. They wouldn't go away.

CHAPTER SIX

THE TAXI DRIVER HAD PROMISED THEM NO RAIN until later in the week, but Rebecca awoke on Monday morning to the sound of rain pattering onto the wooden slats of the gallery and the fat leaves of elephant plants. Now, she thought, snuggling back beneath the covers, they were *really* in New Orleans. The rain was the true sound of this city — maybe because in these old wooden houses, with their flimsy walls, the rain always made itself heard.

But it wasn't a tropical New Orleans downpour, thundering onto the streets and turning gutter puddles into raging torrents. So this meant Rebecca and Ling could wander the Quarter as planned that morning, with just a shared umbrella to fend off the drizzle. Everything was new and different to Ling, even all the things Rebecca had learned, back when she lived here, were just for tourists: the tap-dancing buskers with washboards on the steps of St. Louis Cathedral, the stacks of garish feathered masks in the old French Market, the little stores selling voodoo charms or pralines or Mardi Gras beads or packet mixes of jambalaya.

In the colorful encampment of fortune-tellers, buskers, and painters around Jackson Square, they looked for Aunt Claudia, but she wasn't there.

"I guess a rainy Monday isn't the greatest day to be sitting out here," Ling reasoned. "It's usually much busier than this, right?"

"Absolutely," Rebecca said, steering Ling toward their next stop, Café Du Monde. She'd promised Ling a plate of beignets — delicious hot squares of donut, coated with a snowy blanket of powdered sugar. "She's probably 'making groceries' for dinner tonight. That's what they call going to the supermarket here."

"If we have beignets now and a muffaletta for lunch, I don't think I'm going to be able to eat any dinner," said Ling. "I'm still recovering from that giant burger last night at — what was that place called?"

"Port of Call."

"I loved that street it was on. All those beautiful old mansions. Esplanade Avenue, right?"

"Yup." Rebecca nodded. Esplanade Avenue, where Frank had been *supposed* to deliver the locket entrusted to him back in 1873.

That was another thing she hadn't considered. Even if she managed to rescue the locket from beneath the floorboards of the house in Tremé, how was she supposed to track down the rightful owner? The cousin of the artist must be long-dead by now, and though lots of houses stayed in the hands of one family for years and years, many of the big places on Esplanade were B&Bs these days, or fancy condos. The "Moo-son" family could be long gone.

"Rebecca?" An expectant Ling was looking at her. "The umbrella?"

"What? Sorry, I was in my own world." Rebecca realized she *had* to confide in someone about Frank, or she'd go insane. But could she tell Ling now, in the middle of their fun tourist day? She wouldn't even be sure where to start.

"I know," Ling said. "It's raining again, FYI. What's up? Are you worried about this secret cemetery trip with Anton today?"

Rebecca hadn't even thought about that, but now that Ling mentioned it, she added it to the list of things to obsess over. Anton and Phil were meeting them at the Sixth Street gate of Lafayette Cemetery at four. But Rebecca had been counting on Aunt Claudia still being out at work then, not at home in the little yellow house on Sixth Street, able to look out the front parlor window at any point. Or, even worse, to bustle out and stop them.

"I don't want my aunt spotting us," she told Ling. They were approaching the open loggia of Café Du Monde now, and she could see an empty table. Unfortunately, a pigeon was standing on it and pecking at crispy golden beignet crumbs, its claws making a trail across a tabletop still sprinkled with powdered sugar.

"Why would it be such a big deal going in the cemetery? Is it dangerous?"

"Not really." Rebecca pointed to another empty table, this one pigeon free, and they wended their way toward it.

"Why does Anton have a key to the cemetery? Isn't that weird?"

"It has to do with his family, I think," Rebecca said, playing dumb. "They've lived overlooking it for years and years and . . . well, I don't know the whole story. All sorts of weird things go on here with the old-line families."

"Old line? Is that like a second line?"

"No!" Rebecca laughed. The thought of the snooty Grey family or the Bowmans or the Suttons joining in with a second line was ridiculous. "Old-line just means old. They've been here forever."

"Whatever." Ling scrutinized the very short menu on the back of the napkin dispenser. "I don't know what 'forever' means when you're American. Most of us are immigrants, one way or another. I hate all that high-society snobbery. Like Miss Manners says, 'old money is just new money, the sequel.' How 'old' is Anton's money?"

"His great-whatever grandfather moved here just before the Civil War, I think."

"Hello! The Civil War was, like, five minutes ago," Ling said, making a face. "You know, in the grand sweep of history. If Anton was a descendant of Cleopatra and Mark Antony, say, then *that* would be old-line. Anyway, speaking of Anton — I think you guys need some alone time. When we're in the cemetery later, I'll wander off with Phil, OK? So you two have a chance to talk."

"Thanks," Rebecca mumbled, blushing.

Ling was clearly thinking along romantic lines. But alone time with Anton was exactly what Rebecca needed right now. Anton knew about Lisette. He knew Rebecca could see ghosts. If there was one person she could confide in about Frank, it was him.

There was something surreal about going back to the Garden District almost a year after she'd left. Rebecca felt as though she were wandering through a dream world in which everything was gorgeous and colorful, even on a gray day like this. The voice she could hear telling Ling about the history of the neighborhood was her voice, but it felt disembodied and fake. With all her might Rebecca tried to sound calm, but part of her wanted to scream. *This is the school where I was really unhappy. This is the cemetery gate where Toby Sutton threatened me. This is the street I was dragged along when a bunch of people in masks decided they wanted to kill me. . . .*

"You never said it was this beautiful," Ling was saying, and she was right, of course. Everything about the neighborhood was beautiful and elegant: the lines of oak trees shading the narrow streets, the grand mansions with their cast-iron galleries and ornate gates, the lush gardens, the high white walls enclosing the cemetery, the pristine steps and pillars of Temple Mead Academy.

Things often looked beautiful on the surface, Rebecca thought, but that wasn't the whole story — like the tombs in Lafayette Cemetery, which looked like creamy marble from a distance but were really plastered-over brick.

The lot where the Bowman mansion once stood, gray and elegant and imposing, was now a building site. The burnt remains of the old house were all gone now, and the steel skeleton of a new structure was rising up in its place. The only remnant of what once stood there, looming over the cemetery, was the elaborate wrought-iron fence.

"There are the boys!" Ling waved toward two figures ambling along Prytania Street, still dressed in their school uniforms. "They look like seniors at Hogwarts," she whispered to Rebecca.

"Hey!" Phil called along the street, beaming his wide smile. He'd just started at a strange new school, but he always appeared to be in a good mood, Rebecca thought. When she glanced at Anton, she wished her stomach didn't decide to perform backflips at the sight of him. He made the St. Simeon's uniform look rumpled and dashing, somehow.

"Coast clear?" he asked Rebecca by way of a greeting.

"My aunt may be around," she told him. Ling and Phil were talking to each other naturally and easily, as though they'd known each other for years. Why were things so serious and awkward with her and Anton?

"We just saw her maybe ten minutes ago, driving that way on Magazine." Anton gestured uptown, and then jingled his pocket. "I got the keys. Let's go."

Lafayette Cemetery, surrounded by its white walls, had four different entrances, all guarded by tall iron gates. By this time of day, the last of the tour groups had left, and all the gates were locked. Just standing by the Sixth Street entrance, waiting for Anton to creak open the gate, agitated Rebecca. She wasn't sure if she'd calm down once they were safely inside the cemetery and hidden from prying eyes — they *were* creeping in after-hours illegally — or if there was no such thing as "safe" inside this cemetery. With its long alleys of overgrown foliage and silent tombs, the cemetery felt like an abandoned city, a place of ruins and secrets.

For a while they all walked together, Ling and Phil marveling at the tree-shaded paths and the ornate decorations on some of the tombs, and lamenting the ones that seemed to be crumbling or neglected. Rebecca could barely pay attention.

69

She wanted to see Lisette's grave, but not with everyone else in tow. And she really, really wanted to talk to Anton about Frank and his missing locket.

"You guys must have been in here a hundred times before," Ling said at last, pausing while Phil took a picture of a tomb topped by a stone urn. "Why don't we meet you back at the gate in about twenty minutes? We can just be tourists for a while and take a million pictures."

Before a bemused Phil had a chance to say anything, Ling grabbed his elbow and started steering him down a side path. Anton stood watching them go, then raised an eyebrow at Rebecca.

He didn't need to say anything. They were going to the Bowman tomb.

The tomb was tucked away in a hidden corner of the cemetery where even on a sunny day light struggled to break through the trees. The earlier rain had turned the ground springy underfoot, and muddy in large, slick patches. In the jagged crevices formed by broken slate, murky puddles formed, clogged with leaves.

It had been almost a year since Rebecca had last visited the cemetery. She'd come then to say good-bye to Lisette, laying a laurel wreath on the steps of the Bowman family tomb. Back then, the stone angel that once perched on the tomb still lay in smashed pieces on the ground.

Now the laurel wreath was long gone, and the broken angel had been cleared away. The tomb looked cleaner than those around it, and there was a new name carved into the marble slab covering the vault's door: HELENA BOWMAN. She'd died here that night, killed by the fall of the stone angel. Rebecca swallowed hard at the memory.

There was another recent addition to the marble slab. LISETTE VILLIEUX BOWMAN, 1836–1853.

Someone seeing the Bowman tomb for the first time would have no idea, of course, that for decades Lisette had haunted this very cemetery, visible only to girls of the Bowman family.

"So we're all set?" Anton was talking, but Rebecca hadn't been paying attention.

"Sorry — set for what?" She drew her fingers over the carved letters of Lisette's name. She missed her friend. The cemetery seemed an emptier, lonelier place without her warmth and her dark, sparkling eyes.

"The dance. On Thursday." Anton scuffed at the steps of the tomb with one shoe.

"Oh." Rebecca had forgotten all about it. She still hadn't mentioned it to Ling. She was such an idiot: Neither of them even had anything to wear. "Yeah, sure — I guess."

"St. Simeon's is organizing it this year," Anton said. "So it might be better than usual. And maybe with the four of us going together, we could have some fun."

Rebecca slid down so she was sitting on the steps of the tomb, her back to the cold marble slab.

"Sure," she said again, staring at her damp shoes. "I just don't want to make any problems for *you*. Remember how bad things were at the Bowmans' Christmas party when people saw you'd taken *me*? And after the party, when nobody wanted to talk to you?"

"That was then," Anton insisted. "Things are different now. People have grown up. They've moved on. Marianne and Toby are gone — well, Toby wouldn't show his face there. And Helena . . . well. You know. The old group's all broken up. We don't hang out in the cemetery at night anymore. Everyone's thinking about college now. People like Phil don't know anything about . . . the past. Does Ling . . . ?"

"No." Rebecca shook her head.

"Good." Anton sat down next to Rebecca, so close their arms were almost touching. Almost, but not quite. "Everything having to do with that curse — it's family business. It shouldn't involve anyone from the outside."

Rebecca looked carefully at Anton. "I'm from the outside, really."

"I don't think of you that way. I never did." Anton laid his hand on Rebecca's and they fell silent. The only sound was a car hissing past on the wet road, and the low cackle of insects. Rebecca's hand felt as though it were tingling with electricity;

she dared not move in case Anton thought she was pushing him away. That was the last thing Rebecca wanted to do. She wished this moment could go on and on, but soon they'd have to be back at the gate to meet Ling and Phil. And Rebecca still had said nothing about Frank.

"I need to . . . I need to tell you something," she blurted, desperate to get it all out before she lost her nerve. "I saw another ghost, and I really need your help. His name is Frank and he was murdered in 1873. He dropped this locket under the floorboards of a house in Tremé. . . ."

"Wait, wait, wait. You've seen *another* ghost?"

"Yes. Well, he saw me. It's a long story, but anyway, he talked to me in New York, and now he's down here, and I said I'd help him."

"God, Rebecca, what are you doing?" Anton pulled his hand away. "Didn't you learn your lesson last time? Ghosts are bad news. They're trouble! You have to stay away from them."

"Please, would you just listen for a minute? The locket is in this old house and he needs my help to get it."

Anton wheezed out an impatient sigh.

"I don't even know if I believe in ghosts, OK? This Frank guy — he might just be some weirdo spinning you a line."

Rebecca frowned. "What do you mean you don't believe in ghosts? What about Lisette?"

"That was different."

"What, so you think there's, like, *one* ghost in the whole world? And now she's gone, we can all pretend it never happened . . ."

"Pretty much."

" . . . and pretend that it'll never happen again?"

"I just think that we have more pressing problems right now with the living," he said. "This thing with Toby — it's the main issue on my mind."

"I know that guys aren't good at multitasking," Rebecca said, unable to keep the sarcasm out of her voice. Why was he reacting like this? Why was he being so dismissive?

"We should get going." Anton stood up, dusting off his hands as though he'd been touching something dirty. "Let's talk about this some other time, OK?"

"I don't know when that other time will be." Rebecca pushed herself up. She was blinking back tears. She'd really believed that Anton would understand and help her. Instead he was treating her like a silly little girl.

"Well, we'll see each other on Thursday, won't we?"

Rebecca gazed at him, trying to make sense of what he was saying. She was only here until Sunday. Was Anton really not planning to see her at all until the dance on Thursday night? Was that all she was to him — someone to just bring there so he wouldn't show up alone?

She was furious with Anton, and furious with herself for thinking she could confide in him. As usual, all he cared about were his friends, and his social life.

"Find someone else to take," she said, and stalked off toward the Sixth Street gate.

CHAPTER SEVEN

AUNT CLAUDIA'S WINDOWS WERE STEAMED UP because of the rice boiling away on the old stove. The kitchen was still cluttered and eclectic to say the least, with its mismatched chairs and purple-painted cupboard doors that never seemed to close properly. But all the ripped calendar pages once stuck on the walls were gone, and the old teapot with the chipped spout was now a flower pot on the windowsill. Maybe because it was a special occasion, Aunt Claudia's tarot deck — usually in pride of place on the table, wedged between a salt shaker and a bottle of hot sauce — had been hidden away somewhere.

Rebecca was grateful for the clamor and visual distractions of the house, because it meant she could avoid Ling's meaningful looks. Of course she knew something was up with Anton and Rebecca — she wasn't *blind*. But Rebecca didn't feel like talking about it, and luckily there was the distraction of a house tour by Aurelia, hugging an unwilling Marilyn the cat in her arms.

"This is the parlor," she told Ling, gesturing with one of Marilyn's paws at the array of horse-hair sofas, dusty statuettes, and — a new addition — bronze miniature elephants arranged on top of the TV. "We don't use this room much."

"Does it have bad energy?" Ling whispered, clearly trying to enter into the spirit of the place. Aurelia looked puzzled.

"Stuff sticks out of the sofa and the television doesn't work," she replied, before bouncing off down the hallway.

Rebecca's old room hadn't changed much, though a lot of the freaky items she'd moved to the attic — like the monkey skull that served as a bookend, and the flaking carnival mask from Haiti — were back in position.

"I used to call this the voodoo room, but now we call it Rebecca's room," said Aurelia solemnly. "See?"

She pointed to a framed picture on the bedside table. It was a photograph of Rebecca sitting at the kitchen table and trying to read a magazine — impossible because Marilyn had leapt onto the table and settled herself on the left-hand page.

When Ling was in the bathroom, Aurelia cornered Rebecca in the hallway.

"You know, I *saw* you," Aurelia whispered, and Rebecca's blood ran cold. "Going into the cemetery when it was all locked up."

"Keep it to yourself, OK?" Rebecca whispered back. This was the last thing she needed: a public announcement.

"Of course!" Aurelia was indignant, and speaking so loudly that Rebecca pulled her back into the bedroom. Marilyn took the opportunity to scamper away.

"It's just you know how crazy my dad and your mother get about breaking rules and stuff," Rebecca explained.

"And about going into the cemetery when nobody's supposed to be in there," Aurelia replied. "You could have let *me* in, too, you know."

"But you can go in anytime — when it's open, I mean."

"Not with you and Ling." Aurelia looked hurt. "You said we'd spend time together, but you don't even let me walk around with you when you're right here on this street."

"I'm sorry," Rebecca told her. She hadn't even thought about asking Aurelia to hang out with them that afternoon. "But look — we only arrived on Saturday. We have lots of time to hang out together, OK?"

"When?"

"After school tomorrow. Um, I think. We may be doing . . . something."

"Like what?" Aurelia's eyes watered with tears. "Why is everyone always trying to keep things secret from me? I'm not a little girl anymore. I'm thirteen."

"I know," Rebecca sighed. "But that's still . . . I mean . . ."

"What?" Aurelia was instantly offended. "Like you're so grown up."

"Hey, you two!" Ling poked her head around the door. "What's up?"

"Nothing," they both said, a little too quickly, at the same time.

"Secrets, secrets, secrets," said Ling, narrowing her eyes.

Rebecca glared over at the monkey skull, directing all her — what was it Ling had called it? Bad energy? — at the stupid thing. But when Aurelia flounced off in search of Marilyn, Ling stepped into the room and closed the door.

"Is everything OK?" she asked. "With you and Anton, I mean."

"Sure. Don't worry."

"Well, I *am* worried 'cause you seem pretty upset."

Rebecca took a deep breath.

"It's . . . it's nothing. He's just an idiot sometimes."

"Oh." Ling frowned. "So — well, Phil mentioned something about a dance on Thursday."

"Yeah. I meant to tell you about it, but — well, I'm not going, anyway. You can go if you want."

"I'm not going if you're not," said Ling. "Is this about those girls from Temple Mead? Phil said something about stories he'd heard at school, about Anton being a pariah when he used to hang out with you. Something about a Christmas party? I never realized it was so bad for you here."

Rebecca could barely swallow. Part of her wanted to burst into tears and tell Ling everything — everything about Lisette, everything about Frank. But part of her, the outraged part, wanted to smack each and every boy at St. Simeon's and tell them to shut their big mouths.

"Rebecca! Ling!" Her father was calling them, and Rebecca practically sprinted to the kitchen.

"I don't know why we never make this," he was telling Aunt Claudia when Rebecca walked in, Ling trailing behind. He held plates aloft while Aunt Claudia ladled out a brownish stew of beans and spicy sausage onto steaming mounds of rice. "Those red beans smell so good."

"Red beans and rice, every Monday night," Aunt Claudia told Ling. "This is what people all over the city are eating right now. Nothing changes in New Orleans."

Nothing changes. Rebecca sat down at the kitchen table, her aunt's words echoing in her head. A year was a short time in a city as old as this. Nothing had changed. Rebecca had been deluding herself if she'd thought anything else.

Aunt Claudia insisted on driving them home, and Aurelia insisted on coming along for the ride, so Rebecca was pressed up against a window, her nose almost touching the glass.

It was dark now, and the squat palm trees planted down the narrow median strip — which New Orleanians called the "neutral ground" — looked dense and mysterious. The only other cars driving along Rampart Street seemed to be taxis, but the lack of traffic didn't deter Aunt Claudia from her favorite habits: driving the most circuitous route, driving as slowly as possible, and missing the turn.

"I think that was where we have to turn, back there," said her father, in the front seat. "But we can turn — oh!"

Rather than just take the next right into the Quarter, and wend through the one-way grid of streets, Aunt Claudia pulled one of Miss Viola's maneuvers and performed an abrupt U-turn on Rampart. Aurelia, who was squashed in the middle, lurched into Rebecca, and Rebecca banged her forehead on the window.

"Ouch," she said, staring ruefully over at the other side of Rampart Street, where they should have been driving. There was their corner, with the four grand town houses in a row. Well, three grand town houses and one unloved, derelict one at the end, screaming out for paint and tenants and new window shutters.

Except tonight the top-floor gallery was illuminated by an eerie, silvery glow, stronger than candlelight but not bright enough to be electricity. Rebecca looked closer. It was almost like a mist, or maybe like smoke — but neither of those things made sense, because Rebecca associated mist and smoke with darkness, and this was a soft, wispy light.

She craned her neck, trying to see where it was coming from. Had someone found their way inside? She'd heard about vagrants and squatters colonizing empty houses, but it seemed strange they would head for the very top floor.

Then a girl appeared — practically *wafted* to the gallery's railings — and leaned out. Rebecca gasped.

"What is it?" Aurelia wanted to know.

"Up there — look." Rebecca pointed to the town house. The girl was dark-haired and wore a white dress of some kind, maybe a nightgown. She gripped the railings, looking up and down the street.

"That old house." Aurelia seemed disappointed. "Is it falling down?"

Aunt Claudia made another one of her wide U-turns, and Rebecca couldn't see anything anymore.

"Aunt Claudia!" she called. "Would it be OK if you let us out on the corner of Orleans?"

"That's a good idea," her father said, probably worried they'd spend all evening driving up and down Rampart.

When all the good-byes were said, and they were standing on Rampart waving as Aunt Claudia's car made its dramatic swing into yet another U-turn, Rebecca inched her way to the curb. From here, looking upward, she could still see the silvery light, but to see the girl on the gallery she'd need to walk into the road.

"What is it?" Ling walked over.

"I think there's someone up there. You know, in the empty house. I saw lights up on the gallery."

"You can see lights?" Rebecca's father stood with them now, squinting up. "Really? It looks dark to me."

"And me," agreed Ling. "Maybe we could go stand . . ."

"In the neutral ground — I mean, the median — OK." Rebecca checked for oncoming cars and then bounded toward the neutral ground, before her father could say no.

"Just be careful!" he called, looking up and down the street before he crossed with Ling. "It's getting kind of late to be running around on Rampart."

Rebecca's eyes weren't tricking her: The top gallery was lit in some way, and the girl with dark hair — long curls, Rebecca could see now — was still leaning over the railings. When she noticed Rebecca gazing up at her, she smiled, raising one bare arm in a slow wave.

"Nope," Rebecca's father said. He was standing right next to her on the grassy verge, looking straight at the building. "I can't see any lights on, honey."

"Neither can I," said Ling. "Maybe it was a reflection from car lights or something? It's a shame that building is so messed up. It looks like it's about to fall down at any minute."

"Just as well there's nobody there," said her dad. "If we really did see lights on, I'd have to call the police."

Rebecca stared up at the girl nobody else could see. Her heart was pounding. She opened her mouth to speak, and then closed it again. There was a girl up there, waving at them, and there were lights probably visible from the other side of Armstrong Park. But Ling couldn't see anything and neither could Rebecca's dad. All they could see was a beaten-up town house with dangling rusted galleries and broken shutters. That's why the girl wasn't really waving at *them*. She was waving at Rebecca.

Rebecca's dad urged Rebecca and Ling to come along and head back to the compound. Rebecca complied, but her thoughts were racing. Whatever Anton said, whatever he might choose to believe, ghosts were everywhere in New Orleans. Yet another one was trying to get Rebecca's attention. What was *her* story? Was *she* going to ask for Rebecca's help, too?

CHAPTER EIGHT

O N TUESDAY AFTERNOON, REBECCA STOOD OUT-
side the house on St. Philip Street where Lisette used to
live, wishing she could go inside to take a look. But that wasn't
possible, because it was private property.

"Someone from North Carolina owns it now," her father was
saying. He'd been investigating the house through one of his
contacts at City Hall. "I guess they only visit during the
holidays."

"At least it wasn't demolished," Ling pointed out. All she
knew about this house was that it was one Rebecca had worked
on. She didn't know about the personal connection. She also
didn't know that Rebecca kept looking up and down the street
waiting for Frank to show up, so he could point out the house
where the locket lay hidden.

There were too many ghosts around here, Rebecca thought.
Too many secrets.

The first time Rebecca ever saw Lisette's house, it was in a
terrible state. It looked as though it had been painted with dirty

water, and the roof had buckled. Weeds as big as bushes grew up through cracks in the foundation. It was one of the oldest houses in Tremé, and years of neglect had left it on the verge of collapse.

Eventually she'd been able to go back, with Anton, and help one of the rebuilding crews turn the crumbling, moldy, bug-bitten shell into a house again. Now it looked as fresh and neat as it must have to Lisette and her mother, back before the Civil War, when they lived there.

The stuccoed brick was painted pale blue, the way Lisette had described it, and the shutters were bright yellow. Every slate on the steep roof was new and firmly fixed in place, and the gut-tering and sawtooth detail across the façade were white. New concrete steps, low and broad, led to the front door.

"It's a genuine Creole cottage," Rebecca's father told Ling. "Built back when this was a brand-new neighborhood, and many of the people living here were the community known as free people of color."

People like Lisette's mother, Rebecca thought. She'd come to New Orleans during the revolution in Haiti, and built her own little business as a seamstress, making beautiful clothes for the rich Creole families in the Quarter and on Esplanade Avenue. This neighborhood must have looked so bright and promis-ing then.

Now some of the houses on St. Philip Street looked on the verge of collapse. Three houses in particular were in a terrible state, overgrown with vines, their windows either boarded up or smashed. One was leaning sideways and looked as though one push would topple it completely. Parched boards hung loose from the frame, and the collapsing house had been tagged with black paint. It was amazing those three houses were still standing at all.

"There are more than six thousand blighted properties in the city right now," her father told them. "Some were ruined by the flood waters after the levees broke, but some were in a bad state for years. It's a difficult issue, because people feel really strongly about it."

"They think all the houses should be fixed up?" Ling asked.

"That would be ideal, but it's not really possible. Not here, not anywhere. But some people, naturally enough, don't want to see their neighborhoods decimated, with all the old properties pulled down and replaced with something new that doesn't have any character or history."

"That sounds pretty sensible to me," Ling said. "I think I'm on their side."

"But," warned Rebecca's father, "there are other equally sensible people who don't want their streets ruined by boarded-up buildings, or houses that are dangerous and decrepit. They don't want their kids playing there. They want to live in a neighborhood where they can feel proud and safe and happy, not one that looks empty and unloved."

Empty and unloved, Rebecca thought, thinking of Frank, and his sad-eyed expression.

"How do you think people feel here?" Ling asked him. "Here in Tremé, I mean."

"I think a lot of people probably feel both things," Rebecca's father said. "They don't want the neighborhood stripped bare, with all its history removed. All its *soul*. But you don't want to feel as though you're the only one who cares. You don't want to live in a place that's been left to rot or fall down around you."

Rebecca thought of what Lisette had said to her, the day they walked together to Tremé. Rebecca had been talking about the way people knocked down old buildings and just swept the past away. "The past doesn't go away," Lisette had told her. "You just can't see it anymore." They were standing right here on St. Philip Street, just as she and her father and Ling were doing today.

Rebecca looked at the three falling-down houses. Soon those houses would be gone, and their histories — everyone who'd lived and died there — would be invisible.

"You buying that house?" Someone was shouting at them from the steps of the next house. It was an old black lady, her face poking around her screen door.

"No, ma'am," Rebecca's father said. "We're just looking."

"Looking to buy another house around here?"

"No, ma'am," he said again, walking toward the lady's steps. She pulled the screen door closer, like a shield.

"Good. We don't need any more people like you coming here

and buying up our houses. How can *our* children afford to live here when you trying to make it like the Quarter?"

"I hear what you're saying, ma'am, but really — we're just tourists."

"Tourists?" She humphed. "The man who owns that house now, he's no different from a tourist. Here five minutes at Mardi Gras, and you never see him out sweeping the street. Only time you ever hear from people like him is when they're calling the police, complaining the second line's making too much noise. Complaining when the kids practicing after school! They want the pretty house, but then they decide everyone else in the street too ugly."

"I'm real sorry about that, ma'am." Her father looked quite chastened, as though he were a kid caught doing something wrong.

The screen door closed, and then opened again. This time a teenager stood in the doorway, and Rebecca recognized him right away.

"You're Raphael, right?" Rebecca asked. "We were with your aunt on Sunday. In the car on Rampart Street?"

"I remember," he nodded, smiling. "I'm Raf. My aunt is the only person who calls me Raphael."

"Raf," repeated Rebecca, smiling back at him. "I'm Rebecca, and this is my friend, Ling. And this is my father, Michael Brown."

"Maw-maw, they friends of Aunt Viola!" Raf called into the house. He stood for a moment, a mischievous grin flickering on his face, then stepped out onto the small porch.

"My grandmother says you all should go ahead and buy the house next door, but don't go calling the police when someone plays their trumpet too loud!"

Rebecca laughed, liking Raf immediately.

Raf explained he was on his way back to school, so they agreed to walk together to Basin Street High. Raf and Ling strolled ahead, Ling asking a million questions a minute.

"It didn't sound like Raf's grandmother was too pleased we fixed that house up," Rebecca whispered to her father. "Or maybe she just doesn't like the people who bought it."

"Well," Rebecca's father said, "gentrification improves neighborhoods, but it also changes them. House prices go up, rents go up, and the people who live here, maybe for generations, can't afford it anymore. What makes Tremé a distinctive neighborhood may disappear altogether."

"Becca — I was just telling Raf about the second line we saw here on Sunday," Ling called over her shoulder. "I can't believe some people complain about them."

"Haters always trying to close things down," Raf told them. "The police don't want to give permits. TV news people saying that there's a shooting or a stabbing, or people jumping on cars, and the whole thing has to end. My other grandmother, she says that as well. She says Sundays are for church, not running with second lines. 'One minute they dancing, next they drinking, next they fighting.'"

"Are they really dangerous?" Rebecca asked Raf.

"Sometimes there's trouble," he admitted, shrugging his shoulders. "But sometimes there's trouble at a Mardi Gras parade, and nobody ever says *they* should be stopped. Anywhere you have people, you have trouble. And sometimes people just looking for a time and a place to make it."

Rebecca thought about Toby Sutton, lying in wait for her somewhere in this city. At least, she thought, he wouldn't think to look for her in Tremé.

The ghost girl on Rampart Street was nowhere to be seen, Rebecca was very relieved to observe, when they crossed back into the Quarter. She and Ling were signed up to start work later that afternoon, though even Ling's enthusiasm waned when they were told it was less about gardening and more about clearing rocks and digging up weeds.

A police car sped by, this one with its siren on.

"You girls have to promise me not to go wandering off," said Rebecca's father. "I don't even like you walking over there by yourselves this afternoon."

"It's not far!" protested Rebecca. Her father still thought they were little girls.

"This city has the highest per-capita murder rate in the

country," he said, grim-faced. "And not all the guys you see in Tremé are going to be friendly high school students like Raf. Some of them may want to sell you something, and some may just want to take whatever you have on you."

"Dad!" Rebecca protested, and Ling looked shocked.

"Mr. Brown," she sputtered, "I'm sorry, but that sounds like . . . like racial profiling!"

Rebecca's father kept walking.

"It's common sense, I'm afraid. Wherever you have poor neighborhoods, in any city in the world, you have a whole lot of people who don't want to be poor. Some will get jobs to earn money, some will get it any way they can. It's human nature."

They walked in silence for a while down Orleans Avenue, until Ling asked if New Orleans really had the highest murder rate in the country. Rebecca's dad nodded.

"Wow. This city is messed up," said Ling.

"I guess," Rebecca conceded. For some reason she felt the need to defend New Orleans. "Most cities have their problems, though."

She was surprised at how protective and territorial she felt sometimes toward New Orleans. Rebecca wondered if it was because she'd gone through so much here. What happened last year here had been bewildering and frustrating and difficult, and ultimately, really frightening. But when difficult things happened to you, she realized, they became a part of who you were — like a battle wound, something that showed you'd survived.

* * *

After her father went back to work, while Ling was busy Skyping with her mother, Rebecca made her way back to the corner of Rampart. She was relieved to see that the creepy dark-haired guy — ghost? — wasn't anywhere to be seen today.

All it took was a few minutes of pacing, holding her cell phone up to one ear as a pretext for lurking on the corner, to lure Frank. In the blink of an eye, he materialized by the fire hydrant, smiling at her eagerly.

"I was just down the street," he told her. "Keeping an eye out for you. Delphine told me she saw you last night."

"Delphine?" Rebecca was confused, then remembered the beautiful ghost girl with the curls. "Oh! You mean the girl who lives in this house? The girl on the gallery?" Rebecca was so curious she almost forgot to keep her cell phone clamped to her ear. This was her alibi, after all. People in the street talking to themselves looked crazy. People in the street talking into cell phones were a dime a dozen.

"Pretty, isn't she?" said Frank, and the hazy look in his eyes made Rebecca suspect that Delphine was someone special to him. "I told her you were helping me, and that's why she let you see her. Usually she keeps to herself."

"So you were friends with her back when — you know, you were alive?"

Frank shook his head. "She's been here much longer than I have. You know, she went to school with Lisette."

Rebecca felt her heart leap at the sound of that familiar name. "She was a friend of Lisette's?"

"Yes. She used to ask me about Lisette all the time."

"But why didn't Delphine see her? Lisette walked right along Rampart Street every year."

"Delphine only haunts at night," Frank explained.

"Ahh," Rebecca exhaled. So that was why she saw Delphine last night but not today. Really, the ghost world had more rules than Temple Mead Academy.

"One of the ghosts by the cemetery," Frank said, lowering his voice as though Delphine were around to hear it, "told me that when Delphine was alive, a box of candied fruit was delivered to the house, meant for her mother. But Delphine was greedy, and stole one. The candies were poisoned, so she died. I don't know if that's the true story. You don't like to ask, do you? Especially if you have to shout up three floors."

"I guess." It was odd to think about ghosts gossiping among each other, speculating about how another ghost died. Another way the ghost world was like Temple Mead. "I wonder why they wanted to poison her mother."

"All I know is that Delphine had three sisters, and that her father was a rich Creole with a plantation up on the Cane River. . . ."

"Creoles!" Rebecca had another brainwave. "Maybe she'll know something about the family who lived on Esplanade. You know — the Moussons? The artist's cousins? So we can figure out who should get the locket."

She was about to tell Frank that she had an idea of how to spell the name now, but remembered just in time that he couldn't read or write.

"Maybe." Frank didn't sound persuaded. "She died years before I arrived here — sometime in the 1850s, it was. So I don't think she would know much. She's always stuck up there on the gallery. I think I'm the only person she speaks to. The only ghost, that is."

Frank smiled again, a secret smile. Rebecca felt a little pang, something that almost felt like jealousy. She couldn't possibly be falling for a ghost. That would be ridiculous.

"Um, so — doesn't this Delphine ever come down from the gallery?" Rebecca burbled. She had to pull herself together.

"She tells me that if I ever really need her, she will," Frank said, gazing up at the now-empty gallery. "Perhaps if she could help find the locket, it would make up for the candy she stole. Then she wouldn't be a ghost anymore, either."

It seemed to Rebecca that poor Delphine had already paid a very high price for stealing a piece of candy, and maybe this was just wishful thinking on Frank's part. She checked the time on her phone: She and Ling had to report for duty at the school in twenty minutes.

"I have to get back," she told Frank. "But I wanted to tell you — I'm going to be in Tremé again this afternoon, at the high school that backs onto St. Philip Street . . ."

"St. Philip Street? That's where the house is! The house with the locket."

"Really? So — well, OK. Maybe later you could —"

"I'll see you there," Frank interrupted, and promptly disappeared. Rebecca had wanted to ask him about the dark-haired man she'd seen lurking here on Sunday afternoon, but it was too late.

CHAPTER NINE

REBECCA IMMEDIATELY SAW THE DIFFERENCES between the Big Sweep on Sunday and the Basin Street High after-school cleanup. Here, there were no team T-shirts, high fives, or promises of barbecue. Instead, there were a few dozen high school kids, mostly still in their uniform of blue Polo shirts and pants, some of whom appeared to have been drafted in because they were on detention.

The teacher in charge, Mr. Boyd, preferred shouting to speaking, and clearly had a very low opinion of that afternoon's motley crew of workers.

"Working for your school is a privilege!" he roared. "I want to see smiling faces and calloused hands! Anyone not giving one hundred percent will find themselves back here on Saturday giving two hundred!"

Ling and Rebecca exchanged a worried glance.

"We not on detention," one older boy pointed out, gesturing to his group of friends. "We just volunteers."

Mr. Boyd stared at him so long and so hard, Rebecca thought he was willing the poor kid's head to explode.

"My daddy volunteered in the Korean War," Mr. Boyd said in a low voice, which sounded even more dangerous than his shouting. "Do you think that meant he didn't follow orders at all times? DO YOU THINK HE TALKED BACK TO THE SERGEANT?"

"No, sir." The boy hung his head, and some of the girls tittered.

"The only volunteers we have today are our two UN observers here." Mr. Boyd gestured with his clipboard at Ling and Rebecca.

Everyone else looked at them. The range of expressions ran from bemused to hostile. Rebecca felt her face burning up, and she looked around for Raf and his friend Junior. At least they were smiling.

"I know you think you're do-gooders," said Mr. Boyd, looking from Rebecca to Ling. "But this is no spring-break picnic. No MTV here, filming you dancing on a beach. So, no working for an hour then taking pictures of yourself in a cheerleading pyramid. Got it?"

Rebecca's tongue was frozen to the roof of her mouth, but Ling surprised her by answering right away.

"Yes, sir!"

"I need workers, not shirkers. I got enough trouble on my

hands with American Idol here." He glowered at Junior, whose smile instantly disappeared. "So you, Uptown Girl!"

Rebecca realized he meant *her.*

"You I want ground-clearing on St. Philip with American Idol. If he starts singing, hit him with a rake. And you, Miss Thing!" He nodded at Ling. "I'll start you over there with the Baton Rouge crew, and then you'll be troubleshooting as I see fit. Go, go, go!"

Ling waved a nervous good-bye to Rebecca and scuttled across the school yard after Mr. Boyd.

"Those girls came down here from Baton Rouge?" Rebecca whispered to Raf. They looked as though they were all wearing the Basin Street High uniform.

"No, they're just baton twirlers who march with the band. Ling'll be all right — Mr. Boyd likes them. It's the detention girls he's really hard on. He calls them the Jailbirds. And the boys on detention are the Angolese, because he says they'll end up in Angola Penitentiary if they don't change their ways."

"What does he call *you*?"

"Kermit, like Kermit Ruffins, because I play the trumpet. And because I'm green. Junior is American Idol because he thinks he's gonna be a star. Brando over here is Stanley. We don't really understand that one."

Rebecca didn't get it, either, but she knew that it was best not to ask questions of Mr. Boyd. She followed Raf toward a broad grassy verge where houses possibly used to stand. Now it was a sprawling patch of weeds and tangled vines. A large tarpaulin was spread over a section of land already cleared, and Raf's friend Brando, who was tall and thin, his hair almost shorn off, explained the drill. They had to pull out or dig up everything growing here and throw it onto the tarpaulin or into a trash bag.

Uprooting these giant weeds proved harder than it looked, even though the soil was damp from the recent rain. Rebecca soon found herself on hands and knees, stabbing into the ground with a metal fork and trying to twist up the roots. It was like twirling oversized spaghetti, though the smell was much earthier. Raf worked alongside her, tugging at roots with his hands.

"Have you always lived in Tremé?" she asked him, keeping her voice low in case Mr. Boyd was patrolling nearby.

"Yes. But *we* don't call it Tremé so much," Raf told Rebecca, nodding up at Brando and Junior. "My grandparents call it that, but we say we're from the Sixth Ward. When we play down on Jackson Square or Bourbon Street, we call ourselves the Sixth Sense. That's what we write on Junior's hat, anyway. Don't know if anyone sees it."

"You always go down to the Quarter to play?"

"That's where the tourists are at. They don't come up here into the Sixth or the Seventh Ward. I think the police drive up and down Rampart Street to keep *us* out of the Quarter and to keep the tourists in."

Rebecca nodded, absorbing that. "Do you play on Bourbon Street?" she asked.

"Jackson Square or Royal Street. On Bourbon it's too loud, with all the music coming out of the bars. There's always someone up onstage pretending to be Jimmy Buffett. You want to hear *real* New Orleans music, you need to be out on the street.

"You not gonna hear Kermit Ruffins on Bourbon Street," said Raf. "You not gonna hear Trombone Shorty!"

"Sixth Ward!" whooped Brando, drawing a hard look from Mr. Boyd. Everyone rapidly resumed their weeding, heads down.

When Rebecca finally straightened up, her back aching from too much bending over, she was so startled she dropped her gardening fork.

Frank was sitting on the steps of a green house across the street.

A man wearing an ENTERGY uniform walked up the steps, right through Frank, and knocked on the door. So this couldn't be the derelict house where Frank was killed.

Rebecca didn't know what to do. She couldn't just wander off across the street. Raf was only a few feet away, industriously weeding, and Junior was pushing a wheelbarrow, trying to make the others laugh by swerving it around in circles.

Frank seemed to sense her hesitation. He stood up, and gestured down the street, toward the three collapsing houses she'd noticed earlier that day. He seemed to be pointing to the first house, the one with vines pushing their way through the walls and out the roof, and twisting up along nearby power lines. Its drainpipes were rusted over and the two front windows were sealed with boards. A locked, chained gate protected the front door. It would be incredibly difficult to get in or out of this house, as far as Rebecca could tell. Even the collapsed chimney was knitted over with an entangled jungle of vines.

It hit her then: *This was Frank's house.*

She turned back to look for Frank, but he was gone.

Raf glanced up to see her staring desperately in the direction of the houses.

"Those houses down there look kind of dangerous," she said, thinking quickly.

"Yeah, you right. They going next week."

"Going?"

"The city owns all this land now, and they want to put up some more school buildings. Those houses are coming down on Monday."

Rebecca stuck her gardening fork into a damp patch of ground, pretending to concentrate on shredding her way through the weeds, but her mind was buzzing. Frank had found someone to help him just in time, because the house — and anything hidden within — was going to be smashed to smithereens in a matter of days.

The locket *might* get found in the process, but it was more likely that it would be crushed beneath the wheels, or in the steel jaws, of some giant bulldozer or digger. Or someone would find it and take it, not knowing that this meant Frank would be doomed to the misery of the spirit world for eternity. But how on earth was Rebecca supposed to break in? She wanted to help Frank — she really did. But it all seemed too hard.

"What's the big hurry?" Rebecca asked Raf, trying to sound casual. "I mean, the school year is almost over."

"The school wants those houses gone. All the older people around here, too, they keep shouting about them to the city councilors. One of the houses — the far one, with the graffiti on it? Some drug dealers were using it for a while. There was a shooting, right here in the street. Another time this old man, Mr. Robert we call him, he was sitting in his own house watching TV. Outside they all started shooting at each other and a bullet went right through the screen."

"Was he OK?"

"He was OK, but the TV was shot dead. That's what he went around saying, 'My TV got itself shot dead.' He'd lived here for years and years, long as I can remember. But after that his daughter came to get him, and made him move in with her in Gentilly. My aunt was saying we should all move as well."

"*I'd* want to move," said Ling, walking over to them. She tossed cold bottles of water to Rebecca and Raf.

"Where we gonna go?" Raf asked her, uncapping his bottle. "Where's it any better? Anywhere we can afford, I mean. At least here my daddy can walk to work."

"Maybe someone could fix those houses up?" Rebecca suggested, nervously taking a big gulp of water. "Old houses like those are a piece of the city's history. Sad to think of that history gone forever."

"Better to have a vacant lot than a fixed-up house nobody can afford. Anyway, nobody would want to live in *that* house." Raf gestured with the end of Junior's discarded rake toward the house at the near end of the row — Frank's house. "People say it's haunted."

"Really?" Rebecca tried to keep her voice down. "What do they say? What have they seen?"

"I don't know." Raf shrugged. "Everyone's got stories like that. Most of the houses in Tremé must be haunted, right? People been living and dying here for a long, long time."

"Have *you* ever seen a ghost?"

Raf raised his eyebrows. He was smiling, but Rebecca wasn't sure if he was laughing at her or not.

"This is New Orleans," he said. "Anything is possible."

"A lot of talking going on over here, but not much working." Mr. Boyd seemed to spring up out of nowhere. He stood with his hands on his hips, surveying the remaining patches of straggly weeds with obvious disapproval. "Your average hungry rabbit would have done a better job. You, Uptown Girl! You're distracting my labor force. I'm transferring you to litter collection. But Miss Thing — you have leadership potential. You're promoted to lieutenant of plant-unloading."

Ling scampered off toward a plant-laden flatbed truck, and Rebecca was handed a heavy-duty black trash bag and a stick with a blunt-looking spike. She didn't mind being moved. At least this way she could get close to Frank's house and really snoop around. Maybe there'd be a broken window, or just one plank of wood nailed across the back door.

Rebecca wandered along the chain-link fence that marked the old boundary of the school, plucking litter from the scraggly weeds. Out of the corner of one eye she examined the house. One hard tug on the overgrown vines stretching over the roof, and the whole building would probably come down. Its walls were stripped of any color by the sun and the wind and the rain.

As she edged closer, Rebecca could smell mold, and something else — something awful, like the decaying carcass of a dead animal. Maybe the walls and floorboards inside were rotten. Rebecca shuddered. She poked her spiked stick into a discarded orange juice carton and heaved it into her trash bag. If she managed to get inside the house, what else would she find in there? Raccoons? Snakes? Rats? Roaches? Oh, yes, there'd be roaches everywhere.

Rebecca swiveled to get a better look at the back of the house and gasped so loudly it sounded like a squeak. The dark-haired man she'd seen on Rampart Street on Sunday was sitting on the back stairs of the house, resting on one elbow, and staring straight at her.

He scowled at Rebecca in a way that annoyed and also frightened her. She glanced up the street toward the weed patch where Raf and Brando and Junior were hard at work. If she screamed, they'd hear her. If he made one single move toward her, she'd scream her lungs out and lunge at him with the spiked stick.

Was he a ghost? And could ghosts attack? The only ghosts Rebecca knew were nice ones — Lisette and Frank. But maybe some were mean.

But the dark-haired man didn't move. He just looked at her with contempt, as though he were regarding a roach after he'd crushed it under his shoe.

"Don't you be thinking of trying to get in here," he said.

"I'm not," Rebecca said, affronted. "I'm just looking, that's all."

"Yeah," said the mean man. "I know what you looking for. I seen you talking to him."

"I don't know . . . I don't know what you're saying." Rebecca's heart was thumping so hard, it was about to dance its way out of her mouth and flop onto the ground. Talking to who? Raf? Junior? Mr. Boyd?

"First I seen you walking with *her*, and now I seen you talking to *him*." The man glared up at Rebecca, and she instinctively took a step back. "And that tells me that here's a person who likes to meddle in other people's business. Here's a person who thinks she can interfere."

"Excuse me, but who are you?" Rebecca demanded. The tone of his voice was beyond rude. "I'm here to help the school. I'm not meddling in anyone's business."

He snorted, and shook his head.

"I ain't talking about no school," he said, screwing up his face to suggest she was the crazy one. "I'm talking about *history*. You trying to mess with history. You're trying to mess with *eternity*."

He reached for his jacket lapel, pulling it back in what felt like slow motion. *Scream*, Rebecca told herself. *Run*. But it was too late. He was reaching for a gun, she realized, tucked into the waistband of his trousers. She didn't know what she'd done to make him so angry, but now there was nothing she could do except stand there in a panic, her head swimming, her heart *oomphing* louder than any brass band.

But he was holding open his jacket, she saw now, and there was no gun. No gun, no knife, no weapon of any kind. Just a broad dark splotch of dried blood, like a gravy stain on his shirt. He was showing her his wound. She'd been right the first time she saw him: This man was a ghost.

"If I'm damned for all time," he said slowly, staring at her hard with those mean, bloodshot eyes, "then so is your boy Frank. You understand?"

So this horrible man must have seen Rebecca walking with Lisette, and he must have seen her talking to Frank. And now he was choosing to make himself visible to her, to give her this warning.

"So," he said, closing his jacket again, "unless you're planning on joining us real soon here in the afterlife, best you keep away."

Rebecca opened her mouth to speak, but nothing came out. She felt dizzy and cold, despite the heat of the day, and she had to grab on to the chain-link fence to keep standing upright. She closed her eyes for a moment, fighting back nausea, and when she opened them again the ghost had disappeared. The busted-up wooden steps leading to the back door were empty.

So Frank wasn't the only ghost in New Orleans who knew about the locket under the floorboards. Who was this guy, and why did he hate Frank — and now Rebecca — so much?

CHAPTER TEN

1 DON'T UNDERSTAND," LING SAID TO REBECCA. They were sitting in the kitchen of their rented house while her father talked on the phone in the next room. "Why won't you tell me what's wrong?"

"I just have a really bad headache," Rebecca repeated, staring down at the ridges of the wooden table. "Too much sun today or something."

"It wasn't even sunny." Ling looked skeptical. "Is this about Anton?"

"No. This isn't about Anton. I haven't even thought about him today."

More lies. She'd been thinking about Anton ever since the mean ghost accosted her. She was desperate to call or text him, and tell him what was happening. But there was no point. He'd just tell her to keep away from Frank and have nothing to do with any of this.

"Becca, we've been friends *forever*," Ling said. "Why can't you tell me why you're so unhappy? Is it something *I've* done?"

"No," Rebecca muttered. She stood up, avoiding Ling's frank gaze. She hated hurting her friend like this. "You haven't done anything. Really. I just need some time alone. I'm going for a walk, OK? Tell my Dad I went to the pharmacy or something. I'll be back . . . soon."

On the corner of Rampart Street, she paced up and down, impatiently waiting for Frank. There was more traffic at this time of night, with people driving home from work or arriving in the Quarter for dinner, but — luckily — the usual dearth of pedestrians. Rampart Street wasn't the kind of place anyone went for a dusk stroll.

"I'm here," Frank said, materializing in front of her in a way that might have seemed magical if it weren't so unsettling — especially as the first thing she noticed was the blue gleam of his eyes.

"*You* have been keeping things from me," she said, jabbing a finger toward him. A finger, she realized, that could touch nothing but thin air. "You sit there on St. Philip Street, pointing at a house, and then you just disappear! No warning that there might be another ghost waiting there for me!"

"I'm sorry." Frank hung his head. "I couldn't come over. I just couldn't. He could have hurt me. Ghosts can do that to each other, you know. They go straight for the wound."

"Great." The more Rebecca learned about the world of ghosts, the more it seemed like a dismal and terrifying place. "Who is he?"

"His name is Gideon Mason. I thought if he didn't see me with you, he wouldn't know . . . I mean, he might think you were just some busybody snooping around the back of an old house. Not someone who was trying to help *me* in particular."

Rebecca shuddered. "It's too late. He's already seen me with you. He said he saw me with Lisette last year, and that he thinks I'm some kind of meddler in the spirit world. And now he's threatening to hurt *me*. Is that even possible? Can ghosts hurt people?"

"I don't think so," Frank said, but he didn't look sure. "I know *I* can't. I've heard . . ."

"Heard what?" Frank wasn't reassuring Rebecca one bit.

"I've heard that ghosts can lure people into dangerous situations. To the brink of a cliff, or an open window. But they can't physically attack you, as such. Not that I know of, anyway. Rebecca, I would never put you in that situation. You have to believe me."

"Why do I have to believe you?" snapped Rebecca. "I don't even know you! You could be the most evil and manipulative ghost in the whole world! This whole locket story could be a ruse to — what was it you said? Lure me into a dangerous situation?"

Frank looked hurt.

"Why would I do that? What have I got against *you*?"

"You tell me," retorted Rebecca, her face flushing with anger. "Who knows what goes on in your stupid ghost head? Is there really a locket, or did you just make that up?"

"I've told you everything!" Frank protested. "Please, listen. That man you saw today, Gideon Mason. He's the man who murdered me."

Rebecca caught her breath. It was one thing to know that Frank had been murdered, and another thing to realize she'd come face-to-face with his actual killer. She shivered, thinking of Gideon Mason's angry face, and his threats.

"And then he was murdered himself," Frank went on. He was standing closer to Rebecca now, his blue eyes boring into her.

"Why does he still hate *you*? Why isn't he all aggrieved with the person who murdered him?"

"Let me . . . ," Frank said, pausing as though he didn't know how to go on. "Let me go back a bit. When the artist gave me the locket, Mason was on the dock as well. He must have seen me get the locket, and the money, because he followed me all the way to the house I showed you, the one on St. Philip Street."

"But I don't get it." Rebecca frowned, trying to make sense of the geography of Frank's story. "What were you doing in Tremé? Why didn't you just walk along the river to Esplanade? St. Philip was really out of your way."

Frank was silent. He wouldn't look her in the eyes.

Rebecca shook her head. "Don't tell me you weren't taking the locket to the house on Esplanade," Rebecca said. "Please."

"I was, I was!" he said. "I was walking toward Esplanade Avenue, just as you say, but then — well, I changed my mind. It was wrong of me, I know. But something wicked came into my head, and instead of going straight to the house, I went to look for my friend. His name was Connor, and we'd worked on the docks together. I wanted to find him so we could have a drink with the money I'd been given."

He hung his head and didn't go on. Rebecca couldn't question him for a minute or so because a couple was crossing Rampart Street and about to walk right past her. She stared at her phone as they passed, pretending to check a nonexistent message.

"So you went to this house," Rebecca said at last, when there was no one around to hear her. "And then this Gideon Mason guy attacked you?"

"Yes, in the street," Frank explained, "and then he dragged me into the house. It was a place used by the gang he belonged to, but nobody else was there. He stabbed me and I fell face-down on the floor. The last thing I could manage to do when I was alive was slip the locket out of my pocket and let it drop between the floorboards. I didn't want him to have it."

Rebecca swallowed. Hearing someone talk about their own death was awful. And what must it be like to then see your murderer in the ghost world, roaming the very same streets where he hunted you down?

"He took my money, which wasn't much. That's when two other men arrived at the house. He was boasting about how he'd found a good mark, because I was carrying a silver locket as well as money. They demanded to see the locket, and he didn't have it. They searched my body and couldn't find it. Then they all started shouting. They said he'd stolen the locket, or else he'd made the story up to justify murdering someone in their house and putting them all at risk of detection. The others didn't trust him and they were angry and drunk. There was a fight and he was stabbed."

Rebecca realized she was holding her breath.

"So — you were there — I mean, the ghost of you was there?" she whispered.

"Watching, yes. But when I saw my murderer fall over, bleeding, I left. Straight through the walls and back to Rampart Street. All I could see around me were ghosts. I was terrified. Delphine was the one who calmed me down. She called out to me, and told me that it wasn't so bad being a ghost. She was wrong, but . . . Well. There was nothing I could do about it. Not until now."

"So, Gideon Mason died, obviously," Rebecca said softly, trying not to feel glad that he'd gotten his comeuppance. All these murders! New Orleans must have been a dangerous place in those days.

"Yes, he died. The first time I went back to the house I saw him, and that's when I knew for certain. Another ghost told me his name — I didn't know who he was, of course. And eventually he figured out that the locket must still be inside the house, because I kept going back there. He told me that if I hadn't hidden it, he wouldn't have been murdered that night. He thinks he would have had a chance to redeem himself for the crimes he's committed, and to be a better man. Instead he's a murderer who was murdered himself. He's going to be a ghost forever."

"And that's why he wants to punish you." Rebecca understood now.

"He doesn't want me to be saved. He doesn't want the locket to be found. He wants it to be lost, or destroyed, so I'll never be able to redeem myself for breaking the promise I made." Frank looked stricken. "You have to help me!"

"I want to, really I do," Rebecca told him, and she meant it: He sounded so anguished. But at the same time, she didn't like this new ghost, and she was afraid of what he might try to do, especially if he considered himself damned for eternity anyway. "I'm just. . . . scared, that's all," she admitted.

"You have nothing to be afraid of!" Frank was almost shouting at her. "You have to believe me! He can't hurt you! He's only a ghost!"

"Easy for you to say!" Rebecca raised her voice, too. "He threatened me today, and it was really scary, OK? I want to find this locket. I really, really want to find this locket!"

But she was shouting into thin air, because Frank had disappeared.

This was too much. How dare he just disappear on her? First he only told her half-truths, and now he was running off — wherever ghosts ran off to — right in the middle of a conversation. She swung around on the spot, in case he'd just decided to materialize somewhere else.

"Rebecca? Rebecca Brown? Oh my god, is that you?"

This wasn't Frank's voice. It was a girl's voice, coming from . . . where? Rebecca felt dazed. *Not more ghosts*, she pleaded silently. *Please, no more ghosts*. She couldn't take any more attention from the spirit world.

"It's us, Amy and Jessica. Remember? From Temple Mead."

Rebecca shook her head, the way a dog might shake water from its coat, and tried to get her brain in gear. There was a car parked there at the curb, a silver SUV with tinted windows. But one of the windows was down, and there were two girls sitting in the car, staring at her as though she were naked. Amy and Jessica from Temple Mead. Her so-called friends. The last people — evil ghosts aside — that she expected or wanted to see here on Rampart Street.

Rebecca blinked, realizing that Amy was speaking. "Jessica didn't believe me, but I thought it was you, so I pulled over. Are you OK? You seem kind of upset."

"What? No. I'm fine," Rebecca burbled. She had no idea how long they'd been sitting there, or how much they'd heard.

"Hey, Rebecca!" called Jessica, leaning forward to wave. She'd always been the friendlier of the two, though that was a relative thing. Really, looking back, she'd just been marginally less disapproving.

"Hey, Jessica." Rebecca bent down to wave back. She wished they'd drive off and leave her alone, but she knew that was extremely unlikely. Amy and Jessica could smell gossip from the other side of Lake Pontchartrain.

She couldn't believe how much they'd changed in a year. Jessica's red hair was now in a chic pixie cut, and she wasn't wearing glasses. Rebecca couldn't even tell if Amy was still skinny, because she was completely shrouded by a thick blonde mane of hair. It had to be extensions, Rebecca thought. Amy's hair a year ago was short, and as wispy as a baby's.

"So, what are you doing here?" Amy was looking her up and down, and Rebecca wished she'd changed before running out of the house. Her jeans had grass stains on both knees from the gardening this afternoon, and the hoodie she'd slung on smelled like damp soil.

"I'm just in town for the week with my dad and my friend. We're staying in the Quarter."

"Oh, we know that! Like, everyone saw you on Prytania Street on Monday. What I mean is, what are you doing *here* standing around on Rampart Street? It's totally dangerous, you know. There's a really bad neighborhood just over there." Amy nodded her head in the direction of Tremé.

"I was just . . ." Rebecca couldn't think of a single thing she might be doing here. "Standing around alone like a loser" seemed the answer they expected. "Ah, I just got dropped off. I have to go . . . meet my dad now."

"We're meeting up with Amy's parents," Jessica told her, and Amy's mouth slid into a pout. Rebecca remembered that face well. She used to make it at school when Jessica told Rebecca *anything*, no matter how dull.

"We're going to Arnaud's," Amy said, in a tone that suggested Rebecca would never be admitted to such a venerable establishment.

"So, are you lost?" Rebecca couldn't resist a bit of meanness herself. "The Quarter's that way."

She gestured over her shoulder.

"God, no! We come downtown all the time now — don't we, Jess?"

"Oh. Yeah. We're so *over* Uptown."

"Over it! I was just saying, I wish Peristyle was still open. That was my total favorite."

"If we were going there this would be the best parking spot ever," Jessica observed.

"I know, right?"

Rebecca thought her head was about to drop off her shoulders. She'd forgotten how Jessica and Amy could spout inanities for what felt like hours on end.

"Well, good to see you guys," she said, standing up straight again. "I don't want to make you late for dinner, and I should be . . . getting back."

"Hey, wait!" Amy said before Rebecca had the chance to turn away. "Won't we be seeing you on Thursday night?"

"You know." Jessica was leaning so far forward, her head was almost resting on the dashboard. "At the Spring Dance. The boys have organized it this year. Can you believe that? I bet you they'll totally spike the punch."

"It's at the country club," drawled Amy. She looked at Rebecca with wide eyes, feigning innocence. "So Anton hasn't asked you, then?"

"I was sure he would." Jessica looked disappointed. "Amy said I was totally *deluded*, but . . ."

"Guys move on," said Amy, obviously unwilling to let Jessica's lament continue uninterrupted. "It's horrible, but once you leave town, they just don't remember you. Not if you were just, you know, like a short-term thing."

"Sort of like a summer romance," suggested Jessica.

"You know," said Amy. "A vacation hook-up."

"Actually," said Rebecca, her face burning with anger, "I *will* be seeing you on Thursday night. Anton asked me. To the dance."

"Cool!" said Jessica, but her smile faded so quickly she must have spotted the look on Amy's face.

"So — see you there!" Rebecca gave them a breezy wave, and walked away, suppressing a groan. What had she done? Not only did she not want to go to the dance, she was barely on speaking terms with Anton. She couldn't believe she was going to have to call and beg him to take her. He could easily have asked some-one else by now. Phil might have asked someone else, too, and if that was the case, what was she going to tell Ling? Boys were as slippery as ghosts when it came to getting them to do stuff you wanted them to do. They tended to have minds of their own.

There was only one thing to do, and that was lie.

CHAPTER ELEVEN

I T'S JUST, LING IS DESPERATE TO GO," REBECCA told Anton, pinning her phone to one ear with her shoulder while she unlocked the gate. "She was really upset when I said no. I think maybe she's into Phil or something."

"Really?" Anton sounded dubious. "She met him twice for about five minutes."

"Not just that," Rebecca said quickly. "She's working really hard this week with all the volunteer projects, and this will be our only chance to have fun. She was all excited when Phil mentioned it, and I realize I'm just being really unfair."

"So, do *you* want to go?" Anton asked her. "I don't want you to be forced into it or something."

Rebecca was in the courtyard now, brushing her free hand against the rubbery leaves of a banana plant.

"I do want to go, really," she told Anton, and when she said it, Rebecca knew that she meant it. She wanted to see Anton again. Despite what had happened between them in the cemetery, she knew he would still make her heart skip in that particular way. She wanted to face up to all those Temple Mead girls and show them that she wasn't scared or intimidated. She wanted to dress up and go out with Ling and have some fun.

"If the — if the offer is still open, that is," she stammered. "If you haven't asked someone else. Have you?"

Anton exhaled, something between a sigh and a laugh.

"Who else would I ask?"

"I don't know. Julie Casworth Young?"

"Please. She laughs like a mouse with asthma. And she probably had her date and her dress all organized last October."

"You missed your chance," Rebecca teased.

"Just as well. She'd probably make me wear a pink tie."

"Maybe I'll make you wear a pink tie."

"Maybe I'll make you wear a pink dress."

"Yeah, right." They both laughed, and then fell silent.

"So," Anton said at last. "Friends again, OK? No more arguments between now and Thursday."

That would be easy, Rebecca thought. They weren't *seeing* each other between now and Thursday. And no way was she telling Anton anything about Frank, Gideon Mason, and their all-eternity death grudge.

"But just one thing," Anton added. "Toby is definitely . . ."

"Anton! No Toby, OK? I don't want to hear another word about him." Rebecca had more important things to worry about than Toby Sutton, not that she could discuss them with Anton. "No arguments before Thursday, remember?"

"OK. No arguments."

Back inside the house, Ling and her father were waiting for her, drinking iced tea at the kitchen table.

"How about Cochon for dinner?" her dad suggested. "Ling has never eaten fried alligator."

"I'm not sure I want to," Ling said, screwing up her face. "Don't tell me it tastes just like chicken."

"It kind of does," Rebecca told her. "Hey, I just spoke to Anton. I said we'd go with him and Phil to the Spring Dance on Thursday. If you still want to go, of course."

Ling's face brightened.

"Why not?" she said, smiling up at Rebecca. She looked relieved, probably thinking that Rebecca's bad mood was all about the spat with Anton, and that everything was fine now.

"You don't mind, do you, Dad?" Rebecca turned to her father. "It's the St. Simeon's thing at the country club. It's not a big deal."

Her father, checking e-mail on his iPad, peered at her over his glasses.

"If that's how you want to spend your Thursday night," he said, looking at her as though she was crazy. "I never pictured you two as country club types, but there's a first time for everything. Are you sure?"

"I guess," said Rebecca, even though she wasn't sure at all. "It'll be . . . fun."

"Oh!" Ling gasped and smacked her hand down on the table.

"What's wrong?"

"We don't have anything to wear. All I brought with me were jeans and shorts and T-shirts. I have one sundress, but it's not really Spring Dance at the country club, if you know what I'm saying."

"I don't have anything, either," Rebecca admitted. All the Temple Mead girls would be dressed up like Halloween candy, she was sure, shining and rustling and sickening. She looked over at her father, still studying his phone. "I guess we won't be able to go then."

"All right, all right," he said without even looking up. "Tomorrow morning. Shopping for dresses. One hour only. Price limit to be agreed in advance."

"Thanks so much, Mr. Brown!" Ling was all smiles.

"Thanks, Dad. Um — we might need shoes as well. But we can totally do our own hair and makeup!"

"We might need some makeup," Ling whispered to Rebecca.

Rebecca's father rolled his eyes.

"I'm glad it's not a big deal," he said. "Actually, if this *isn't* a big deal, I'd hate to see what a big deal looks like."

* * *

Ling and Rebecca bustled into Miss Viola's small, overstuffed vintage store as soon as it opened at ten. Within five minutes Miss Viola had sent Rebecca's dad out to buy himself a coffee at CC's, because, in her opinion, men "cluttered up the shop." She pulled a series of '80s party dresses from the rack for the girls to try on.

"Now *this* one is very Madonna," she announced, flapping something short and black at Ling. "But *this* one is more *Falcon's Crest*," she said, holding up a poufy purple dress with big sleeves. "Not that you girls will remember that."

In one of the changing rooms, pulling off her jeans, Rebecca's phone kept buzzing. Aurelia was sending her text after text. After much wheedling and negotiating, Aunt Claudia had said Aurelia could join the volunteers at Basin Street High for one afternoon only. Both St. Simeon's and Temple Mead were ending classes early that day, and Aurelia was catching the streetcar into the Quarter.

"You'd think they'd let them out early on Thursday," Ling shouted through the curtained divide after Rebecca told her the news. "So they could spend the time getting reading for the Spring Dance."

"They probably booked the entire Belladonna Spa this afternoon for mani-pedis," Rebecca said. "You won't be able to drive down Magazine Street for all the illegally parked SUVs."

"Tell me what you think," said Ling. Rebecca peeked out

behind her brocade curtain to see Ling step out in the Madonna number, which was short and black, with a peplum. Ling looked lovely in it, walking around on her tiptoes.

"Just the right length for a petite young lady," said Miss Viola approvingly, twirling her finger in the air to get Ling to turn around. "A little big around the waist, but I don't have a smaller size. That's no problem. We can take that in for you."

"Is there time?" Ling asked.

"Baby, my family are Indians. We're the fastest sewers in New Orleans."

Ling was looking puzzled — Miss Viola was *Indian?* — so Rebecca thought she should explain.

"She means Mardi Gras Indians," she said, zipping up her dress. "It's a big African-American tradition here. Some people mask as Indians, and wear amazing costumes and big head-dresses made of feathers and beads. I read a book about it."

"You never seen Mardi Gras Indians in person?" Miss Viola asked. Rebecca shook her head. "You had to read a *book*?"

"Last year during Carnival all I saw were the big parades. The ones down St. Charles."

Miss Viola looked appalled. "Tell that nephew of mine to take you inside his daddy's house. Now, how about *your* dress?"

Rebecca stepped out fully from her fitting room. Her dress was jade green, with narrow shoulder straps and a flouncy skirt. Rebecca twirled, admiring her reflection in the mirror. The green looked good with her dark hair, she decided. She wondered what Anton would think.

"That color looks beautiful on you," Ling said. "Maybe silver shoes?"

Rebecca's dad returned to admire their purchases, and to pay Miss Viola. Rebecca expected him to head straight downtown for one of his endless meetings, but outside in the street he surprised her.

"How would you girls like to take a walk around a cemetery with me?"

"When?" Ling said, with no enthusiasm in her voice.

"Which cemetery?" Rebecca asked, hoping that it wasn't Lafayette. She really didn't feel like going back there.

"Whoa — no need to thank me!" Rebecca's dad teased. "I thought you guys were history buffs? I've got an hour free, and I thought we could go to St. Louis Number One. It's the oldest cemetery in New Orleans."

"Oh — now? Great!" Ling's face relaxed. "That's the place the Voodoo Queen is buried, right? Marie Laveau?"

Rebecca's dad nodded.

"So let's go," Rebecca said. She didn't know what else to do now, anyway, except avoid scary Gideon Mason, and obsess about how impossible it would be to get into that boarded-up derelict house. And Aurelia wouldn't be descending until after two.

"I just thought if you meant later on," Ling was burbling, "it would be a problem, because I'm meeting someone for a coffee. . . ."

"Who are you meeting?" Rebecca asked. Ling didn't know anyone in New Orleans.

"Just . . . ah, Phil," she said, suddenly engrossed by the poster display in a shop window. "At the Croissant d'or. You don't mind, do you?"

"Of course not," Rebecca said.

Well, well, well. Those two weren't wasting any time. Then she remembered her lie to Anton, about Ling being desperate to go to the Spring Dance. He'd probably told Phil. Did boys talk to each other like that? Who knew?

"I thought you could spend some quality time with Aurelia and then we'd walk over to the school together," said Ling, still looking in the shop window. Her cheeks were pink. "If that's OK."

"So — cemetery, yes?" Rebecca's dad asked, looking faintly amused. "Let's drop your bags off and go. You never know — maybe there's a surprise waiting for you there. And I'm not talking about the tomb of Marie Laveau."

"What kind of surprise?" Rebecca asked. Probably a carriage ride, or some other hokey tourist thing.

"You'll have to wait and see," said her father, all mysterious and self-important. "But I'll give you one clue. I was wrong about the spelling of the name you asked me about the other day. It's M-U-S-S-O-N."

"What is your dad talking about?" Ling murmured. Rebecca froze, but her father smiled.

"Rebecca was asking me the other day if I knew of a local artist by the name of Musson here in New Orleans. Well . . . let's just go to the cemetery. All will be revealed!"

The St. Louis Number One Cemetery had the same high white walls as Lafayette Cemetery. But it was much older, smaller and mazelike, with less room for avenues of trees or vast, fancy tombs like the Bowmans'. The paths underfoot were damp and sandy, and the view over the walls was of redbrick projects and high-rise hotels. It was crammed in every direction with graves — some so neglected they were just crumbling piles of brick, others freshly whitewashed and etched on both ends with family names. The unmarked tomb said to be Marie Laveau's was scarred with graffiti kisses, tributes of flowers, candles, and trinkets heaped at its base.

"Man, we're never going to find this tomb," Ling muttered to Rebecca. They crunched up and down rows, trying to be methodical, but it wasn't easy. This wasn't an orderly place: It was a jumble of over three hundred years of burials. "How do you spell the name again?"

"I think it's over this way," Rebecca's father said, checking the time. "It better be. This place is closing in ten minutes."

Tour groups were filing out, and the caretaker wandered around jingling his keys.

"I think we missed some over here," Rebecca said in desperation, though she was certain they'd already circled this exact spot. How could they miss a tomb in such a small cemetery? She stopped to shake a pebble out of one shoe, feeling guilty about leaning against someone's tomb in order to prop herself up.

"Rebecca!" Ling called. "Here it is!"

Rebecca tugged on her shoe and raced over to where the others were standing. A railing and elaborate gate enclosed the tomb, and Rebecca pressed against it, scanning the names engraved on the marble slab.

Musson, Musson, Musson — one after another. The very second name was a Desirée — the name Frank had said! — but she'd died in 1819, so it couldn't be the same one. Toward the bottom of the slab, however, another Desirée Musson was listed. Born December 1838, died April 1902. Rebecca did a quick calculation. This Desirée would have been thirty-four years old the day Frank was entrusted with the locket. Could she have been the cousin living on Esplanade Avenue?

"You know, there's something much more interesting about this tomb than the railings," Rebecca's father said. "Have either of you noticed the famous names here? See up at the top, Desirée Musson née Rillieux? This was a famous Creole family in this city. One of the Rillieux had children with a free woman of color here, and their son, Norbert Rillieux, became a famous engineer and inventor."

"That's super-interesting," said Ling, leaning in to take another photo. Rebecca was still focused on Desirée's name.

"And the other name you can see further down," Rebecca's dad went on. "The line that reads Henri, Jeanne, Pierre De Gas. They all died young, and probably close together, because their names are all on that one line. Yellow fever maybe. Anyway, they were the children, I believe, of this lady here, Estelle Musson. See? Her husband isn't buried here, because he left her at some point and moved back to France. His name was René De Gas. And he was the brother of — who?"

"Cemetery closing!" shouted the caretaker. "Closing in two minutes! Anyone not out in two minutes, you gonna be sleeping here tonight!"

Rebecca's dad smiled at her. "I'll give you a clue. His brother spelled it as one word, not two. D-E-G-A-S."

Rebecca couldn't believe what she was hearing.

"You mean," she said, "*the painter* Degas?"

Something was clicking together in her head.

Her dad nodded proudly. "The only one of the French Impressionists ever to visit the U.S.," he said. "And he came here to New Orleans, to visit his brother, and his uncle's family. They lived somewhere up on Esplanade. There might be a plaque outside the house. . . ."

Rebecca's heart was beating so fast she thought she might fall over. The painter who gave Frank the locket was *Edgar Degas*. Desirée Musson was Degas' cousin! That little picture inside that Frank had mentioned: That could actually have been painted by one of the great French Impressionists. It could be worth millions of dollars!

"Come on — we better go before we get locked in," Rebecca's dad said. "More interesting than Marie Laveau, right? I told you I had a surprise."

"Right," Rebecca agreed. Her arms and legs felt weak; her head was stuffed with cotton wool. She followed her father and Ling out of the cemetery in a daze. Degas. Degas. Degas. One of her favorite painters. One of the most famous painters *ever*.

She had to rescue that locket.

CHAPTER TWELVE

WHEN LING FINALLY SKIPPED OFF TO MEET PHIL at the Croissant d'or — a café in the premises of a nineteenth-century ice cream parlor — Rebecca raced straight to the corner of Rampart Street. Aurelia would be arriving soon, so there wasn't much time. But she had to talk to Frank.

For the first time Frank was actually waiting there for her. As she ran up Orleans, she could see him, and he started talking when she was still a few strides away.

"I went to Carondelet Street," he said, his blue eyes gleaming. "And I talked to this ghost who used to work as a porter there. He remembers the names of all the cotton offices where he worked. He said the one I was talking about never paid him for his last day's work. He said other things, too, that I can't repeat in front of ladies . . ."

"Frank!" Rebecca said. She was desperate to interrupt him with her news, but she'd never seen him so animated.

"He said the company was called Musson, Prestidge, and

Co." Frank was looking very pleased with himself. "I knew I remembered it right!"

"Frank," Rebecca tried again. "The man who gave you the locket, the artist . . ."

"Yes, I've been thinking about him as well," said Frank. He paced the corner, the angles of his face sharp under his chalk-white skin. "I remember that he had a long, thin nose and a short beard. He spoke French with his brother in New York, and with the men at the cotton office. When he spoke to me in English, he had a strong accent, and —"

"I think I know who he is. Who he was!" Rebecca had to interrupt. "He was a very famous French painter named Edgar Degas. The Mussons were his cousins."

Frank gazed at her, as though nothing she said made sense. He'd never heard of Degas, she realized, but why would he? How could he hear of anything much, apart from fires or floods, things he could see with his own eyes? The life of a ghost must be so monotonous.

"So you know who should have the locket?" he asked her. "Is that what you're saying?"

Rebecca opened her mouth to say yes, sort of — in that she knew much more than she did yesterday — though still had no idea of how to rescue the locket itself — but she was distracted by the sound of pounding footsteps.

Someone was running along Rampart Street toward them; she'd have to stop talking to Frank until the danger had passed.

Really, they needed to find somewhere less public to meet. It had been so much easier with Lisette, hidden deep within Lafayette Cemetery.

"Hang on a minute," she whispered to Frank. Then she remembered Aunt Claudia's various warnings about bag snatchers on Rampart Street. She shaded her eyes and squinted down the street to get a better look at the person pounding toward her. If she didn't like the look of him, Rebecca decided, she would start running herself, down the middle of Orleans Avenue.

"Oh my god," she said. The person running toward her, looking terrified and frantic, was Aurelia. And in the distance, rounding the corner in hot pursuit of her, was a boy with a shock of bright red hair.

Toby Sutton.

"What's wrong?" Frank wanted to know.

"Don't disappear!" she snapped at him. "Seriously. I need your help."

"How can I . . ."

"That's my cousin. Someone's chasing her." Rebecca, her heart thumping, could barely get her words out. "You have to help. Take my hand!"

There was a moment's hesitation from Frank, and then he reached for her. Rebecca knew she'd disappeared from view because of the panicked look on Aurelia's face. She was crossing Orleans, and gazing at the spot where Rebecca had been standing just a moment ago, but, of course, she couldn't see her now. Frank's touch had rendered Rebecca invisible.

"Now," she hissed at Frank. "Grab her!"

"But . . ."

"Do it!"

As Aurelia hesitated at the corner, Frank grabbed Aurelia's hand and pulled her toward the wall. Seeing Rebecca again, holding the hand of a disheveled stranger — just as Aurelia herself was doing — was too much for Aurelia. Her eyes looked ready to pop out of her head, and she opened her mouth as though she was about to scream.

"Shhh," Rebecca whispered. "Keep your mouth shut, and stay very still! Toby can't see us, but you *have* to keep still."

A trembling Aurelia gazed from Rebecca to Frank, her little face pale with fright, but at least she wasn't speaking. The three of them stood pressed against the building's rough walls. The only sound was Aurelia's agitated breathing. Rebecca gripped Frank's hand, trying to concentrate on how substantial it felt, how real — like a living hand, except much colder. Her own breathing was heavy, too, and she had to get it under control. She didn't want anything to give them away to Toby.

Because he was standing on the corner now, just a few feet away, bent over and panting. It was more than a year since Rebecca had seen him. He was taller now, and heavier. Acne had exploded across his chin, as livid as his hair. The scowl on his face made him ugly, she thought. His eyes were wild, like some kind of feral creature's.

Toby straightened up. He looked down Orleans and then along Rampart Street, shaking his head in disbelief. Rebecca gripped Frank's hand even tighter, willing Toby to walk away.

But instead he marched over to the boarded-up front door of the town house and hammered on it.

"Where did you go, you stupid girl?" he shouted, kicking at the door. "Where did you go?"

Rebecca held her breath. Toby was just inches away from her now. She didn't dare look at Aurelia; all she could hope was that Aurelia was standing still and not about to do something stupid, like panic and drop Frank's hand.

Instinctively Rebecca wriggled closer to Frank. They might be hidden from sight right now, but Rebecca and Aurelia weren't ghosts. They were still corporeal beings, and if Toby reached a hand out he could touch her. Rebecca knew from her ghost walk with Lisette that though the living couldn't see you, they could certainly bump into you. She'd gotten bruises trying to navigate the streets of the Quarter, when the living blithely walked into her or smacked at her with bags and elbows. If Toby managed to grab her — or Aurelia — he would be too strong, she thought. In a tug-of-war with thin, waifish Frank, Toby would win. Rebecca had no idea what he planned to do once he'd caught Aurelia, but she didn't want to find out.

Toby kicked the door again — once, twice, three times.

"I saw you with *her*!" he roared, smacking his fists against the planks nailed across the door. "I know you're here somewhere!"

He staggered back toward the curb and glared up at the building's rusted galleries. It took all Rebecca's will to stop her teeth from chattering, with fear and with cold. *Just go away*, she thought. *Leave us alone.*

As though he could hear her thoughts, Toby gave up. He walked away down Rampart Street, shoulders hunched, head down. Even when he disappeared around a corner three or four blocks in the distance, Rebecca was still standing with her back to the building, holding Frank's hand, afraid to move. Anton had been right about Toby. He was back, and he wanted revenge.

None of them knew what to do or say. That was pretty obvious. Frank was holding the hand of a girl he'd never met before, no doubt confused about who she was, why some angry guy was chasing her, and how they were going to explain this whole invisibility thing to her. Aurelia, on the other side of Frank, was still — uncharacteristically — silent. Rebecca leaned forward to look at her.

"Relia — are you OK?" she whispered. Aurelia nodded. "Don't be afraid. This is Frank. He's . . . good. He's on our side."

She didn't know what else to say. Frank gave her a questioning look, probably wondering what "our side" meant.

"But . . . b-b-but . . ." Aurelia was trying to speak.

"What is it?" Rebecca said softly. Poor Aurelia. First she'd been chased by Toby, and now a ghost was holding her hand. It was probably her most traumatic afternoon ever.

"Who are all these people?" Aurelia bleated, and Rebecca turned to follow her gaze. There was Rampart Street, studded with replica gas lamps, scraggly crepe myrtles, and miniature palm trees. Someone was walking into the tattoo place. A bus chugged by on the far side of the street. A few cars passed, and a taxi made a U-turn.

And then there were the ghosts. Rebecca had forgotten all about that. Aurelia was seeing the world of ghosts for the first time, and unfortunately, Rampart Street was home to hundreds of them. Slaves and soldiers, gentlemen and gang members. People who'd been run over, people who'd been stabbed, people who'd died in burning houses and car wrecks and shoot-outs. People from the 1760s and the 1860s and the 1960s. It looked like a cross between a costume ball and the Halloween parade in New York, except everyone was sort of wandering around aimlessly, or clustered in strange era-defying groups, a grotesque range of fatal wounds on display. No wonder Aurelia was in a state of shock.

"Um," Rebecca said, wondering for the briefest of moments if she could get away with a lie. Impossible. Aurelia wasn't stupid. "These are ghosts."

"No way," Aurelia breathed.

Rebecca was feeling calmer now. Toby was gone. Aurelia didn't appear to be freaking out. There were two hundred ghosts walking by and looking at them, but none of those ghosts seemed to care that much. Ghosts were always thinking about themselves.

Then Frank dropped their hands, and the ghosts all disappeared.

"Oh, man!" Aurelia complained. "Where did everyone go?"

"He's here," Frank told Rebecca.

"Who?" Rebecca was panicking again. Toby was back? Why was Frank exposing them?

"Gideon Mason. He was standing over there looking at us. At you and your cousin."

"No," Rebecca groaned. Gideon Mason had seen Aurelia with Frank. Was he going to start threatening *her* now, too? Wasn't it bad enough that she was getting chased in the street by a maniacal Toby Sutton?

"Who are you talking to? What's going on?" demanded Aurelia. She couldn't see or hear Frank anymore, Rebecca remembered. As far as Aurelia knew, she and Rebecca were the only ones standing on this corner. "Where's that cute boy with the dirty clothes and the blue eyes? Why was he holding our hands?"

"He's still here," Rebecca told her. This whole thing was a

mess. Of course, Aurelia was going to have a million questions. "It's just — it's just, you can't see him."

"Well, then how do you know he's still here?"

"*I* can see him. He's made himself . . . visible to me." Rebecca wanted to tell Aurelia as little as possible, to protect her from the world of ghosts, but that wasn't going to be easy. "He's a ghost, too, OK? And when he holds our hands, we can see all the other ghosts. And they can see us."

"Oh." Aurelia pondered this latest piece of information, eyes narrowed.

"But why couldn't Toby see us?" she asked. "He was looking straight at us."

"When a ghost holds your hand, you're invisible to living people," Rebecca explained. Giving Aurelia all this information made her extremely nervous. Who knew where it would end up? Blathered about online during some marathon IM session with Claire? Announced over macaroni and cheese in the junior lunchroom at Temple Mead, perhaps? "When he lets go, you're not invisible anymore."

"But *he's* invisible."

"Yup. That's right."

"So tell me again — how come *you* can see him?"

"I . . . I just can, OK?"

"So," Aurelia drawled. "You can see this ghost the way you could see that other ghost last year, the one who killed all the girls?"

"She didn't *kill* anyone," Rebecca said. She hadn't realized that Aurelia knew even this much about Lisette. Aunt Claudia wouldn't have told her. "It's much more complicated than that."

"*She* was the one who was murdered," said Frank, coming to Lisette's defense. He nodded at Aurelia. "Tell her."

"I know, I know." Rebecca told him. "I can't get into all that with her."

"Are you talking to him?" Aurelia demanded, her eyes wide. "Are you talking to him *right now*? Can he hear me?"

"Yes, he can hear you."

"And he can see me?"

"Yes." Rebecca sighed. Why did this have to happen? If only Toby hadn't been stalking Aurelia in a completely insane way, Rebecca wouldn't have panicked and asked Frank to grab her hand, and Aurelia would have been none the wiser about all this. Keeping secrets was a difficult and sometimes dangerous business. But secrets getting out could be much, much more dangerous. Especially with a mean ghost and an even meaner Toby Sutton on the loose.

"So," Aurelia said, hands on hips, "what I don't get is how come *you* can still see him but I can't, when I could five minutes ago? It's not fair!"

"Look." Rebecca didn't even know where to begin. "The thing with ghosts is, they don't appear to *everyone*. They haunt specific places, and choose to appear to specific people. For a reason."

"And what's the reason he 'appears' to you? That you really love ghosts?"

Rebecca blushed. "It's because I'm . . . I'm trying to help him with something, OK?"

"Well, I could help him, too. I know this city really well. Much better than you do." Aurelia was getting sulky.

"Could she?" Frank asked. "Do you think she could help?"

"No, I don't," Rebecca told him.

"No, you don't, do you?" Only hearing half of the conversation, Aurelia misunderstood what Rebecca was saying. "You don't know New Orleans at all. I could help you look for this locket. . . ."

"What?" Rebecca shouted. How could Aurelia possibly know anything about the locket?

"She could help with the locket?" Frank was all excited now as well.

"No, she can't. She doesn't know what she's talking about."

"I do, too!" Aurelia was indignant. "Someone told me all about it at school this morning. They said that someone had seen you on Rampart Street, and you were all ranting and raving about a locket you needed to find."

Rebecca's stomach dropped. Amy and Jessica. Unbelievable. They *had* been sitting there in the car for a minute or two before

Rebecca noticed them, and this was the juicy piece of gossip they'd taken back to Temple Mead.

"One girl thought that maybe you'd stolen it and then lost it, and if you didn't find it, the Mafia in New York would kill you. But someone else thought that you'd dropped the locket at the Bowmans' house the night you burned it down, and that's why you were desperate to find it again, before the police did, because that would be evidence and you'd go to jail."

Rebecca was beyond exasperated. "I didn't burn down the Bowmans' house, and — this is the most ridiculous conversation." She hated being the subject of speculation at her old school, and it didn't escape her that every speculation involved criminal activity of some kind. "Aurelia, come on. We should go."

"Just tell me about the locket," Aurelia pleaded. "I'm sure I could help."

Before Rebecca realized what he was doing, Frank took Aurelia's hand again, and she gasped, eyes bright with excitement.

"I'm the one looking for the locket," he told her. "My name is Frank O'Connor. Do you really think you could help?"

"No, she cannot!" Rebecca exclaimed, wrenching Aurelia's hand free.

"Becca! He wants me to help him!"

"Don't listen to him," Rebecca said. She started walking

away, dragging a reluctant Aurelia along the sidewalk, and shooting Frank the angriest of looks.

"I'm sorry," he called after her. "Please don't be upset with me!"

Rebecca ignored him. She kept hold of Aurelia's hand and pulled her as hard as she could down Orleans Avenue.

CHAPTER THIRTEEN

Y OU'RE SO SELFISH, BECCA," AURELIA WAS COM-
plaining. "You just want to keep all the ghosts to yourself,
so you can be the special and important one."

"That's not true," Rebecca told her, but the criticism stung.
Maybe there was some truth in it. Was that why she hadn't
breathed a word of any of this to Ling? "I just don't want
anything bad happening to you, OK? I'm just trying to protect you."

"Protect me from what? Nobody ever tells me anything."

"I'll explain, I promise. I'll tell you everything. Just not
right now."

Aurelia muttered and sulked all the way to the Croissant
d'or, and once they were there, would only speak to Ling and
Phil. She even refused Ling's offer of a cookie, sitting with her
arms folded and her bottom lip stuck out. Rebecca knew she was
going to have to make peace with Aurelia before things got even
more out of hand.

Phil insisted on walking them up to Tremé, even though it would make him late meeting his mother at the World War II Museum. Rebecca fell back a little, so Phil and Ling could keep chatting away to each other, and so she could grab her chance with Aurelia. It wasn't easy, because her cousin was still fuming.

"Relia," Rebecca said in a low voice, reaching for Aurelia's hand. Aurelia pulled it away and kept looking straight ahead. "Relia, I'm sorry. I promise I'll tell you everything."

"When?" Aurelia demanded. "Tonight?"

Rebecca's dad was taking them to Commander's Palace for dinner, and Aunt Claudia and Aurelia were invited as well. Even though the restaurant was only on the other side of Lafayette Cemetery, Aunt Claudia hadn't been for years. Rebecca didn't remember her *ever* going to restaurants.

"It might be tricky tonight."

"Then you'll say it's tricky tomorrow, and it's tricky the day after, and then you'll go home."

"OK. I'll try my best tonight. Straight after dinner, all right?"

"You promise?" Aurelia still sounded sulky.

Rebecca nodded. What she was going to tell Aurelia she didn't know, but at least she had some time to think about it.

"And you have to promise me something," she said. Ling and Phil had already crossed the street, but Rebecca dawdled long enough to miss the crosswalk light. "You can't say a word about the ghost. . . ."

"Frank?"

"Yes, Frank. You can't say a word about him, or what you saw today, to anyone. Not to your mother, not to Claire, not to Ling, not to my dad — promise?"

"All right." Aurelia jabbed at the crosswalk button. Ling and Phil didn't seem to have noticed that Rebecca and Aurelia had fallen behind. How did they find so much to talk about?

"And you never told me why Toby Sutton was following you," said Rebecca, "or why you ended up on Rampart Street."

Aurelia sniffed.

"I'll tell you tonight," she said, sticking her nose in the air. "After dinner."

That afternoon's work on the Basin Street High land seemed harder and dirtier; the sun was more punishing; and Mr. Boyd was even more of a taskmaster.

"Curly Sue!" he bellowed at Aurelia. "Get your Uptown behind over here. Now, try to be a good influence on the Jailbirds. Show them how you like your gardens to look on St. Charles Street. I want to see every piece of trash GONE."

Ling and Rebecca made trip after trip to a giant rented composter with armfuls of stinky, prickly vegetation. Råf, who arrived late, not wearing his school uniform, was working on the far side of the playground with Brando. Junior was nowhere to be seen at all. Rebecca tried not to look at the falling-down house where the locket lay hidden, but she couldn't help glancing over there, especially when Aurelia and the Jailbirds were stationed nearby to pick up litter. Gideon Mason, Frank's murderer, had seen Aurelia with Frank that day. What if he decided to accost her and threaten her, the way he'd done with Rebecca?

Ling must have noticed Rebecca's constant looking over at the house, because she nudged her, nodding to Aurelia.

"What was up with her at the café?" Ling muttered to Rebecca. They were both turfing weeds into the composter, and they needed to keep their voices down to avoid incurring the wrath of Mr. Boyd. "She's in a major huff about something."

"She's annoyed with me," Rebecca whispered back. "She thinks I'm not including her in . . . stuff."

"Well," said Ling, gesturing with a bulbous weed toward Mr. Boyd. He was busy confiscating the cell phone of one of the Jailbirds and shouting. "After this afternoon she may not *want* to be included."

Mr. Boyd stared over in their direction.

"Man, he must have bionic ears," Rebecca muttered, and they hustled back to the mound of waiting weeds.

After a steady, arm-aching two hours of work, Raf ambled over. He was carrying two cold bottles of water for them.

"Mr. Boyd says to tell you that the word 'volunteer' comes from the Latin *voluntarius*. He says it means 'of one's free will.'"

"And he's telling us this . . . why?" Ling opened her bottle of water and splashed a little over her head.

"He means you free to go whenever you like," Raf explained. "He's not as nasty as he seems. He knows you guys work hard, and this isn't your own school or anything."

"We can keep going for a while," Rebecca said, glancing at Ling to make sure that was OK. Ling, glugging down water, nodded. "Tomorrow is the last day we can help, and we'll need to finish early. We're going to this — thing."

She felt shy about telling Raf what "this thing" was exactly. He might look at them differently if he thought they hung out with the Temple Mead/St. Simeon's crowd. If St. Simeon's needed to clear ground for a schoolyard expansion, it would hire landscape gardeners. It wouldn't need to rely on willing — and not-so-willing — teen labor.

"No problem," Raf said. He started walking away, then stopped. "You going to the country club, right?"

Rebecca and Ling exchanged bemused glances. How could Raf possibly know this?

"Ye-es," Rebecca said slowly. Raf laughed.

"My aunt told my grandmother you were in her store this morning." He laughed again, backing away. "Uptown, downtown, everyone's in your business."

"I guess," said Rebecca, shaking her head. Unbelievable. Next Raf would be telling her that he'd heard she'd burnt down the Bowman mansion and was looking for a missing locket.

"You might see my brother," Raf called over his shoulder. "He'll be there."

"Your brother goes to St. Simeon's?" Ling asked.

"No, he's at college. Xavier. He works banquets at the country club. He'll be bussing your table."

"Well," said Ling, when Raf had gone. "This thing tomorrow night is going to be weird, isn't it?"

"It's going to be awful," Rebecca said. "Sorry. But we already bought our dresses."

"As everyone knows, apparently." Ling threw her water bottle toward the recycling bin and raised her arms in triumph when it dropped straight in. "It's the talk of New Orleans. Uptown Girl and Miss Thing have bought their dresses!"

The sky was clouding over by the time Aunt Claudia, her day of fortune-telling in the Quarter finished, came by to collect Aurelia.

"Rain coming in for Jazz Fest," Aunt Claudia sighed, rubbing her bracelets the way she always did when she was anxious. Rain was bad for her business, Rebecca remembered. Nobody wanted to sit out in the pouring rain having their tarot cards read.

Aurelia waved good-bye to her new BFFs, the Jailbirds, with much more enthusiasm than her halfhearted "see ya" to

Rebecca, but she seemed bouncy enough getting into Aunt Claudia's car, her usual good humor restored. If Gideon Mason had menaced her, Rebecca reasoned, she wouldn't look so cheerful. And now the crisis was over, more or less, because Aurelia had ballet class after school tomorrow, and wouldn't have time to come downtown.

Half an hour later, with their mound of decaying weeds successfully transported, Rebecca and Ling set off back to the house on Orleans Avenue. Rebecca was looking forward to a hot shower, hoping the steam would help clear her head.

Usually they would be walking past people sitting out on their porches or front steps, or even in a fold-up chair on the sidewalk, but it was quiet outside this afternoon. The sky was dark with clouds by now, thunder rumbling in the distance.

"Do you think we'll make it home before the rain?" Ling asked. "I can't believe how dark it got all of a sudden."

"Yeah, I . . . ." Rebecca couldn't finish her sentence. There, on the other side of the street, was Gideon Mason. He glowered long and hard at Rebecca, then started crossing the street toward them.

"I saw you today," the ghost said, quickening his pace. "You and that other girl. Pretty little thing. Dumb like you. Didn't I warn you? Didn't I tell you to keep away?"

Rebecca's heart was pumping. She wanted to scream at the ghost, but she couldn't: Ling was here. She started walking faster, refusing to turn around and look at him. He was freaking her out. She just wanted him to leave her alone.

"You can't get away from me!" he called, and Rebecca, panic surging, grabbed Ling's arm.

"I think maybe we should run," she said.

Ling hesitated, looking up again at the sky.

"Really? You think it's that . . ."

"Run!" cried Rebecca, and took off down the street, praying that Ling would follow. She ran so fast her heart felt as though it were exploding in her chest; her face was boiling, and even her ears throbbed. Behind her she could hear Ling's footsteps pounding, but Rebecca didn't dare look around. She didn't want to see the ghost. She didn't want to know if he was following as well.

On Rampart, Rebecca darted across the street without looking, noticing too late a car that had to swerve to avoid her, and only stopping on the island because Ling was shouting at her.

"Rebecca! That car almost hit you!"

Rebecca buckled over, wheezing. Ling thudded across the road and placed a protective hand on her back.

"I'd rather be soaked to the skin than get ourselves killed," Ling gasped. "This is crazy."

"Sorry," Rebecca managed to spit out. Still breathing hard, she straightened up. Thunder rumbled again, longer and louder this time. The sky was charcoal. She blinked back tears, annoyed with herself for feeling so scared. The ghost couldn't hurt her — wasn't that what Frank said? But if that were true, why did Gideon Mason keep threatening her?

A light shone into her eyes, which didn't make any sense: The sun was hidden behind the swarming mass of dark clouds. But when Rebecca looked up, she saw the source of the strange light. The top gallery of the corner town house was illuminated by the same silvery glow Rebecca had observed the other night. And there, like a wisp of smoke, was the ethereal girl she'd seen before, bending over the railing. Delphine.

"What is it?" asked Ling, following Rebecca's gaze.

"Nothing," Rebecca said, transfixed by the eerie half-light radiating from the gallery. Didn't Frank say the girl only haunted at night? It was still late afternoon, but maybe the dark sky had triggered her reappearance.

"Hello!" Delphine called down to Rebecca. "Hello!"

Rebecca stared up at her, openmouthed.

"Dude," said Ling, who had no idea what Rebecca was looking at. "You're scaring me."

"Be careful of that bad man," the girl on the gallery cried. Her lilting accent reminded Rebecca of Lisette. "The man with the dark hair and the angry face! He's a very, very bad man!"

A crash of thunder made Rebecca jump, and then the ghost girl and her mist of light were gone, like a movie someone had turned off. The town house was in darkness again, closed-up and shabby.

Ling was staring at Rebecca, obviously worried. "Becca, I think you had too much sun today or maybe you're dehydrated — I don't know. Let's just get you home, OK?"

Rebecca nodded. She didn't think she could speak anymore, let alone take another step. Rain was falling now, pattering onto her head, and through the watery blur she couldn't make out anything — neither the derelict town house nor the cars hissing along both sides of Rampart. Other lights flashed and winked at her: the crosswalk signal, a flickering streetlight, a darting bolt of lightning.

Two blue eyes, like cold, crystal lakes, searing into her from the other side of the street.

Frank.

"No," Rebecca said, closing her eyes. "No more."

"Becca!" Ling's voice echoed and faded. "You're really scaring me!"

Rebecca swallowed, trying to pull herself together.

"Let's go," she murmured. "We have to go. We have to run."

The crosswalk light flashed green, and Rebecca took off, pelting across the final stretch of Rampart and down Orleans Avenue. Rain swooshed into her face, half blinding her, and she staggered the last few steps to the gate, grasping for its railings. *No more ghosts*, she wanted to say. *No more.* It was all too much for her today. She could barely stand up, let alone search for her key. Ling's hand was on her arm.

"Everything's OK," Ling said to her, her voice gentle. "Don't worry. Nobody's chasing us. Everything's OK."

"But it's not OK," Rebecca said. She was crying now, tears mixing with the rain until she felt her face was drowning. "You don't understand. It's not OK."

"Let's go inside and get out of the rain," Ling said softly. It was easy for *her* to be calm, Rebecca thought. To Ling, this was just a beautiful old city. It wasn't *Night of the Living Dead*. "And you can sit down, and tell me everything that's upsetting you. Just tell me everything, and we'll figure it out. Things are easier when there are two of us to talk them over. Uptown Girl and Miss Thing, right?"

Rebecca sobbed even harder. She really did want to tell Ling everything. She was tired of keeping all these secrets, of talking to these ghosts. Everything was too hard.

"You won't believe me," she said, smearing rain and tears out of her eyes. "I know you won't."

"Try me." The rain was heavier now. Ling pulled Rebecca's bag toward her and fumbled inside for the key to the gate.

"I know you won't. I wouldn't believe it if you told me." None of this would make sense to a normal person. Sure, Aurelia had believed her, but Aurelia had seen the ghosts for herself.

"Well, maybe I'm not as skeptical as you are. I promise to believe you, whatever it is you're about to say."

Rebecca sniffed, rubbing her face.

"The thing is," she said slowly, blinking at poor bedraggled Ling. "The thing is, there are ghosts everywhere in this town. And I can see them."

CHAPTER FOURTEEN

THE RAIN WAS LOUD ON THE OLD ROOF OF THE slave quarters, thundering onto the flagstones of the courtyard, but at last they were dry and safely inside. Rebecca lay on the bed in her little room, gazing at the steamy windows. Although she'd taken a hot shower, and was dressed in clean sweatpants and a hoodie, she still felt shivery. She'd told Ling everything — well, she'd told her a lot. Ling had listened intently, saying very little. Maybe she thought Rebecca was crazy.

Ling walked in now, carrying a towel, and helped Rebecca to sit up and wrap it around her wet hair. Then Ling pulled a white wicker chair close to the bed and sat down.

"OK," said Ling. "While you were in the shower, I was thinking. Certain things have to happen."

"First thing," Rebecca croaked, "you have to believe me."

"I believe you."

"Really?" Rebecca wasn't even sure if she believed herself anymore. She wriggled into a seated position again, propping herself against a pillow.

"Yes. Why wouldn't I?" Ling looked dumbfounded. "We've been friends forever. Why would you start lying to me?"

"I didn't tell you lots of stuff about what happened to me here last year. With seeing ghosts, I mean. And anyway, I could just be going crazy, right? You might think I'm out of my mind."

"Look, do you want me to believe you or not?" demanded Ling. She put her feet on the bed and slouched in her chair. Rebecca nodded. "All right, then. Let's review. There's a ghost named Frank who wants you to rescue a locket he hid under the floorboards of a house in Tremé sometime in the 1870s."

"Eighteen-seventy-three."

"And not only do you have to retrieve it, you have to return it to the descendants of the person to whom it rightfully belongs. And that person is . . ."

"Was."

". . . someone named Desirée Musson, and she is — was — the cousin of an artist. And, as we learned this morning, that artist is probably Edgar Freakin' Degas."

"Right." Rebecca slumped down again. Thunder crashed overhead, shaking the roof. Both she and Ling looked up.

"Eek," said Ling. "That sounds angry. Speaking of which, there's a second ghost. Gideon Mason? He murdered Frank to steal the locket, and when he couldn't find it, got murdered himself. So now he's all bitter and twisted, and trying to get in the way."

"Pretty much."

"Hmmm." Ling crossed her ankles, then uncrossed them. Rain drove against the windows, almost drowning out the buzz of Rebecca's phone. She pulled it out from under her pillow.

"Text from my father," she reported. "He's on his way home. He says we should get ready for dinner."

"You know, if you don't feel up to going out tonight . . ."

"No, I'll be OK. Just hearing you talk all this through makes me feel better. Everything was getting so mixed-up in my head. Anyway, I need to talk to Aurelia tonight, which is a whole different complication — but whatever. Go on."

"Where were we? Two ghosts. One seems good, one seems bad. As far as we know."

"As far as we know," Rebecca repeated. "And then there's the third ghost. The girl up on the gallery. Delphine."

"And her deal is . . . ?"

Rebecca shrugged. "She's a friend of Frank's. I think they may . . . like each other or something." Rebecca felt her cheeks warm up and she shook her head; she didn't want Ling thinking Rebecca had feelings for Frank, too. Not that she did. Right? "She wants to help him in some way, but she's stuck up on that gallery all the time, from what I can see. Tonight she was trying to help. She was warning me about Gideon Mason."

"But she could be dangerous herself, right?"

"I guess," Rebecca admitted. "But I don't think so. She was friends with . . . this other ghost. One I knew last year. That's another story."

160

Ling raised her eyebrows.

"Who knew your life was this complicated? This is like *The Sixth Sense* on steroids. Anyway, the inevitable conclusion is: We *need* to help Frank. Don't you think?"

Rebecca liked the sound of that "we." Things would be much easier now that Ling was in on all this. At least Rebecca wouldn't have to sneak around quite so much.

"Yes," she said, trying to get her thinking straight. "Because if we don't find the locket, it may be destroyed. And something that belonged to Degas, something possibly incredibly rare and valuable, may get crushed to pieces."

Ling's eyes widened.

"And," Rebecca continued, "because Frank needs someone living to help him. Until the locket is found and handed over to its rightful owners, he's stuck being a ghost. If the house gets demolished next week, and the locket disappears, Frank is, basically, doomed to be a ghost forever."

"Oy." Ling slid even further down in her chair until she was almost parallel with the ground. "And the house in question is that one by the schoolyard?" Rebecca nodded forlornly. "And it's all boarded up, and not exactly in the world's safest neighborhood, so we can't just pop in anytime to look around. Not to mention it's guarded by Caspar the Unfriendly Ghost."

"Exactly."

"So," said Ling, in the kind of voice that suggested she was a detective who'd just solved the case. "I know what we have to do."

"What?" Rebecca sat up.

"Tomorrow you need to introduce me to Frank. Then we can grill him until he's, like, toasted on both sides."

Rebecca laughed. She was feeling so much better now.

"Then we need to talk to Raf."

"Raf? Really?"

"If anyone can help us, he can."

Rebecca wasn't so sure. They might not get a chance to talk to Raf tomorrow. He might not believe them, or want anything to do with this. But she didn't have any better ideas, and at least Ling seemed to be approaching this whole nightmare with gusto and determination. Rebecca was all out of gusto.

"We should get ready." Ling checked her watch. She was the only person under forty Rebecca knew who actually wore a watch. "I'm starving. But one last thing. Who else knows about any of this?"

"Anton," Rebecca told her. "Well, he knows a little piece of it. I tried to talk to him about Frank on Monday, but he doesn't *want* to know. So he won't help us, I don't think."

"Whatever! We might need him for an alibi or decoy at some point, though. You don't think he said anything to Phil?"

"I doubt it. He's not going to start talking about ghosts if he doesn't even really believe it himself."

"OK — so the only people in on all this are you, me, Anton, and various crazed ghosts."

"And Aurelia." Rebecca wanted to hide behind her pillow.

"WHAT?"

"It's a long story. . . ."

"They always are, with you."

"And the thing is, she doesn't really know anything. Just that there's a ghost, and that he's looking for a locket. She really, really wants to help. But I don't think that's a good idea. It would be like bringing . . . I don't know, a pirate as a date to the Spring Dance. Chaos would ensue."

"Rebecca! Ling!" Her dad was out on the gallery, tapping at the door. The noise of the rain had drowned out his footsteps on the usually creaky stairs.

"Almost ready!" Rebecca called, tugging the towel off her hair and throwing it onto the ground.

"Ten minutes, OK?" he shouted, and then he was gone.

"This session of ghost court is adjourned," said Ling, already out of her chair. "Second session when we get back tonight. Agreed?"

Rebecca nodded. Things were not any easier now, but they *felt* easier. She'd been stupid to hide all this from Ling. She wouldn't dread waking up tomorrow, now that Ling was on her side.

Rebecca was glad she hadn't opted out of the dinner at Commander's Palace. She'd seen the distinctive turquoise-

and-white striped awning many, many times when she was living in the Garden District, and observed the young valet parkers sprinting up and down Washington Avenue in the rain, but she'd never been inside.

Anton lived just on the other side of the cemetery, and part of Rebecca hoped he would walk in at some point with his parents: The Greys were certainly rich enough to eat here every night of the week. Maybe she should have even told him they were all coming here tonight. Her father wouldn't have minded Anton joining them. But right now her head was too full of Frank — even though *he was a ghost*, as Rebecca had to keep reminding herself.

Ghosts had complicated problems, as she'd learned, but even so, things seemed less complicated with them, in a way, than with real flesh-and-blood relationships. Frank was always pleased to see her. And when he held her hand it didn't *mean* anything — apart from instant invisibility. If only she could be invisible tomorrow night at the Spring Dance. The closer it got to the night, the more nervous Rebecca grew. Sure, lording her presence over Amy and Jessica would be gratifying. But she wasn't looking forward to walking through a sea of hostile faces. No one from Temple Mead would be very happy to see her again. Would it just be the social freeze of the Bowmans' Christmas party all over again?

"It's like a floor show," Ling was saying. They'd been seated at a round table upstairs in the busy Garden Room, and a swarm of waiters was delivering the first course, lifting silver covers off each plate at exactly the same time in one choreographed swoop.

"I feel kind of bad eating turtles," Ling said, studying her soup bowl.

"If you've already tried alligator, you'll be fine," Aunt Claudia said. She had dressed for the occasion in an almost normal outfit: a long black dress with a draped paisley scarf, which she called her "Arabian stole." Aurelia was gussied up, too, in an expensive-looking polka-dot halter dress. It made quite a change from her usual after-school wear of castoffs.

"It's from Ballin's in the Riverbend," she told an admiring Ling. "It's Claire's sister's. Claire lent it to me."

"Does Claire's sister know?" Rebecca asked. Aurelia ignored this question. She was still giving Rebecca the cold shoulder.

"She lent me these shoes as well," she told Ling, pushing back the tablecloth so they could see her gold strappy sandals.

"Your feet are soaking," sympathized Ling. She'd had the same bad luck on the way in, climbing straight out of the taxi into a giant puddle.

"Why don't you invite Claire to come along to Jazz Fest with you on Friday?" Rebecca's dad suggested. But Aurelia told him Claire was leaving right after school that day, to visit her grandparents in Jackson.

165

Rebecca had forgotten all about Jazz Fest. She'd been excited when she first heard they were going: Now it was just another complication. Time was running out. When exactly would they get the opportunity to find a way into that boarded-up house and rescue the locket? For the hundredth time she considered telling her father everything, and for the hundredth time decided it wasn't a good idea. Sure, he knew about Lisette and believed in *her*, but that didn't mean he'd believe all Rebecca's stories about Frank and Delphine and Gideon Mason, let alone a lost Degas hidden beneath the floorboards of a house in Tremé. Like Anton said, Lisette was a family ghost. Frank was just some unknown guy from another century with a sob story and a stab wound.

Ling must have had the locket on her mind, too, because she kept bringing up the subject of derelict houses on the verge of collapse.

"That town house on the corner of our street, for example," she said, slurping the last of her soup. "It's such a beautiful building, with all that ironwork on the galleries. But nobody's living there."

"I wouldn't live on Rampart Street," Aunt Claudia said firmly. "It's bad enough using the parking garage there."

"But gentrification will keep pushing its way out of the Quarter, don't you think?" Rebecca's father asked her. "When we were in Tremé on Tuesday, I couldn't believe how much money people are spending fixing up historic houses there now. In some streets you'd think you were in the Quarter."

"Except mostly black people live there," Aurelia said. "What? Why are you all looking at me like that? I'm just saying the truth."

"Those houses by Basin Street High are coming down next week," said Ling, with a significant glance at Rebecca.

"I guess you have to weigh what's more important to a neighborhood — the people who live there now, or the people who used to live there," said Rebecca's dad. "And much as I love the craftsmanship and history of some of those houses, a neighborhood isn't just about pieces of wood. As we saw after Katrina, those things can get swept away by floodwaters, or blown to pieces by the wind. A neighborhood, a community — it's about the people."

Rebecca thought about the burned-down Bowman mansion, a landmark for more than one hundred fifty years in the Garden District, but now gone forever. Just thinking of that night last year reminded her of Toby lurking in the city again, chasing Aurelia through the streets. What was he planning this time? Another fire? Given how much he apparently loved New Orleans, he didn't seem averse to burning half of it down. It was bad enough dealing with ghosts without Toby entering the fray.

"But I do see your point, Ling," Rebecca's father was saying, "about the importance of legacy in a neighborhood. You're absolutely right. How much of it can you remove or replace without destroying it altogether? Like Storyville, the place that witnessed the birth of jazz. Places where Louis Armstrong and Joe Oliver and Jelly Roll Morton lived and played — all gone."

"Do you remember Storyville, Mama?" Aurelia asked, her mouth full.

"Baby, I'm not *that* old," said Aunt Claudia. "Storyville was knocked down when my grandmamma was a tiny little girl."

"So that's what I'm saying." Ling waggled her fork in the air to help make her point. "When you take away the buildings, you take away the history of a place."

"But history lives in people as well as buildings," Rebecca's father pointed out. "In traditions and customs."

"Red beans and rice," said Aunt Claudia, smiling.

"Gumbo," said Aurelia, her mouth still full.

"So when we're talking about Tremé," said Rebecca's father, "a much bigger concern is the one Rafael's grandmother was talking about the other day. Prices going up may be a bigger threat to the history of the neighborhood, and to the history of the city, than houses coming down. If you take the people out of Tremé — the social clubs, the musicians, the Mardi Gras Indians — then you disperse that living, breathing culture.

Maybe you even kill it off. So you'll be left with pretty streets lined with pretty houses, but those streets'll be empty. Or else it'll be like the Quarter, filling the void with tourists. And the story the neighborhood is telling, its own particular history that draws on tradition and invents new ones, like jazz, will go quiet. The soul will be gone."

Rebecca sighed.

"This is a very depressing conversation," declared Aunt Claudia.

"Miss Viola says her family mask as Indians," Rebecca told her father. "She said we should ask Raf about it. Ask to see his dad's house."

"You don't need to go to anyone's daddy's house to see Indians," said Aunt Claudia. "You can see Indians on Friday at Jazz Fest. I don't know — you girls, running around in Tremé!"

She raised an eyebrow at Rebecca's father, and he nodded, as if they'd agreed something in advance.

"You know, I've been hearing stories at City Hall today," he said, cutting a piece of flaky white fish piled high with buttery crabmeat. "About some things going down in Tremé at the moment. I'm wondering if you girls really need to go back tomorrow."

"Oh, but we have to!" Rebecca exclaimed. They *really, really* had to go back to Tremé. Her father had no idea. Aurelia, on the other hand, was watching Rebecca intently, her pretty face screwed up into a frown.

"We promised we would," added Ling. "Just one more day."

"I'm sure they won't miss you," said Aunt Claudia. "They seemed to have a lot of helpers this afternoon."

"And it's just not a good place for you two to be wandering around," Rebecca's father said.

"We're not really wandering around," Ling pointed out. "We're on school property and completely supervised the whole time by Mr. Boyd."

"And he is *really mean*," said Aurelia. "Every single girl on my litter squad was a victim of Mr. Boyd's unfair detention policies. They said it was practically a violation of their human rights."

"So really, we're *more* safe there, if you think about it." Ling was on a roll. Rebecca could only sit back and marvel at her ingenuity. "Anyone engaging in crime within two hundred yards of a public school — well, that's a federal offense."

"I should have insisted on driving you home today!" Aunt Claudia said. "I wouldn't have forgiven myself if something had happened after I left."

Rebecca didn't look at Ling in case a guilty expression gave them away.

"Maybe I'll come over in a cab and get you tomorrow," Rebecca's father said. "I can finish up early."

Rebecca stared down at her napkin, wishing everyone would stop freaking out. She and Ling had a lot to accomplish tomorrow, and adult interference would only make things more complicated.

Her phone buzzed in her jacket pocket, and Rebecca surreptitiously pulled it free. Maybe it was Anton. Maybe he'd seen them walking into Commander's, though — she had to admit — he'd need to be sitting on the roof of his house with a telescope to manage that.

Her dad had a strict no-texts-at-dinner policy back in New York, but everyone was preoccupied right now with the orange juice Aurelia had just spilled all over the table. Rebecca glanced at her cell phone screen and frowned: It wasn't Anton. It was a number she didn't recognize.

enjoying commanders?

Rebecca was puzzled. Who *was* this? The phone buzzed again. Caller ID unknown.

looking for a locket?

Rebecca stifled a gasp. Her blood was roaring in her ears. Could this be from Amy or Jessica? But the menacing tone of the texts didn't seem to fit.

Her phone buzzed a third time; another message was blinking.

how bout looking on st philip, stupid girl????

Stupid girl. The exact thing Toby had said to Aurelia.

171

Toby Sutton. This had to be Toby Sutton. Rebecca glanced around in terror. How did he know they were at the restaurant: Was he watching them? Following them? How did he get ahold of her number?

And how could *anyone* possibly know about the house on St. Philip Street?

CHAPTER FIFTEEN

THE RAIN HAD STOPPED, BUT THE STREETS WERE still drenched. They walked back to Aunt Claudia's the long way around the cemetery because, Rebecca suspected, her father and aunt didn't want her to have to pass the Coliseum Street gate. Bad stuff from the past, Rebecca thought. They had no idea of all this bad stuff in the present.

Everyone moved at a glacial pace along Prytania, wind rustling the oak trees and showering them with a spittle of raindrops. Aurelia was walking with Ling, jabbering away a mile a minute, and Aunt Claudia and Rebecca's father were deep in conversation. Rebecca's heart was pounding. Was Toby somewhere nearby, hiding, waiting to pounce? Why was everyone walking so slowly? Her head was jerking in every direction, following every shadow, every rustle, every passing car.

There was too much to think about. Someone — most likely Toby Sutton — was threatening her. Gideon Mason, the nasty ghost, was threatening her. Aurelia was The Girl Who Knew Too Much, and highly unlikely to stay quiet for long. It was Wednesday night, and they were leaving on Saturday, which meant there was almost no time left to get into the boarded-up house in Tremé and find the hidden locket. Tomorrow night they'd be at the dreaded Spring Dance; much of the next day would be consumed by Jazz Fest. This was the most stressful spring break ever.

Because everyone was still dawdling while Rebecca strode ahead, she rounded the corner of Lafayette Cemetery before the rest of the group. A silver Audi was zooming up Sixth Street, so fast it took Rebecca's breath away. It swerved left onto Prytania without stopping or even slowing down, and Rebecca could make out the color of the driver's hair — bright red. The car then screeched off into the distance, skidding a little on the wet road.

A yellow moon glinted between cracks in the clouds, beaming a sickly light onto the cemetery's pale walls. Rebecca stood still, trying to compute what she'd just seen. An expensive car that looked a lot like the one usually parked in Anton's driveway, driven by someone with bright red hair. Toby Sutton.

And standing on the other side of Sixth Street, looking at her with a mix of dismay and dread, was Anton.

* * *

Everyone else had gone inside the house on Sixth Street, hustled in by Aunt Claudia, despite Aurelia's protests.

"Rebecca promised she'd talk to *me* after dinner tonight!" she grumbled as Ling steered her up the front steps. "You guys are going to see Anton tomorrow. Why does she need to talk to him *now*?"

Everyone else thought they were being so tactful and discreet, letting Rebecca and Anton have their romantic moment together out there in the moonlight while the rest of them hurried inside for a cup of Aunt Claudia's weird herbal tea. They had no idea — not even Ling — that Rebecca was almost speechless with indignation.

She stood, arms folded, on the sidewalk, staring at the empty parking space in the Grey mansion's cobbled yard.

"Toby was visiting *you*, wasn't he?" she demanded. "This afternoon he was in the Quarter, chasing my cousin through the streets! And now he's sending me abusive texts!"

"That *was* Toby," admitted Anton. He looked utterly dejected. "He texted me and said he wanted to talk. I don't know how he got hold of a car. I think his parents cut off his credit card so he couldn't rent one."

Rebecca didn't care about Toby's car. He was dangerous enough on foot.

"Why is he chasing my cousin? Why is he *stalking* me? What is his problem?"

"I don't know." Anton shook his head. "But like I've been trying to tell you — I think he's really losing it. I'm trying to calm him down. Believe me."

"I don't know why I should believe you," Rebecca said, fighting back angry tears. "Remember what you were saying last Sunday up at the lake? About how it's impossible to break with the past?"

"I didn't say it was impossible," said Anton softly. He sidled toward her, but Rebecca backed away. "And I wasn't talking about *me*. Toby's the one who can't let this thing go. He's still really upset about what happened last year — probably because of what happened to *his* family and *her* family after Helena died. They don't even live in New Orleans anymore. The old group is broken up. Everything is over. Maybe that's why he can't forgive you. Why he's blaming you."

"That stupid curse had nothing to do with me." Rebecca kicked at the curb. "It wasn't me who brought that thing down on our heads. It was all about what happened a century and a half ago! And whose fault was that? *His* family and *your* family and *Helena's* family!"

"But Rebecca," Anton said softly, "Helena's family *is* your family. You're really a Bowman, just like Helena is. Helena was, I mean."

He bowed his head, his face pale. Rebecca may not have liked Helena much, but she'd been Anton's friend since childhood.

"I . . . I . . ." Rebecca didn't know what to say. He was right, of course. She was part of the Bowman family, whether she liked it or not. The Suttons, the Greys, and the Bowmans were all bound up together in the curse. Now, even when the curse had ended, they were still bound up together, one way or another. They would be for the rest of their lives.

"I should go in, I guess," she said, swiping at her face to wipe tears away. "Everyone will be waiting. . . ."

"Not yet." He came close, and this time she didn't back away. She wanted to trust Anton. She wanted to believe him. When he stood this close, it was hard to breathe. His shirt smelled of pine.

"There's something you should see," he said in a low voice. "In the cemetery."

Rebecca darted a look back at Aunt Claudia's house. The curtains of the front parlor were closed, and no one seemed to be peeking out. Everyone was probably in the kitchen, sitting and talking around the table.

"Just for, like, five minutes. I don't want anyone coming out to look for me and getting all worried when they can't see me."

"Maybe they'll think we eloped," said Anton, sighing when he saw Rebecca's face. "Joke, OK? I'm joking."

He beeped open the trunk of the black BMW and pulled out a flashlight.

"It won't take long," he promised. He glanced down at Rebecca's shoes. "It may be kind of muddy, though."

Rebecca's nerves were chattering. Everything, from the squeakiness of the cemetery gate to the sodden darkness under the canopy of trees to the slipperiness of the damp path, was freaking her out. After she stumbled on a patch of wet leaves, Anton, leading the way, took her hand. All she could think of was the contrast with the bitter cold of Frank's hand, which she'd held this afternoon. Anton's was warm and soft and strong.

Even in the dark Rebecca could tell they were walking toward the Bowman tomb. What was so important that Rebecca had to be dragged into the cemetery at night to see it? She'd just visited the tomb on Monday.

"Here," said Anton. He dropped her hand and shone the flashlight onto the white tomb.

"No!" Rebecca cried. The marble slab where Lisette's name was carved had been defaced, sprayed with swirls of black paint. Someone had tried to remove her name from the family tomb in the most base way. All the other Bowman names were untouched. Only Lisette's had been vandalized.

"I'm really sorry," said Anton. "I knew you'd be upset."

"It's disgusting. Despicable."

"I saw it just a little while ago," Anton told her. "This is where I met with Toby. He thought this would be a safe place for us to talk."

"So *he* did it?" Rebecca was spluttering with rage. *How dare he? How dare Toby Sutton commit such a sacrilege?*

"Yeah, I think he did. It was already like this when I arrived, and he denied any knowledge of it, but it's pretty obvious. He has so much anger right now, it's . . . it's nasty."

"Nasty? He's psychotic. Why would he do something like this?" Rebecca was struggling to hold back tears, thinking of her friend Lisette, still persecuted even now that she was dead. "Why can't he just leave her alone?"

"I think he blames Lisette for what's happened." Anton lowered the flashlight, maybe so Rebecca didn't have to look at Toby's vile handiwork any longer. "Her death brought about the curse on the Bowman family, and that led to . . . you know. What happened to Helena. The problem is, Lisette isn't around to punish. So he's going to take it out on you, somehow."

"And *this* is taking it out on me?"

"Lisette's dead. She's not even a ghost anymore, right? The only person this could hurt is you, because you were closer to her than anyone else. I thought about not showing you, to protect you from it. But I wanted you to understand how Toby is dead set on revenge. How he's not thinking straight at all."

"You don't have to tell me. I believe you," she said. Her voice sounded far away, she thought, as though it belonged to someone else. Today had been too much: too many nasty surprises.

Now Rebecca just felt weak, completely spent. She wanted to crumple into a ball at the foot of the tomb.

Rebecca felt herself sliding down the cool marble, landing with a bump on the damp stone steps. Even with her eyes closed, sticky with tears, she could sense Anton sitting down next to her; she was intensely aware of the weight of his knee leaning against hers, the press of his shoulder. Even in this state of weepy exhaustion, Rebecca couldn't ignore the thrill rippling through her, every place where their bodies touched.

Anton eased an arm around her shoulders, pulling Rebecca close. She rested her head against his shoulder, inhaling the pine smell of his shirt, listening to the wind swishing through the trees. Her feet seemed to be sinking into mud. She wanted to be close to Anton, she realized. So much came between them all the time. They let other people get in the way.

She lifted her head, to tell Anton she was sorry for being mad, but before she could say anything he pressed his lips to hers.

It had been a long time since Anton had kissed her, but Rebecca remembered how soft and sweet it was — the first time, the second time, every time. Nothing else seemed to matter when he kissed her. The trees whispered around them, as liquid as rain. Rebecca's heart thudded. She wanted more than anything to stay like this, hidden away in the cemetery. Anton holding her, Anton kissing her. Just the two of them, exactly like this.

A car alarm sounded in the distance, and the moment was broken. Rebecca buried her face in Anton's sleeve, grateful for the darkness: She felt suddenly shy.

"We should go soon," she said, her voice muffled. She had no idea how much time had passed since they entered the cemetery. If only they could sit here all night, huddled together on the steps of the tomb.

"I guess," Anton murmured into her hair. "You know I'm going to work this out, don't you? This thing with Toby. This has to end once and for all."

"I hope so," she whispered, entwining her fingers with Anton's.

"And I don't know how, but he knows you're looking for a locket. How could he have found that out?"

Rebecca felt like banging her head against the tomb. "I was talking to the ghost," she told Anton. "The one I was trying to tell you about on Monday. We were on Rampart Street, and two idiots from Temple Mead drove up. Jessica and Amy. I guess they heard my half of the conversation."

"Which means half of Temple Mead got to hear about it as well." Anton sighed. "And someone probably told Marianne, and she told Toby. He may be on the run from his parents, but I'm sure he's in touch with his sister."

"Someone sent me this text tonight," Rebecca said, pulling out her phone. She held up the screen so Anton could read the second message. Anton winced.

"So he talked to you about it tonight?" Rebecca asked, slipping the phone away again.

Anton nodded grimly. "As soon as he mentioned it, I had an idea and I kind of ran with it. I think it might be a way out of all this."

"Really?" Rebecca felt a surge of hope.

Anton squeezed her hand. "I told him that I knew all about it, even though I don't. All I know is what you said on Monday night, something about a ghost."

When you didn't want to listen, Rebecca thought, but she didn't say anything. She wanted to hear the rest of Anton's idea.

"The thing is, I don't think Toby has much idea about it, either. He just has some vague Temple Mead gossip to go on."

"But he sent me another text, mentioning St. Philip Street." Rebecca clicked onto the next text and waved it in front of Anton. "That's where the locket is hidden, in this house that's about to be demolished. How would Toby know that?"

"Isn't St. Philip Street the place you've been volunteering?"

"Oh. Yeah." That made sense. For all Rebecca knew, Toby had been driving up and down the street observing her all week. "I was helping to clear weeds and litter."

"Maybe he thought you were looking for something buried there. I don't know. But I really don't think he knows a whole lot more. So I told him that the locket was something that belonged to Lisette. It was real special to you, and that's why you'd come back here to New Orleans, to find it."

"What?" Rebecca wriggled free of Anton's grasp. This idea sounded nuts.

"Hear me out!" pleaded Anton. "I told him you'd found the locket this week. That your dad had all these contacts at City Hall, and that someone at the Historic New Orleans Collection had it."

"They don't have jewelry there! They only have books and maps and things!"

"Toby won't know that," Anton assured her. "The only library he's ever been into is the one at St. Simeon's, the day he tried to burn it down."

"Please tell me how this helps," Rebecca said, trying not to panic. Suddenly the swampy darkness of the cemetery felt oppressive.

"OK. Toby thinks you have the locket now, and he thinks that it's super-precious to you. When I told him you had it, he got this crazy look in his eyes. He said: 'Not for long.' I think if he can take his revenge by getting the locket from you, it'll all be over. He'll leave you alone. He'll leave this tomb alone. So I'm going to get you a locket tomorrow."

"*Get* me a locket?" Rebecca's head was spinning.

"Yeah, buy an old one from an antiques store. I'll drop it off at your place, and you can wear it to the dance tomorrow night. One text from Marianne, and I bet you Toby will show up in the parking lot."

"To mug me, basically."

"Basically. But don't worry — I'll be there to make sure it doesn't get out of hand. And then it'll all be over."

"You really think this will work?" Rebecca asked. She wanted to trust Anton and his plan, but her heart was sinking.

The kiss they'd just shared seemed like a hundred years ago. Now all she had was another reason to dread the Spring Dance.

CHAPTER SIXTEEN

LING KNEW EXACTLY WHAT SHE THOUGHT ABOUT Anton's fake locket plan.

"It's the stupidest thing I ever heard," she said.

They were in their shared bathroom back on Orleans Avenue. Rebecca sat on the edge of the tub, watching Ling take off her makeup.

"Really?" That was discouraging. Rebecca had almost convinced herself the plan might work.

"The whole thing hinges on Toby showing up tomorrow night at the dance. Why would he do that? Everyone who's going knows him, right? So if he's trying to hide out so his parents can't find him, why would he show his face there?'

"I don't know." Rebecca squirted toothpaste onto her brush. "Maybe because he knows for sure I'll be there, and thinks nobody will try to help me if he steals the locket. He remembers that I wasn't exactly popular at Temple Mead."

"That's possible," Ling conceded. "But what if he doesn't

185

show up? What then? He still hates you, and he's still plotting revenge, and . . ."

"I don't know. He comes over here and tries to burn down the house." Rebecca wasn't joking. Who knew what Toby would do?

On Thursday morning she woke up heavy with dread. The day seemed to promise nothing but awkward situations, tricky conversations, and potential confrontations. Ling was adamant that she needed to "meet" Frank. And she still thought they should talk to Raf, to see if he could help them get into the house on St. Philip Street.

At breakfast another complication presented itself. Her father had rearranged his entire schedule so they could all have what he called "a fun morning together." They were going, he announced, on a carriage ride around the Quarter, then to the African American Museum on the Bayou Road.

When her father suggested picking up po' boys later at some lunch place on Poydras Street, Rebecca heard herself squawking "No!"

"Can't we grab some lunch back here?" she pleaded. "Just so we can have a break and then get into our work clothes, OK?"

"OK," he agreed, humming as he rinsed the breakfast dishes. "I don't know how we'll do it, but we'll pack it all in!"

So that was how, with the day seeping away, she and Ling found themselves with fifteen minutes of father-free time. Back at the house after the morning's activities they bolted down a chunk of the giant muffaletta her father had bought at Central Grocery, and then plotted their escape. As soon as her dad said he needed to make a few calls, Rebecca signaled to Ling.

"Just going out to get some soda!" she called, and then they ran for the gate before her father could point out, quite sensibly, that there was some in the fridge.

When they reached Rampart Street, Rebecca realized that Frank would never appear if he saw someone else standing with her, so she told Ling to wait around the corner.

"Frank!" Rebecca bellowed, not even caring if anyone nearby heard her. "Frank! Get over here!"

He was so slow materializing that Rebecca wanted to kick the fire hydrant in frustration. This wasn't the time for him to be all elusive.

"Rebecca?" Ling called forlornly from around the corner. "Should we give up? I just had to stand here watching a guy pee in the street."

"One more minute," Rebecca told her. "FRANK!"

"I'm here," said a voice behind her.

"Good grief," she said, spinning around. "Don't do that! Why can't you just appear in front of me like a normal ghost?"

"Are you all right?" he asked, his blue eyes intense. *Those eyes*, thought Rebecca. They had some strange kind of power over her.

"Look," she said, trying to breathe evenly and not lose it, "I have, like, five minutes before I have to be home. And I need you to do something for me, right now. You need to meet my friend. To make yourself visible to her."

"I don't think that's a good idea," Frank said, backing away.

"You did it yesterday, with my cousin!" *Please don't disappear,* Rebecca thought.

"That seemed like a life-and-death situation," he said. His face was paler today, more sunken-in. "Making myself visible, it just puts more people at risk. He'll *see* you all."

"Who?"

"Gideon Mason. You said he's threatening you, making your life miserable. Now he's seen your cousin with me as well. . . ."

"But you said no real harm could come to us, right?"

"I suppose." He didn't sound very sure of this now, but it was too late to worry about that at the moment.

"Please. My friend knows everything. She's trying to help us find the locket. Ling!"

Ling came creeping around the corner. "Where do I stand?" she asked Rebecca.

"We should move closer to the building," Frank said. "We're too much out in the open here."

"Just by the door," Rebecca told Ling. "And don't freak out, OK?"

She could tell by Ling's saucer eyes and stunned expression that Frank was visible to her now as well. How did he do that? She'd ask him, but there wasn't time.

"Oh my god!" Ling exclaimed. She clapped a hand over her mouth to stifle an excited giggle.

"Ling, Frank. Frank, this is Ling."

"Sorry to be so . . . wow!" said Ling. "You just appearing like this, from invisible to — here in the blink of an eye. It's like *I Dream of Jeannie!*"

"I think I know that song," Frank told her. "A ghost down on the docks sings it."

"I only know the TV show," said Ling. Now they both looked confused.

"He doesn't know about TV. Look, we don't have much time." Rebecca didn't want them to get sidetracked. "Frank — any more information we could use?"

Instead of answering, Frank vanished.

"How does he *do* that?" Ling wanted to know. She grabbed Rebecca's hand and they scampered back down Orleans Avenue. "By the way, you never told me he was so good-looking. Have you got some kind of thing for him?"

"Please. He's been dead since 1873," said Rebecca.

"Better not let Anton see him," Ling advised. "He might get jealous."

"I don't want anyone else to see him," said Rebecca. "He's right about that. I wish Aurelia had never seen him."

Sometimes Rebecca wished *she* had never seen him, but now it was too late. It was too late for everything. In forty-eight hours, they'd be on their way back to New York and if they didn't come up with a plan fast, Degas' locket would be smashed to smithereens. If they talked to Raf this afternoon and he was unable — or unwilling — to help, she'd have to work on Anton again. How could they manage this by themselves?

When they got back to the house, her father had finished his phone calls and was waiting for them in the courtyard.

"You just missed Anton," he told Rebecca. "He dropped this off for you."

He tossed her a small yellow package. Rebecca resisted the urge to rip it open on the spot. Ling stood dead still, staring at it as though it contained explosives.

"He said he and his friend'll be over around seven to collect you two. Everything OK?"

"Yeah. Why wouldn't it be?"

"I get the feeling you're up to something," said her dad, but Rebecca could tell by the tone of his voice that he was joking around.

"Us? No. God, no," said Ling. "Um, Rebecca, maybe we should leave that — upstairs? Before we go?"

"What is it?" her father wanted to know. He scraped his chair back from the metal table and stood up.

"Just something to wear tonight. A necklace, I think." Rebecca was trying to sound nonchalant.

"Really? That's kind of an expensive gift, isn't it? Do you really think you should accept something like that from Anton?" Her father wasn't joking around anymore. He was frowning.

"You're so right," Ling told him. She was already halfway up the stairs of the slave quarters. "Miss Manners says that you should never accept a personal gift like jewelry or clothing from a man unless you're engaged to him."

Rebecca looked up at Ling, willing her to shut up. How was this helping?

"But luckily," Ling continued, beaming her widest smile, "this isn't a gift. Is it, Becca? The necklace belongs to Anton's mother. It's just on loan for tonight. His mother thought it would look perfect with Rebecca's dress."

"Really?" Her father glanced from Ling to Rebecca. "How does his mother know what your dress looks like?"

"Um, she came out of the house last night," Rebecca said. She wasn't such a smooth liar as Ling. "You know, after dinner. When I was out on Sixth Street talking to Anton. And we had sort of a chat about it, and she mentioned this necklace that she thought would look nice and all."

"Oh. Well." Rebecca's dad still looked puzzled. "That's nice of her."

"Super-nice!" Ling said, and bounced up the remaining

stairs. Rebecca dashed up after her, eager to get away from her father before he came to his senses.

Ling was waiting inside, ready to pounce on the package.

"Why didn't Anton just bring it over tonight?" she asked Rebecca. "Boys are not thinkers, are they?"

"I guess he didn't realize Dad would be here," said Rebecca, slitting the package open with her finger. There was no note inside, just a blue box that opened with a clunk. Inside the box lay a large silver locket attached to a long, heavy chain. Something that vaguely resembled the letter *V* was engraved on the outward-facing side of the locket, though the engraving was so fussy and ornate the letter was hard to make out. Lisette's last name was Villieux. That was probably why Anton chose it.

"It's kind of ugly." Ling made a face. "And it'll look weird with your dress. But you only have to wear it tonight. Just long enough to get mugged."

"Don't remind me," Rebecca groaned. "Come on. Let's go pull some more weeds."

Mr. Boyd was on a rampage this afternoon. There was no way Rebecca was going to get the chance to speak to Raf. She couldn't even speak to Ling. Rebecca was on painting duty, working on a breezeblock wall the far side of the yard. Her group was so far away from everyone else, "we're almost in the Seventh Ward," as one of her fellow painters said.

"Is this a work party or a talk party?" Mr. Boyd was roaring. "Kermit, you're no more use to me than an actual frog!"

LeLe, the girl next to Rebecca, told her to paint faster.

"I want this finished today," she said. "Tomorrow after school I'm going to Jazz Fest. All I dream of is crawfish bread."

Rebecca slathered on paint, keeping a wary eye on the sky. If it started raining, all their work would be wasted. But it would mean work could stop for the day and there'd be time to talk to Raf before her father came back.

"It's not gonna rain," LeLe told her. "God loves Mr. Boyd too much. That's why it only rains after we finish, and all weekend long."

The rain wasn't cooperating, but finally Mr. Boyd seemed to be. He strode over to inspect the wall, and seemed pleased, more or less. A little too much grass painted for his liking, he said, but he told Rebecca that she and Ling could finish up.

"You've done plenty," he said. "Thanks for your help this week."

"Thanks for . . . having us," Rebecca said. Mr. Boyd, walking away, held up his clipboard in salutation.

Ling had finished her planting duties and was one step ahead of Rebecca, as usual.

"I told Raf I had a splinter," she whispered, "and he said we can come back to his house to use some tweezers. You can text your dad to meet us there."

"Do you really have a splinter?"

"A little one. I could pull it out with my fingernails. But this is a good plan, right? Walk and talk, my friend. We can walk and talk."

Rebecca had assumed they were going to his grandmother's house farther down St. Philip, but Raf led them in a different direction, along Marais Street to his father's house. Everyone was there this afternoon, he said, working.

"We need to ask you something," Rebecca said, not wanting to waste any time. She was keeping an eye out for Gideon Mason, to make sure he wasn't anywhere around, listening in. "We need your help. But you have to promise to keep it secret. Really, it's top secret."

"Can we rely on you?" Ling asked so seriously that Raf looked alarmed.

"Are you two undercover Feds or something?" he asked, stopping dead in his tracks. "I don't wanna get involved in other people's business. People who get involved in other people's business around here end up shot dead on their own porch."

"No, no! This is just *our* business," Rebecca reassured him. *And a ghost's.* She didn't know how much to tell him. "It's about one of the houses on St. Philip — the ones coming down next week. We need to get into it this weekend, to look for something."

"Look for what?" Raf still sounded suspicious, but he started walking again.

"Something that — someone we know lost there."

"Who do *you* know in Tremé?" Raf asked. "Is this something Junior told you? He always spinning lines to girls. Don't listen to him."

"No, it's someone else. Someone — look, it's just really hard to explain." Rebecca looked over at Ling, flanking Raf on the other side. How much could they tell him? How much would he believe?

"It's a sort of historical mystery," Ling improvised. "We've been doing some research, and it seems as though something was hidden away in that house over a hundred years ago. Something of historic importance."

"Hidden where?" Raf seemed skeptical. "Those houses have been empty a long time. If anybody left something in them, somebody else would have taken it by now, believe me."

"It's under the floorboards." Rebecca wondered if it was a good idea to tell Raf any of this. If Anton didn't want to know, why would Raf? He didn't even seem to be listening anymore, shouting out to some friends of his cruising by on bicycles. But after they'd wheeled away around the corner, he asked Rebecca which house she was talking about.

"The one at the near end. The haunted one."

"You want to break into that house and start pulling up floorboards? Even though that place might be falling down around your head?"

Rebecca and Ling both nodded.

"Tomorrow, early evening," Ling told him. "When it gets dark, so people don't see us. We really need your help getting in."

"Will you help *me* when the police charge me with criminal trespass? Sorry — but no way."

Rebecca and Ling looked at each other. Anton wouldn't help them, Rebecca thought. Raf wouldn't help them. They were going to have to manage the locket rescue on their own.

CHAPTER SEVENTEEN

"LET'S JUST FORGET IT," REBECCA SAID QUICKLY. It was a lot to ask of someone else, she knew, especially someone who'd just met them. Maybe she should just tell her father about the whole thing and see if he could get the demolition halted. He knew about Lisette, so maybe he'd believe this ghost story. Maybe, maybe not.

"You won't say anything about this to anyone, will you?" Ling asked Raf.

"I'll say nothing," Raf assured her. "I see nothing, I say nothing. This is it."

He gestured to a white shotgun double, and turned to climb the stairs.

"I should warn you," Raf said, grasping the door handle. "It's gonna be crazy in here."

Raf's father's house looked quiet and ordinary from the outside, but opening the front door revealed something like Aladdin's cave. The small front parlor, crammed with people, was an explosion of color. Rebecca had never seen so much yellow in her life — yellow feathers, yellow satin, yellow sequins, all of it heaped on a table in the middle of the room.

Propped against one wall was a giant feathered headdress that spread into vast wings. It had to be seven feet tall, and almost as wide, studded with panels of gleaming fake jewels, pale as Easter eggs, and twinkling sequins. People were sewing, she realized, men as well as women, some sitting around the table and others perched wherever they could find a place. A little girl stood on a chair while a smaller headdress, fluffy with soft feathers, was tried on her head for size. She rolled out her lips in a pout and tried to push it off.

"Everyone, these are my friends Rebecca and Ling!" Raf shouted; the little girl was wailing now. "This is my father, my grandfather, my grandmother, my aunt Cissy, my aunt Angela, my cousin . . ."

"Can you sew?" Aunt Cissy called out. "Can you thread needles?"

"They're from New York," Raf announced. "They've never seen Indians before."

"I can thread needles," Ling offered, her splinter forgotten, and Raf's cousin Jackie waved her over. Jackie was wearing a jeans and a Liuzza's-By-The-Track T-shirt. Everyone was just in T-shirts and jeans, Rebecca noted, but the scene looked insanely glamorous to her, like an old-time Hollywood musical.

Alongside the giant headdress, pieces of costumes sat propped against the wall: an intricately beaded sleeve, tall feathered boots, some kind of outsized feathered bib encrusted with jewels. She'd never seen anything like this in her life.

"Why you crying?" one of Raf's aunts asked the little girl, tugging on one of her long braids. "You say you want to be a little queen tomorrow, and now you crying!"

"They fixing everything up for Jazz Fest tomorrow," Raf told Rebecca. "Some of the suits got torn and messed up on St. Joseph's, and then my aunt's grandbabies decided they want to mask with the rest of the tribe at Jazz Fest, so everyone's sewing."

"I can't sew but I can use a glue gun," said Rebecca, and soon she was seated at the table, decorating staffs for the children to carry. This wouldn't bring her any closer to rescuing the locket, but at least she could sit down for a while.

She didn't want to ask a million questions, but Ling, sitting on the floor, wasn't quite so shy. They spent all year working on new "suits," Raf's father said, in time for Mardi Gras, and then they wore them again on St. Joseph's Day, otherwise known as Super Sunday.

"For some Indians, that's all," he told them. "A year of paying and sewing for two days of wearing. But you'll see us tomorrow at Jazz Fest. Everyone looking real pretty."

"So during Mardi Gras you have a big parade?" Ling asked. Raf's father shook his head and grinned, looking just like Raf.

"We're out on the backstreets," he said. "You gotta come find us. You gotta come to our neighborhood."

"I never go to parades." Aunt Cissy bit on a pin.

"Sometimes I catch a bit of Zulu up on Broad," said Aunt Angela. "But otherwise I'd never walk out to watch a Mardi Gras parade."

"Why?" asked Ling, threading another needle and pinning it, yellow thread dangling, onto the cushioned back of an armchair.

"My daddy got himself beaten right out there on Canal Street," Raf's grandfather said, "for daring to stand and watch a parade. And people want to know why we make our own carnival?"

Rebecca couldn't believe how quickly the time passed. She was concentrating so hard, it was impossible to think about anything but the task at hand — even if Aunt Cissy's grandbaby looked profoundly unimpressed with Rebecca's decoration of her staff. Before long her phone was buzzing; her father had pulled up outside in a cab, and it was time to say good-bye.

Raf's father walked out with them, and Rebecca's dad climbed out of the cab, which was stopped on the other side of the street. The two men stood in the road, talking. Raf had followed them out of the house as well, and he grabbed Rebecca's arm at the bottom of the stairs.

"I really want to help you," he said in a low voice. "But it just sounds too . . ." He shook his head. .

"I understand," Rebecca told him, though she wished he would change his mind.

"Can't your dad help you? Doesn't he know people who could stop the demolition?"

"Maybe," Rebecca agreed.

"Because on the one hand you got an old white guy — no offense — who can talk to people at City Hall. And on the other you got a black kid from the Sixth Ward trying to smash his way into a house. Which you think is better?"

"Ready?" Rebecca's father called to them, shaking Raf's father's hand. Ling was trotting along the sidewalk, chasing a drifting yellow feather.

"Well — see you," Rebecca wished Raf would change his mind, but there wasn't any time left to persuade him. She stepped into the road, waiting for Ling to catch up.

"Look for us at Jazz Fest tomorrow afternoon!" Raf called. "And wear some rain boots!"

Rebecca had turned back to smile at him when she heard the screech of a car. The sound came out of nowhere. One minute the street was quiet; the next she was deafened by the roar of someone accelerating toward them at top speed. Someone grabbed her arm and tugged, sending her staggering back onto the curb. She was conscious of a flash of silver metal, of Raf's father shouting.

"Lunatic!" Ling was shrieking. "Becca, are you OK? That

guy was parked just down there and then all of a sudden he swerves out and . . ."

"I think your dad got hit," Raf said, and he took off across the road. A nauseous panic swirled through Rebecca: Her Dad? Hit? She couldn't even see him.

"Dad!" she cried. Where was he? How could this all have happened so quickly?

"I'm OK!" called out a creaky voice, and she ran toward it blindly. Raf and his father were leaning over her own father's prone form. He was sprawled on the ground, clutching his ankle, and looked white as a sheet.

"That crazy fool nearly killed you," Raf's father was saying.

"I got out of the way in time," said Rebecca's dad, wincing with pain. "Think I just twisted my ankle. Don't cry, honey. Everything's fine."

He smiled up at Rebecca, but it looked more like a grimace. She rubbed away her hot tears and tried to breathe. He was OK. They were all OK. Still, Rebecca couldn't stop shaking. Something very bad could just have happened to her father, to any of them.

Ling was by her side, a supportive arm around Rebecca's waist. Rebecca was conscious of people out of their houses now, up and down the street, people standing on their porches, more men coming forward to help.

"This child needs to sit down," Miss Angela was saying, and Rebecca allowed herself to be led back to the stoop. Her nerves felt torn to shreds. Someone was handing her a dewy glass of iced tea, and Ling slid onto the step beside her.

"Shouldn't we call an ambulance?" Ling asked, and Miss Angela looked at her as though she were speaking in Mandarin.

"I tried to see the license plate," Ling told Rebecca in a low voice, "but it all happened way too fast. I did see *something*, though."

"Something?" Rebecca sipped at her tea. It was insanely sweet, but it was making her feel better. Across the street two men were hoisting up her father, carrying him to a plastic chair on the sidewalk.

"Some*one*," Ling muttered. "Didn't you say that kid Toby Sutton has red hair?"

Rebecca nodded, and took another gulp of tea. She looked at Ling, knowing exactly what she was going to say.

"That was all I saw," Ling told her. "The driver was a young guy with red hair. You know, if he wants to drive around trying to kill people, he should at least have the sense to wear a hat or something."

Toby Sutton didn't have any sense, Rebecca thought. That's what Anton kept telling her. He was deranged right now. Doing things that only a deranged person would do.

Raf's father, who'd sent the cab away, insisted on driving them back to the Quarter in his van. When they got there, he helped Rebecca's dad hobble into the house on Orleans Street. The foot wasn't broken, Raf's dad said; the assembled medical opinion on Marais Street had reached that verdict, and Rebecca's father agreed. Miss Angela had sent them home with some pain tablets and a few bags of frozen vegetables to use as ice packs.

After Raf's father left, Rebecca bustled around getting her father comfortable.

"I'll call Anton and tell him we can't go to the dance," she said, but her father shook his head.

"I'll be fine." He lay on the sofa with his foot up on two pillows, a glass of water and some painkillers next to him on the coffee table. "I just need some rest this evening. You need to go out and have a good time. Forget all this. What are you going to do — sit around the house, moping? And what about the boys?"

Ling gave Rebecca a hard look. Rebecca knew what her friend was thinking: *What about the locket*?

Rebecca bristled at the thought of seeing Toby; all of the stress of the last few hours had hardened into an indignant rage. She wanted to smack him in the face.

"You go start getting ready, Ling," Rebecca's dad said. "You, too, Rebecca. Go on! Those boys'll be here soon."

"I'm going to get you the ice pack," Rebecca told her father. "And I'm calling Aunt Claudia!"

"You don't need to do that," her father argued. "Just leave me a bag of chips and the remote. I'll be fine."

Ling went back to their little building to shower, and Rebecca pulled a bag of frozen corn out of the freezer.

"Honey?" her father called.

"Are you OK, Dad?" Rebecca walked back in brandishing the bag of frozen corn, wrapped in a dishtowel. "Really, please let me call Aunt Claudia."

"I'm fine — really. I was just going to say that I think you girls may have to go to Jazz Fest without me tomorrow. We'll see how I feel in the morning, but if it's a sprain I should keep off it. Now go put on those expensive dresses, OK?"

Up in her room, Rebecca shook out the green dress and then trudged to the bathroom for the briefest of showers. She thought about her conversation with Raf, just before Toby had pulled his stunt. There was no point now telling her father about the actual locket, the one in the house in Tremé, or asking for his help. They were only in New Orleans for another day and a half, and it looked as though he'd be spending all that time lying half asleep on the sofa.

Rebecca slipped on the green dress, noting again how flattering the color was. But this time she didn't feel excited or glamorous. She brushed out her tangled hair, hoping it didn't look too frizzy. She was slipping on Anton's locket when Ling peeked into the room, looking fabulous in her short black dress.

"Yikes," Ling said, walking in with her makeup bag. "I wonder why Anton's mom thought that would look so good with your dress?"

"Very funny," said Rebecca. The locket chain was too long and way too heavy.

"You could hang a pocket watch from that chain," Ling observed. "And the locket is huge. Maybe you could keep your lipstick in it?"

"The main thing is that it's old," said Rebecca, "so Toby believes it could have belonged to Lisette."

Ling peered into Rebecca's mirror and dabbed some glittery eye shadow on her lids. "Is Anton sure he'll turn up tonight? What if he just tries to run you down again?"

"I hope he's waiting for us when we arrive," Rebecca said, reaching over to pull a container of blush out of Ling's bag.

"And then we can beat him up, right?"

"I wish."

"Hurry up then!" Ling commanded, passing Rebecca a tube of lip gloss. "The boys'll be here soon. And you want to look stunning in front of all the Temple Mead dumb — what does Aurelia call them?"

"Dumb Debs. Give me some of that glitter."

They checked on Rebecca's father, who was contently watching The History Channel while icing his ankle. When the doorbell buzzed, Rebecca went to open the gate for Anton and Phil.

But only Phil was standing there, looking slightly more grown-up than she remembered him. He was wearing a blazer and khakis, and reeked of aftershave.

"Anton's in the car," he explained. "He's illegally parked just up there, so if you guys are ready?"

"I'll go get Ling." Rebecca leaned out to see where Anton was waiting. A black BMW, its brake lights bright, was stopped a little way up the street.

As they approached, Anton got out of the car, racing around to open the front passenger door open for Rebecca. At the sight of him, Rebecca felt her composure crack.

"Your friend Toby tried to kill us today!" she told him. "My father is injured! He can't even walk!"

Anton paled. "What . . . what happened?"

She slid into the car and sat seething while Anton got back in.

"We were in Tremé, about to get into a cab, and he drove up at top speed. He was trying to knock us down. Ling pulled me out of the way just in time."

"It was Raf, actually," Ling volunteered from the backseat.

"Is your father injured really badly?" Anton asked. He looked upset, but not all that surprised.

"Well, he can't walk. He might need to get X-rays."

"Do you want me to call my dad?" Phil offered. "He could fast-track him through Truro."

"I just want to get tonight over and done with," Rebecca said, folding her arms. If Toby really *did* want this stupid locket, he could have it. After this evening, she never wanted to see him again.

"Rebecca, I promise you." Anton's voice was breaking. He hadn't started the car yet. "If Toby tries anything tonight beyond taking the locket, I'll hit him. And after tonight, I will never, ever have anything to do with him again. After tonight, if I ever see him again, even from a distance, I'll call his parents and I'll call the police. I swear."

Rebecca said nothing. This wasn't Anton's fault, she knew. But how could he *ever* have been friends with someone as mean as Toby Sutton? Why didn't he call the police when he knew where Toby was hiding out?

They all sat in silence until a taxi driving up Orleans honked at them to get out of the way.

"Come on then," Rebecca said. "Let's get this over with."

CHAPTER EIGHTEEN

THE COUNTRY CLUB WAS NEAR THE LAKE, AT THE end of a long driveway lined with oak trees. Anton had parked on the far side of the lot, near the golf course, but nobody tried to run them over as they walked to the building. Rebecca's nerves were buzzing; she felt completely on edge. But if Toby was planning on making an appearance tonight, he wasn't here yet.

The ballroom was long, with French windows down one side and a dance floor — presided over by a squat DJ — at one end. The chandeliers and busy carpet made the place feel like a casino, Rebecca thought, though she'd only ever been in one casino in her life, years ago in Atlantic City. A tiny bar was tended by a very short elderly man with slicked-back hair and big glasses, who poured Cokes and Shirley Temples slowly, as though he'd never done this before in his life and was worried about dropping the bottles.

Rebecca walked past girls with elaborate hairstyles and shiny short dresses, and boys wearing jackets from Brooks Brothers or Perlis. Tuxes, Rebecca remembered, were not allowed at the Spring Dance, so nobody would get it confused with Senior Prom. All that meant was that lots of boys turned up in their fathers' blazers, which made them look even younger and skinnier than they really were.

Anton reached for her hand, and Rebecca felt her face reddening. People were staring at them: Of course they were. Especially the girls. Anton looked so much more grown-up than most of the boys here. He was wearing an actual suit, dark blue and slim fitting, and his tie wasn't a stupid Saints tie — Rebecca had counted three of those just walking through the lobby — or something decorated with tiny crawfish or alligators. She was too nervous and self-conscious, so after gripping his hand way too hard she just let it drop.

"OK," said Ling, catching up with her. They walked toward a vacant table while the boys fell behind. "I've seen two girls with those weird fishing feather things in their hair. I have to say, I kind of like them."

"The humidity is going to your head," said Rebecca. She was trying not to look too closely at the crowded tables in case she saw someone she recognized from Temple Mead.

At some tables every single person was either talking on their iPhone or texting. Anton told Ling that there were numerous after-parties at various people's houses and at clubs, and a lot of people were probably trying to decide what they'd do next.

Rebecca didn't get it. Girls at Temple Mead talked all year about what a big deal the Spring Dance was, but so many of them seemed eager to move on. Maybe when they finally made it here, they discovered that all school dances were essentially the same, and not that glamorous after all. It was just the same girls from school, sitting with the same boys they'd known all their lives.

Servers in black and white ferried food out to a big round table in the middle of the room. One of them was probably Raf's brother, but Rebecca couldn't see anyone who looked particularly like Raf, and it was hard to see much in this room anyway, because the lights were so dim. Ling insisted on them both walking over to the buffet to check out what was on offer, expecting it to be good: Food was usually *really* good in New Orleans. In fact, Rebecca had promised Ling that it would be a cut above the usual school-dance fare. But actually it was a weird mix of kiddie food, like mac-and-cheese and slimy hot dogs, with heavy grown-up stuff, like braised pork belly and oyster dressing.

Phil seemed delighted with the food, piling up his plate with sticky barbecued shrimp and hamburgers, but Rebecca had realized that Phil was one of those people who made the best of everything. He was a cheerful person who liked to join in, take part, and look on the bright side.

"I think Phil might be kind of weird," she muttered to Ling after he came back from the bar with another round of Shirley

211

Temples and said they were the best he'd ever tasted. "It's like he's in some kind of cult."

"He's not weird. He's just from the West Coast." Ling nudged her. "What *is* weird are these cupcakes. I swear they're from a Betty Crocker mix."

"Everybody go whoop, whoop!" boomed the DJ. "Put your hands in the air, and give it up for the Milkshake song!"

"I love this song!" Phil licked barbecue sauce off his fingers. "It's, like, so retro!"

"I know, right?" agreed Ling, and they raced off to join the throng on the dance floor.

"Want to dance?" Anton asked Rebecca without any enthusiasm.

"No," she said. It was happening again. The night Anton took her to the Bowmans' Christmas party it was just like this — the two of them sitting by themselves, glum and awkward, while other people had a good time. She wondered if he would kiss her again tonight, but it seemed unlikely. There was a tension between them now, not to mention way too many Temple Mead girls staring.

"I feel sick about what happened today," Anton said to her in a low voice, as conscious as she was, it seemed, of other people overhearing.

"It's not your fault," said Rebecca. Anton was leaning in so close, their foreheads were touching. She wished everyone else in the room would vanish — like ghosts. Unfortunately, Rebecca had just spotted Amy and Jessica only three tables away. They were looking over, and probably trying to eavesdrop as well. Wishing they'd set wiretaps in all the floral displays, no doubt.

"The locket looks good," said Anton, and they both smiled, knowing it was a big lie. The locket was beyond ugly. Rebecca couldn't wait to be rid of it.

Ling staggered back off the dance floor, laughing and whooping, and persuaded Rebecca to walk with her to the ladies'.

"If I get through this without running into anyone," she whispered to Ling as they waited in line, "then I . . ."

"Rebecca!" Jessica lurched out of a cubicle, the door banging behind her, and practically ricocheted into one of the sinks. "I'm so glad you came!"

Rebecca and Ling exchanged glances. It sounded as though Jessica had been drinking more than Shirley Temples. She turned on the faucet and water splashed all over her lacy blue dress.

"Weeee," she giggled. "Oh my god, Anton Grey looks hot! You are so lucky!"

Ling gave Rebecca a "told you so" look.

"Oh, um, Jessica. This is my friend from New York, Ling."

"Ling?" Jessica held out a soapy hand, almost falling over. "Ling-A-Ling! Ding-A-Ling! That's a cute name!"

"Thanks," said Ling, raising an eyebrow. "You having a good time?"

"The best," sighed Jessica. "Oh my god, you won't believe who else is here tonight. Marianne Sutton! She came all the way from Miss . . . Mississ . . . Mississippi. It's like — the old days!"

Rebecca felt her smile straining. *The bad old days*, she wanted to say.

"Amy says," Jessica stage-whispered. "Amy says that Toby Sutton is around, too. Somewhere."

"What? Here, at the country club?" Rebecca instinctively put her hand to her neck.

"Who knows?" Jessica shrugged, then half flounced, half stumbled out.

When they left the ladies' restroom, Rebecca was on high alert. Toby might be here. And his sister, too. Rebecca remembered the warning Jessica and Amy gave her when she first started school at Temple Mead. *Watch out for Helena Bowman and Marianne Sutton. They could make a lot of trouble for you if they don't like you.* Helena might be gone, but Marianne was still around.

In fact, she was right there in the lobby, smiling at Rebecca as though they were long-lost friends.

"Hey, Rebecca," she said, and Rebecca felt herself blushing. There'd always been something about Marianne — Marianne and Helena — that had made her feel awkward and ungainly, at some kind of disadvantage. Marianne looked even thinner these days, Rebecca thought, and her eyes were the palest washed-out blue. She was smiling at Rebecca but there was no warmth to the smile, no warmth in her eyes. It was that same haughty, appraising look she'd given Rebecca the first time she'd ever spoken to her, on the stairs at Temple Mead. Rebecca felt inept, unable to speak.

Ling, however, wasn't intimidated at all.

"So, is this the one with the insane brother who likes to burn things down?" she asked, staring at Marianne. "The one who tried to run your dad over in the street this afternoon?"

"I don't know anything about that," Marianne protested, her smile fading. "What Toby gets up to has nothing to do with me, OK? I don't even know where he is."

She stepped closer to Rebecca, as though Ling weren't there, and held out a hand.

"Everything else is in the past, yeah? Let's make peace, and be friends. You and me."

Rebecca gazed at Marianne's pale hand. She really didn't want to shake it. She just wanted to walk away.

"That's an . . . unusual necklace," Marianne said, stepping even closer.

"It's a locket, actually," Rebecca said. *As if you didn't know,* she wanted to snap. Marianne was almost bending over to stare at it, drinking in every detail. Marianne might say that she had no idea where Toby was, but Rebecca didn't believe that for one single minute. She was feeding Toby information. Anton's guess was probably right: Marianne had heard about the locket from her old cronies at Temple Mead and had let her crazy brother know right away.

"Did you buy it here?" Marianne asked. Rebecca couldn't believe that Marianne had managed to fool her last year, pretending to be her friend when they were getting ready to ride in the Septimus parade together. Right now she was utterly transparent.

"I didn't buy it," Rebecca told her. "I guess it's . . . it's really a family piece. It has huge sentimental value."

"Well, I didn't think you were wearing it because it was pretty." Marianne grimaced. Some of the other girls standing nearby tittered.

"I'm wearing it," said Rebecca, resisting the urge to slap them all, "because it will always remind me of a very dear friend I made in New Orleans last year. Needless to say, I didn't meet her at Temple Mead."

Julie Casworth Young sashayed over, turning to stand at Marianne's elbow as though she were a Miss America contestant taking her appointed spot on the stage. Rebecca hadn't seen her for a year, but of course, she remembered Julie — blonde, pretty, spiteful. She was one of Helena's exclusive set, one of the girls who used to hang out with Anton and Toby in the cemetery. As far as Rebecca could remember, Julie had never, ever spoken to her directly before.

"Rebecca, isn't it?" she squeaked. Anton was right: She did sound like a hyperventilating mouse. "And that's . . ."

She was peering at the locket as well. Really, these girls would make terrible spies. They weren't subtle at all.

The strangest look passed over Julie's face, like a cloud passing across the moon, and Rebecca wasn't sure how to read it. But she'd put up with their scrutiny long enough.

"Let's go," she said to Ling, and they marched away, back toward the ballroom.

"Have a good time at Jazz Fest tomorrow!" Marianne called.

"How do they know we're going to Jazz Fest?" Rebecca hissed at Ling.

"Keep walking," Ling murmured, and they wove through the obstacle course of tables as fast as they could. "Man, these girls are mean. You know why they hate you, right?"

"Because I'm an outsider. I'm not one of *them*."

"Doesn't matter where you come from," said Ling, dodging a waiter carrying a tray of dirty plates. "You stole their number-one man."

"Anton?" Rebecca said, pretending to sound surprised.

"Duh. Look around you. It's like Brad Pitt surrounded by the seven dwarves. He's like the crown prince of St. Simeon's."

"He's just a guy," muttered Rebecca.

"There are guys," said Ling, sighing, "and then there are *guys*."

She nodded toward their table, where Phil was in the middle

of some long and apparently hilarious story — though he was the one doing all the laughing.

"If I were you," she went on, leaning close to whisper in Rebecca's ear, "I would dance with that guy of yours and drive these witches even wilder with jealousy. Why not? What have you got to lose?"

Ling was right, Rebecca decided. So the next time Anton asked her to dance, she said yes. It was a slow number, which was better in almost every way. Slow dances were much easier for most guys to manage, because they basically involved walking and hugging. A slow dance also meant she could be close to Anton, feel his arms around her again. And, of course, Rebecca couldn't help wanting to annoy the sneering Temple Mead girls.

Anton pulled her close, and Rebecca relaxed into the warmth of his chest. The song playing was cheesy, but she didn't care — everything about this dance was cheesy. She felt Anton's lips on her hair and her skin flushed with delight.

"You look real pretty tonight," he whispered to her, and she hid her smile against his jacket lapel.

She wanted to close her eyes and block the rest of the world out. But even if she could zone out the eyes boring into her, and all the muttered comments, it was hard to enjoy the moment. Too many distracting concerns were beeping in her brain like unanswered messages. Toby. Frank. The fake locket. The real locket. The house on St. Philip Street. Her father. Aurelia. Gideon Mason . . . *beep beep beep beep.*

The dance let out around midnight, and she and Anton walked out with Ling and Phil. She held Anton's hand again, squeezing it gratefully. Things were easier when they faced them together. And who knew what they'd have to face in the parking lot?

Their little group walked slowly to Anton's car, everyone trying to act casual but, Rebecca knew, intensely aware that Toby might pop up at any minute. Ling pulled Phil away for a moment, showing a sudden interest in a vintage Jag parked in the middle of the lot.

Rebecca knew what she was doing. Toby was more likely to confront Rebecca if the only person with her was Anton: He thought Anton was on his side.

The stupid locket was so heavy, it was giving her a neck ache. Rebecca couldn't wait to be rid of it. It bounced against her dress with every step. She peered into the dark trees lining the golf course. Where was Toby? What was he waiting for?

Anton was nervous, too, she could tell. He even checked the trunk of the car before they got in, as though Toby might be hiding inside. But there was no sign of him, and soon Ling and Phil rejoined them.

"Well, so much for your brilliant plan," Rebecca said to

Anton when everyone was safely in the car, doors locked. "Marianne was interrogating me in there, but where's Toby?"

"I have no idea," Anton admitted.

"I'm still wearing this locket. What happens now?"

Anton started the engine, staring straight ahead.

"And Marianne knows all about us going to Jazz Fest tomorrow," Rebecca added.

"That means Toby knows it, too," said Anton.

Rebecca felt a stab of fear. "He's not going to attack me in public, is he? Not with thousands of people around."

Anton frowned. "Easy to get lost in a crowd. Easy to steal things as well."

"I went to Times Square last New Year's Eve," said Phil, "and someone stole my wallet."

"You're such a tourist," said Ling. "Who goes to Times Square on New Year's Eve? And who would go to Times Square on New Year's Eve and carry a wallet?"

"I'm coming with you tomorrow," Anton announced, looking at Rebecca. "You have to wear the locket. But don't worry — I'll be there the whole time with you. I'm not letting you out of my sight."

"I'll come, too," volunteered Phil from the backseat. "Because, dude, whatever's going on, I think you need my help. I never told anyone here this, but I totally know judo. Three years when I was in elementary school, my friends. Three years!"

"I take back all those mean things I just said," Ling told him. "You're clearly a superhero."

Any sort of hero was better than nothing, Rebecca thought. She *did* feel slightly better, knowing that Anton would be with her tomorrow. Whatever Toby was planning next was sure to be very, very bad.

CHAPTER NINETEEN

REBECCA'S FATHER WAS IN NO SHAPE TO COME TO Jazz Fest and walk around the fairgrounds all day. His ankle was throbbing and swollen, and Aunt Claudia was coming over to take him to the hospital. Friday could be a busy work day for her, especially with all the tourists in town for Jazz Fest, but it was a wet morning, threatening to develop into a truly sodden afternoon.

"Miss Cissy's grandbaby is going to be a wet little chicken today," said Ling, gazing out the kitchen window at rain plopping onto the banana leaves.

"At least Anton or Phil can use my ticket," Rebecca's dad said, wincing with pain. "And you'll keep an eye on Aurelia, won't you? Claudia said she's been acting up this week. Something about not getting to spend enough time with you. Maybe 'cause Ling's here . . . ow!"

Rebecca felt a pang of guilt. She'd forgotten all about the one-on-one talk with Aurelia that never happened. On Wednesday night, by the time she and Anton left the cemetery, the little party at Aunt Claudia's was breaking up, and her father had already ordered a cab to take them home. Aurelia had seemed a little sulky, but Rebecca had other things on her mind — mainly, she had to admit, that long kiss with Anton. Since then so much had happened that she'd barely given Aurelia a second thought.

"I'll spent lots of time with Relia today," she told her father. She *did* want to talk to Aurelia, but part of her wished her little cousin wasn't coming at all that afternoon, not with Toby on the loose. Whatever went down with Toby today, he *had* to leave Aurelia alone. She'd done nothing, absolutely nothing, to make him want to hurt her.

Beep beep beep. Rebecca's brain was in overload again. What about Frank and the locket in the boarded-up house? By this time tomorrow, she and her father and Ling would be packing up, about to fly out of New Orleans. She needed someone's help. Someone with a clue.

Rebecca knelt by the sofa, seeing if her father's shoe would go on despite his injured ankle. It wouldn't.

"Dad," she said, standing up and handing him the useless shoe. "Tonight when we get home, could you and I talk about something? It's about Tremé and those houses that are going to be demolished next week."

"Sure, honey," he said. "Whatever you want to talk about — I'll be here. I'm going to have to hop to Claudia's car, aren't I?"

"Mr. Brown," Ling called from the kitchen. "I texted Phil, and his father is going to make sure they take care of you at the hospital. He's going to come down there himself."

"I just feel so useless," Rebecca's dad said. "I was really looking forward to today."

"So was I," Rebecca lied.

"You should have brought rain boots with you," he said. "It's going to be bad out there. If it's too wet and you're not having a good time, you just come home, OK?"

Rebecca wanted nothing more than to stay home all day, with the doors and shutters closed, hiding from the world. But there was the matter of a locket that needed to be stolen, and another locket that needed to be found. Time was running out for both.

The threat of heavy rain wasn't putting off the crowds at the Fair Grounds Race Course. Anton had to park a twenty-minute-walk away, taking care to find a space on the "high ground" side of the street in case the gutters flooded. When they reached the pedestrian entrance, thousands of people were making their way through the turnstiles, many of them laden down with backpacks, baby strollers, folded ground tarps, collapsible chairs, and golf umbrellas. Some people were already wearing transparent rain ponchos, alert to the dark clouds swirling overhead.

"At least it's not all sandy and dusty here," Anton told them as they crossed the racetrack. "Some years I go home all covered in grit."

This year, Rebecca soon realized, they would go home covered in mud. The combination of overnight rain and thousands of trampling feet had turned every stretch of grass into a slushy mire. Aurelia — given permission to leave school at lunchtime, thanks to a note from Aunt Claudia — was the only one in their group wearing rain boots with her shorts and T-shirt, but soon all her bare skin was flecked with dirt. Anton and Phil, both in jeans, looked like they'd been wading in a swamp. Rebecca and Ling were wearing the sneakers they'd worked in this week, already dirty. Even though the day was warm, Rebecca kept her hoodie zipped up, so only the chain of the locket was visible around her neck.

After the rain returned in a series of emphatic bursts, girls in flip-flops or Crocs found themselves suctioned into the mud. Many gave up, walking around barefoot, up to their ankles in oozing dirt. Phil, soaked to the skin in the first downpour, threw away his shirt and bought a dry souvenir T-shirt and a rain poncho. He also managed to buy and eat — within the first two hours of arriving — crawfish bread, sausage and jalapeño bread, boudin balls, alligator pie, a soft-shell crab po'boy, and a shrimp flauta.

"I don't know even know how you're still standing," Ling said to him, sipping on a huge rosemint iced tea. Whenever the rain stopped, the muggy heat seemed to intensify. Rebecca's hair was frizzing into an unruly mane.

"They should rename this Food Fest," said Phil. "I think even *my* digestive system is in overload."

Rebecca hadn't realized there'd be so much to see here, or so many ways to spend money. There were tents where you could buy CDs or books or posters, and stalls selling crafts or jewelry or paintings. They wandered in and out of music tents where people were listening to gospel choirs, blues guitarists, and jazz acts. There were Cajun fiddlers on one stage, a Caribbean reggae band on another, a tribe of Mardi Gras Indians on another; they even sat awhile to listen to a barbershop quartet in one of the smaller tents, waiting for the rain to pass.

The area in front of the biggest stage was packed with people sitting on plastic sheets or fold-up chairs, banners, and flags marking their spot. From a distance it looked like a medieval tournament, multicolor banners fluttering in the wind, spectator stands lined along the side ready to watch the jousting. These stands, striped like circus tents, were for VIP ticket holders, Anton told them.

Aurelia was in a strange mood. She wasn't as chatty as usual, or as bouncy, but occasionally Rebecca caught her smiling to herself, as though she were thinking of some glorious secret.

"I'm really sorry I haven't had much time to hang out," Rebecca told her. It was midafternoon and they'd spent an hour listening to Lucinda Williams on the Gentilly stage. Rebecca loved Lucinda Williams, and standing next to Anton, swaying along to the music, singing along with "Car Wheels On a Gravel Road," she could almost forget about everything going on right now. Almost.

Rebecca hung back from Ling and the boys, so she and Aurelia could walk together. She put a protective arm around her cousin's shoulders.

"Whatever," Aurelia said, shrugging off Rebecca's arm.

"You can't still be mad at me!"

"You promised we'd talk on Thursday, but then you just went off with Anton."

"I'm really sorry about that. We were talking about Toby Sutton. I told Anton that he'd been chasing you in the Quarter. How did that all happen, anyway?"

"I was walking up from Jackson Square," Aurelia told her. "And I saw him, and thought he was following me, maybe so he could find out where *you* were staying. So I decided to take a weird route, trying to lose him, but when I started running he did, too. I didn't know what to do, so I just kept running all the way up to Rampart. I was trying to help *you*! And you're not even grateful."

"I really am," Rebecca told her, quickening her step so they didn't lose sight of the others. With so many people trying to squeeze onto the pathways, which were marginally less muddy than the grass, it would be easy to get separated. Toby might very well be here somewhere, watching and waiting.

"Well, if you were, you would tell me more about the cute ghost boy and what this whole locket thing is about. Instead of letting me hear about it from someone else."

"Who? Oh, you mean at school. Don't listen to all that tittle-tattle. They don't know what they're talking about. I'm sorry that you had to get embroiled in all this."

"I'm not sorry." Aurelia was smiling again, and that made Rebecca nervous.

"The thing is, this whole locket thing is much bigger and crazier and possibly more dangerous than you realize," said Rebecca. Aurelia could be so stubborn and willful sometimes.

"You're not the only one who can see ghosts, you know," snapped Aurelia.

"One ghost! You've seen one ghost!"

"I saw hundreds of ghosts, actually, right there on Rampart Street."

"OK, but what I mean is, you've only talked to one ghost."

"You don't know that," Aurelia said enigmatically. "You don't know anything. Maybe I know more than you do — have you ever thought of that?"

She scampered ahead to catch up with the others, and Rebecca was forced to push her way through the crowd: She didn't want to be alone if Toby *did* manage to find her.

"I almost lost you," she said to Anton, out of breath more from agitation than exertion, and he took her hand without saying a word.

Near the Heritage stage they were pushed off the path by an effusive crowd of second-liners who continued dancing and hollering even after the band they were trailing stopped playing.

"It's Raf!" Ling shouted, pointing. Light rain was starting to fall, and she, Phil, and Aurelia seemed to be eddying away in the crowd. Raf, looking damp in a white shirt and dark tie, was marking time at the end of a row of musicians, dabbing at the mouthpiece of his trumpet. Rebecca pushed her way toward him, dragging Anton in tow.

"Hey!" she said. "I didn't realize you were *playing* here today."

"I got the call," he grinned. "Thanks to Brando."

Rebecca looked for Brando: He was in the back row, almost completely obscured by a tuba.

"Why did you guys stop?"

"Nobody moving," he pointed out. Whenever one of the big acts finished playing, Rebecca had observed, people swarmed from one end of the grounds to another, clogging the concrete arteries of the racetrack. The social club members up ahead, dressed in vibrant orange, couldn't find a way through the crowd. Rebecca introduced Anton to Raf, and they did one of those silent, eyebrows-raised, head-nod greetings that boys seemed to go in for.

"So you got into the house already?" Raf asked Rebecca. "You didn't waste any time."

"What are you talking about?" Someone passing by shoved Rebecca, and she let go of Anton's hand.

"The house on St. Philip. I went over there to take a look this morning, see if there might be an easy way in for you. That's when I saw."

"Saw what?"

"The boards off the back door. You didn't do it?"

"No!" Rebecca was shouting to make herself heard over the crowd noise. "You mean someone broke in?"

"I guess. I thought it was you."

Rebecca felt her pulse begin to race. "I haven't been back to Tremé since we were at your house. I was going to talk to my father about it tonight."

"Well, if you're looking for something in there, you better hurry," Raf said, raising his trumpet. "Anyone can get in there now. *Anyone.*"

Someone was beating a drum: The second line was on the move again, taking Raf with it. Rebecca stood watching them march away, a familiar panic surging through her. If anyone could get in, they could find the locket. Maybe the floorboards had rotted away, and it was easily visible. Maybe she should go to the house right now and look for the locket herself before it was too late.

"Rebecca!" Anton was shouting at her. "Come on, it's starting to rain. I think the others went that way."

It wasn't easy going *any* way, with crowds pushing in both directions, everyone surging along the flooding pathways. Rebecca pulled up her hood, which meant she could only see straight ahead. People bumped her, and one particularly hard knock pushed her straight into a vast puddle. Mud oozed up over her shoes and into her socks. It felt disgusting.

Rebecca splashed around, confused, trying to get her bearings. They were close to the big stage area, and the crowd was enormous. Rain was coming down hard now. Food stalls were rolling down their plastic blinds, the trees fading into blurry dark shapes. She thought she could see Anton up ahead, near one of the big VIP stands, and she stood up and sloshed toward him, her feet weighed down like anchors in the sticky mud.

Someone pushed her hard from behind, and Rebecca had to reach out to steady herself on the back of the stand. Its striped canvas skirt was flapping open, all the ties hanging loose. And then she was pushed again, so hard it took her breath away. Rebecca fell against the flapping canvas and when it gave way she staggered sideways, slamming into a thick wooden post under the covered bleachers.

Toby Sutton smacked a hand over her mouth, pinning her against the post. Rebecca squirmed and kicked, but he was strong, and she was trapped against the post.

Above them people were stomping and cheering; the act onstage was blasting into a song. In her pocket, her phone buzzed and vibrated. But there was nothing Rebecca could do. Nothing at all.

CHAPTER TWENTY

TOBY'S FACE LOOMED WAY TOO CLOSE, HIS EYES
enlarged and gleaming, like some feral creature. Rebecca
shook her head from side to side, trying to squirm free, or at
least to make herself heard. But between rain drumming on
the stand's roof, and the band booming from the nearby stage,
her tortured murmurs, Rebecca knew, made about as much
impression as the whir of a moth's wings.

"You got that locket?" he said in a low voice. Rebecca nodded. His damp hand was pressed so hard against her mouth,
she was finding it hard to breathe. "You want me to take my
hand away? Here's the deal. I take my hand away so you can
breathe, but if you dare scream, if you make the slightest peep,
I'll kill you. No ghost here to save you now. Understand?"

She nodded again. But Toby did nothing. He was waiting,
Rebecca realized. Waiting, just in case, for a lot of noise.

The song ended and the crowd above them erupted into
cheers and applause. In a flash Toby slid his hand from Rebecca's

mouth to her neck and wrenched the chain hard. Without meaning to she cried out with the burning pain of it, and Toby's hand was back on her mouth.

"You must think we're real stupid down here," he hissed at her, his red face still terrifyingly close. "You think we'll fall for one of your pathetic little tricks. We're not all as stupid as Anton Grey."

Rebecca could barely see him now; her vision was blurred with tears. She was afraid. Her neck felt sliced open.

"You seem to think," he said, "you can fool me with this!"

He held up the locket. Rebecca blinked back tears, trying to focus. What was he talking about now?

"Last night, you were so pleased with yourself. Flouncing around like the Queen of New Orleans, when nobody wants you here. Nobody! You got your claws into Anton, but nobody else is fooled. Especially not Julie."

Rebecca's mind raced. What had she said to Julie Casworth Young? What could she possibly have done to give the game away?

"There you are, showing off your locket. Thinking I'll be waiting outside to snatch it from you, and then you can wander off feeling all smug and clever, like you've tricked dumb old Toby. But you're the dumb one, aren't you?"

Rebecca squirmed again, desperate to break free.

"You're so dumb," whispered Toby, "you think you can buy something from an antiques store in Old Metairie and pass it off as a family heirloom. Julie was in that store with her mother last weekend. They saw this butt-ugly thing and laughed at it!"

Rebecca felt sick to her stomach. Sometimes New Orleans was too small a town. She should have known they wouldn't get away with this. Anton should have known.

Rain thundered overhead; drums pounded. People were cheering and stamping and clapping. There was no point to any of this, no point at all. All the will to fight back against Toby was seeping away. Rebecca's body felt limp and weak. Tears dribbled down her burning cheeks.

Toby must have thought she was beaten, because he seemed to relax a little as well. He took his hand away from her mouth and hurled the locket into the dirt.

"Anyway," he said. "I already knew that locket was a fake. My man Gideon told me where the real locket's at." His eyes twinkled with malicious pleasure.

"Gideon?" Rebecca was incredulous, but she had to think fast. "You believe some story that a stupid ghost tells you?"

"Ghost?" Toby screwed up his face. "He's no ghost. What are you talking about? Don't think you can trick me with all your stupid ghost talk. None of this locket stuff is about your little friend Lisette. You're just trying to steal something valuable and take it back to New York with you. You and your stupid cousin. Gideon told me all about it. Well, we have other plans."

An angry panic seared through Rebecca. She knew she wasn't as strong as Toby. She knew that nobody above would be able to hear her scream. But she was a girl, and she knew how to fight like a girl. She reached up and grabbed two handfuls of his hair, pulling them with every last bit of her strength. She tugged his head to her left and smacked it against the wooden post. Toby howled, almost falling over, and Rebecca knew she had seconds, just seconds, to get away. She half ran, half staggered outside into the rain, crashing into a group of people walking past. Rebecca dropped onto her knees, her hands squishing into the mud.

"Girly, are you OK?" someone was saying, and Rebecca nodded mutely, rain dribbling down her face and into her mouth. She was wet and filthy, but she was free of Toby — for now, anyway.

Anton found her at the medical tent. She'd asked the people she'd smashed into how to get to it, wanting a dry spot to sit down and gather her bearings. There, she was able to get cleaned up a little and send Anton a text. One of the paramedics dabbed antiseptic on the chain burn on her neck: It stung so much Rebecca cried out.

The sound of Anton's voice, calling her name, was a huge relief. She wanted to get out of here as soon as possible.

He hurried over, white-faced, to the cot where she was sitting.

"I lost you," he called, his voice cracking with emotion. "I looked everywhere for you!"

Rebecca reached up a hand so he could help her up.

"Toby," she croaked. Her neck was throbbing. "He took the locket. But . . . where are the others?"

"I gave Phil the keys, and he's bringing the car up to Gentilly Boulevard. Well, Ling is. Phil can't drive a shift. That's why she had to go with him."

The rain had stopped. Rebecca felt better out in the fresh air, though she was glad to have Anton's arm around her as they trudged across the wet sand of the racetrack.

"What about Aurelia?" she asked.

"I don't know where she's gone off to. None of us had her number, but I thought we'd call or text her on your phone. Don't worry — I'm sure she's not far away."

"No, no, no." Rebecca's heart was pumping again, sending shots of pure panic into her brain. "We have to find her right away. Toby said some stuff. . . ."

"But why would he care about Aurelia?" Anton looked confused. "He has the locket now, right?"

"He doesn't have the locket." Rebecca stared into Anton's face, willing him to understand. "He ripped it off my neck and threw it away under the bleachers. He knows it's a fake!"

Anton frowned. "But how would . . ."

"He knows, OK?" Rebecca fumbled for her phone. A message was blinking; it was from Aurelia.

dont worry i hav to meet smone dwntwn. big secret. c u 2morro.

"Oh my god." Rebecca's knees buckled. "I don't believe it."

She passed her phone to Anton so he could read the message.

"Who's she meeting?" he asked.

"You're not going to want to hear this, but I think she's meeting Frank." Rebecca started walking as fast as she could in the direction of the nearest exit gate, but hordes of people were leaving now, walking in what seemed like slow motion, and the gate seemed a mile away. Thunder grumbled, and the sky was growing dark again.

"Who is Frank?" Anton was next to her, his arm around her back, steering her through the crowds.

"The ghost. The ghost I was trying to tell you about the other night. The ghost who lost the locket in the house in Tremé."

"And you told Aurelia about this . . . this ghost?"

"She *saw* him. On Thursday, when Toby was chasing her, Frank grabbed her hand so Toby couldn't see her anymore. Remember last year, when I explained all that to you?"

"A ghost holds your hand and you're invisible or something," said Anton. He still sounded skeptical. "I didn't really believe that was true."

"Well, it's totally true," Rebecca snapped. Why would he think she would make this stuff up? "And just now Toby said something about her — it's too complicated to explain. Basically, everyone knows that the real locket is in the house on St. Philip Street. Aurelia knows, and I think she wants to be the big hero and rescue it by herself. But Toby knows, too. That's the problem."

"You're sure about this?"

Rebecca rubbed her forehead. She wasn't sure about anything. Aurelia wasn't supposed to be downtown at all yesterday, but maybe she'd blown off her ballet class and caught the street-car down to the Quarter. She knew where to wait for Frank, on the corner of Rampart Street. If Aurelia said she wanted to help find the locket, he'd tell her *everything* — of that Rebecca was perfectly sure — because he was so desperate right now. The house was about to be demolished. Rebecca was about to return to New York. Frank was staring down eternity.

"You know which house?" Anton asked, pushing through the turnstiles behind Rebecca. She caught her breath: This was new. Maybe he *would* help after all.

"Yes." Rebecca nodded. "It's really near the school — there are three houses that are empty and all boarded up, and it's the one at the end. But here's another weird thing — remember what Raf was saying today, about someone breaking into the house?"

"I didn't hear any of your conversation," Anton said. "I didn't like to listen in. You might be making a date or something."

Rebecca laughed in disbelief. Anton, jealous?

"Is that why you let go of my hand?" she demanded.

"Don't be ridiculous," he said. They were on Gentilly now, the sidewalks crammed with street vendors selling bottled water and umbrellas, police out in the road directing traffic and shouting at taxis. Anton leaned out to look for his car.

"Or maybe you lost me on purpose just as we got to the spot you and Toby had agreed on." Rebecca had just thought of this, but suddenly it made sense.

"*What?* Rebecca." Anton turned to face her, grabbing her by both shoulders. "Tell me that you don't believe I'm in leagues with Toby. Please. Tell me that you don't think I'm that crummy and conniving and despicable a person."

"I don't know." She hung her head. Her neck smarted on one side, where Toby had tugged the chain until it broke. Why had Anton left her alone? Why? After all this time, she still didn't really trust him.

"You have to know," he said. He leaned his head toward her. "God, why do I have to keep proving myself over and over? You have to know by now that I care about you much more than any of my old friends. More than Marianne and Toby and . . ."

"More than Helena?" Rebecca gazed straight at him. Anton looked as though she'd punched him in the stomach.

"Helena was only ever a friend," he said softly. "You're . . . much more than a friend. You have to believe me when I tell you that. And I have to believe *you* when you tell me there's some ghost who's hidden a locket, and you have to find it before Toby kidnaps your cousin or whatever. . . ." He took a deep breath. "OK. I believe you. Now, before we do anything or go anywhere else, do you believe *me*?"

Rebecca looked into Anton's eyes. She thought back to the night one long year ago when they stood outside the Bowman mansion, the night Helena was killed. Anton had fought with Toby right there on the sidewalk, and then Toby had set fire to the Bowman's house. He'd gone against his friends and his family, everyone important in his life, just for her.

She leaned forward to kiss him, aiming for his cheek, but he twisted, kissing her directly on the mouth. Rebecca kissed him back, holding tight to him. They had to trust each other. They had to believe each other. They were in this together.

CHAPTER TWENTY-ONE

As soon as they found Ling and Phil, crawling along in stop-start traffic, Anton took over the driving. Rebecca told him to head for Rampart Street.

"I could kill Toby!" Ling ranted. "Becca, I'm *so* sorry we lost you. The crowd was too crazy. He must have been waiting for his moment."

"I'm OK," Rebecca told her. "I think I might have pulled some of his hair out, at least." She had to laugh. "Phil got a T-shirt at Jazz Fest. I got two handfuls of Toby Sutton's hair."

"And what does Aurelia think she's doing, running off like this, making us all crazy with worry?" Ling spluttered.

"She thinks she's helping," Rebecca said, wishing she could turn around to face Ling without her neck zinging with pain. "By the way, Raf told me that the house on St. Philip Street has been broken into. The boards are off the back door, and he said anyone could walk in right now."

"Who did that? Toby?"

"I have no idea how he would break into a house if it's all boarded up," said Anton, zooming down a side street to try to avoid traffic, but getting stuck again at the end. "He doesn't have any money to buy supplies."

"He had enough money to get into Jazz Fest," Ling pointed out. "Maybe Marianne gave him money? Maybe that's why she came down from Mississippi for the dance?"

"You know, I should call my dad," Rebecca said. "I should have told him all about this today, or last night, or — or right away yesterday in the cemetery when we found out that the locket might contain a Degas."

"What Degas?" asked a startled Anton.

"Wait a minute," interjected Ling. "How would Toby know which house?"

"Gideon Mason," Rebecca told her.

"No," groaned Ling.

"Who is Gideon Mason?" Anton demanded. "And what's this about a Degas? You mean, the French painter?"

"I shouldn't have kept all this a secret from my dad," Rebecca said, ignoring Anton's questions. "If I call him now . . ."

"What could your dad do?" Ling demanded. "Hop to the corner on his sprained ankle? Call the police and tell them to be on the lookout for a girl and a ghost? Two ghosts, actually."

"Who is this Gideon Mason?" Anton was shouting.

"Another ghost," Rebecca told him. "The one who murdered Frank. Toby's talked to him, but I don't think he realizes that Gideon Mason is a ghost."

"OK, so this ghost thing is totally a new development," said Phil, who'd been sitting quietly until now. "Maybe someone could bring me up to speed?"

"Actually, *Degas* is the new development," said Anton. "I don't know who this guy Raf is, I don't know what some dead French Impressionist has to do with anything. . . ."

"Don't forget the ghost!" Phil called out.

"Two ghosts," Ling reminded them.

"I don't even know why we're driving to Rampart and not St. Philip Street," Anton said.

"We can't explain it all now," Ling snapped. "Can't you drive any faster?"

"Look," said Rebecca, "here's the deal. Please, just listen."

She twisted her whole body to protect her sore neck, so she was sort of facing Anton, and Phil could see more than the back of her head.

"The main ghost is a young guy named Frank who was murdered in 1873. The day he died, he dropped a locket through the floorboards of a house on St. Philip Street so the guy murdering him couldn't steal it."

"And the guy murdering him was this Gideon Mason guy," Phil said.

"Yes. And we have reason to believe that the locket was entrusted to Frank by the artist Degas, who spent some time here in New Orleans."

"Cool!" said Phil.

Rebecca talked as fast she could. "The house is being demolished next week, so this is incredibly urgent. If the locket isn't rescued and returned to its rightful owners — the descendants of Degas' family, I guess — then Frank is condemned to being a ghost for eternity. Plus something that belonged to Degas is completely destroyed."

"Not cool!" said Phil, and Ling shushed him.

"Raf is a guy who lives near the house, and Ling and I have been volunteering at his school this week." Rebecca shot Anton a be-jealous-if-you-dare look. "Yesterday I asked him if he could help us break into the house to find the locket, but he was really not happy about that, because he thought it would be dangerous, and he might get into trouble, and . . ."

"At least someone here is using their brain," interjected Anton, and Ling kicked the back of his seat.

"Hey!" she said. "You have no intellectual high ground! You had the fake locket idea! That worked out, huh?"

"But," Rebecca continued, "as I was saying, when I saw Raf today, he told me someone has already broken down the back door of the house. This could mean various things — that Toby's trying to get in to find the locket, that someone else is trying to get in to find the locket, that, say, drug dealers have been using the house . . ."

"This gets better and better," muttered Anton.

"But it also means *we* can get in now, right?" Ling asked. "If we ever get through this stupid traffic."

"Right," said Rebecca. The busted-down back door was the only semi-good news of the day, as far as she could see.

"Permission to speak, Team Leader," asked Phil, raising his hand. "Please explain the missing cousin."

Rebecca sighed.

"My cousin got wind of this whole locket-under-the-floorboards story the other day. She saw Frank, and got really overexcited. She wants to help him, and thinks I'm just trying to stop her, to keep all the great ghost stuff for myself. I think she went down to the Quarter yesterday to talk to Frank again, and that she's planning — I don't know what. Maybe to go to the house right now and look for the locket?"

"Permission to speak again. What do we think Toby is planning?"

Just thinking of Toby and his plans made Rebecca's stomach turn. "All he knows is that I'm looking for a locket." Rebecca and Anton exchanged looks. "He knows that the one I was wearing last night was a plant. So today he ripped it off my neck and threw it away. He also knows, I guess, that Aurelia is part of the whole locket-search thing."

"And we're driving to Rampart Street because . . ." This was Anton.

"Because when I want to find Frank, that's where I go. And that's where Aurelia met him, so I think she'll probably go back there today. I just sent her a text telling her to wait for us on Rampart Street. Whether she will, I don't know. If she had to walk there, we might even get there first."

"I'm keeping my eyes peeled," Ling said. "It's easier to make things out now that it's stopped raining."

"So, best-case scenario," said Phil. "We get there first and intercept her before she runs into a drug dealer or Toby."

"Yes," said Rebecca, her nerves starting to chatter. "And worst case, we're too late. Toby gets the locket and destroys it or runs off with it, just to spite me. And he hurts Aurelia." Rebecca's throat tightened. "Anton, really — you just missed that light! Can't you get us there any quicker?"

"This isn't the Batmobile, you know! I have to, like, drive on the road!"

"But maybe if we're not too late, I'll get to meet one of these ghosts?" asked Phil. "Good ghost, bad ghost? Whatever?"

"Probably not," Ling told him. "Ghosts are very picky. They don't make themselves visible to just anybody."

"Man! I'd rather see a ghost than a drug dealer."

"Well, it's a good thing you know judo," sniffed Ling.

"Judo's not so great when the other people have guns. They

never told us that in elementary school, but I figured it out for myself."

"Could everyone please stop talking?" Rebecca asked. Anton was flying along Rampart Street now, swooping into a U-turn. "This is it! We're here."

Rebecca was out of the car before it came to a complete halt, sloshing through the flooded gutter. The sky looked menacing, brimming with rain. Another downpour was on its way. Aurelia was nowhere to be seen.

"Frank! Frank!" Rebecca bellowed. Ling was on the sidewalk now as well, striding up and down, shouting Frank's name. The boys had stayed in the car, probably at Ling's request. That was good thinking. Rebecca didn't want to scare Frank off by turning up with strangers.

But where was Frank? Fat raindrops were falling now, plopping onto Rebecca's head. With every moment that passed, it was getting later and darker; the house in Tremé would be even more difficult to navigate. Getting in was one thing; finding the locket was another. They needed Frank.

"He's always found me before," she told Ling frantically. "I've never had to wait this long when I wanted to see him. But he could be anywhere — down by the river, on Carondelet, somewhere in the Quarter. Over by the cemetery. I just don't know."

"What should we do?" Ling asked her. "Go straight to the house on St. Philip Street and see if Aurelia and Frank are there already?"

Rebecca walked to the curb, balancing at the very edge and staring up at the derelict town house.

"I have another idea," she told Ling. "Delphine! Delphine! Please! I need your help!"

"Who is Delphine?" Ling asked, puzzled.

"That ghost girl, remember? She comes out on the top gallery when it's dark."

"How can *she* help?"

"She likes Frank."

"You mean, *likes* likes?"

"Maybe. I don't know — Delphine!" To Rebecca's immense relief, a pearly light beamed from the top gallery, transforming its rusted railings into a sparkling jewel box. It was hard to believe no one else could see this, Rebecca thought; in the gloomy, sodden twilight, Delphine's ghostly light swirled out into the sky like dry ice pouring from a stage.

"Yes? " Delphine was there, smiling her sweet smile, leaning so far over the railings she looked as though she might tip over.

"Delphine, I really need your help!" Rebecca shouted up.

"You can see her?" Ling asked. "Really?"

"Allo, Rebecca!" Delphine was waving, but Rebecca really needed her to focus. This wasn't a social call.

"I have to find Frank!" she shouted, rain hitting her upturned face. Anton and Phil in the car would have had no idea what she was doing or who she was talking to. She'd forgotten to mention there was a third ghost. "I think he may have met up with my cousin, Aurelia, right here on the corner. She's younger than me — short dark hair, about this tall . . ."

"Oh!" Delphine looked dismayed. "You know that girl? The skinny girl with the curls?"

"Yes! Have you seen her?"

Delphine nodded slowly.

"When?"

"Just five, perhaps ten minutes ago," Delphine called, stretching over the railings. "But Rebecca — she was not with Frank!"

"Really?" Rebecca wiped raindrops out of her eyes. Maybe Aurelia got tired of waiting for Frank as well, and just headed off to the house on St. Philip.

"She was with that other ghost," said Delphine. "That nasty man, the one I warned you about. Monsieur Mason. I saw them talking together, and then he took her hand and they walked away. That way."

Delphine pointed toward Tremé.

"No," groaned Rebecca. This was a worst-case scenario she hadn't considered. The ghost Aurelia was talking with yesterday — it wasn't Frank. It was Gideon Mason. And maybe he hadn't been so mean to Aurelia. Maybe he'd been very, very nice. He was working Aurelia; he was working Toby. One way or another, he meant to get to that locket before Rebecca and Frank could.

"Rebecca, what's going on?" Anton was standing next to her now, staring up at the town house. "What are you looking at? Who's Delphine? What's happened?"

"OK." Rebecca was trying to pull herself together. She pushed damp hair out of her face, and stood with Phil, Anton, and Ling in a little huddle on the curb. "I've just been talking to another ghost named Delphine."

"What do you mean, another ghost?" demanded Anton. "You never mentioned another ghost!"

"So now there are three ghosts?" Phil asked. "Whoa!"

"Three who matter to us, anyway. Delphine says she saw Aurelia walking up to Tremé holding the hand of a ghost, but the problem is, the ghost wasn't Frank. It was Gideon Mason, the murderer. He wants the locket destroyed. He's been following me this whole week and threatening me. . . ."

"Why didn't you tell me?" Anton demanded.

"What could you have done?" asked Rebecca, wincing; her neck ached. "Ghosts can only hurt each other, anyway."

"So that means he can't hurt Aurelia, right?" Raindrops dribbled down Ling's face. This was the second time this week, Rebecca realized, she'd made poor Ling stand out in the rain talking about ghosts.

"I don't think so. But he *can* get her or Toby to find the locket and then maybe destroy it. Throw it into the river or something — I don't know. He could be spinning Aurelia some line about how the locket is cursed. Aurelia doesn't know the whole story. Toby doesn't, either, but he'll destroy anything if he thinks I want it."

"They're on their way to the house now?" Anton asked, and Rebecca nodded. "Then let's go!"

"Hang on!" Ling grabbed his arm. "Becca, didn't you just say Aurelia and the ghost were holding hands? Doesn't that make Aurelia invisible?"

"It does." This just got worse and worse.

"So I won't be able to see her, and neither will Phil or Anton."

"I won't be able to see her, either," said Rebecca, "unless Gideon Mason makes himself visible to me. And ghosts can pick and choose when that happens. If Frank was here, two of us could hold his hands, but without him, we won't be able to see Gideon or Aurelia or anything. . . ."

"Unless . . ." said Ling. She turned to face the town house. "Ghost girl! Delphine! Can you hear me?"

Delphine, arms resting on the railings, gazed down with interest.

"I can't see you, but I know you're there!" Ling bellowed. She was looking up toward the wrong end of the gallery, but Rebecca was sure Delphine could hear her. They could probably hear Ling in Congo Square. "We need your help! Please come down!"

"Please, Delphine!" Rebecca pleaded. Frank had said Delphine was a friend of Lisette's, that they'd gone to school together. Delphine must have walked through the streets of Tremé all the time when she was alive, and that meant she could haunt them now. If she chose to come down from the gallery. "For Frank's sake — please!"

"Shouldn't we try to find a guy ghost?" Anton asked. "I don't want to be rude, but if there's going to be a ghost fight . . ."

"Excuse me," Ling said, giving him her coolest stare. "Why is this about boy power all of a sudden? Who fought off Toby Sutton today? Rebecca here. All by herself. And she doesn't even know judo."

"It means 'the gentle art,' " Phil explained.

"Not to mention that because of your *brilliant* idea about the fake locket," Ling said, turning on Anton, "we now have to deal with a psycho arsonist as well as an evil ghost!"

"Could everyone stop arguing, please!" They were running out of time, Rebecca knew. If they couldn't find Frank, they needed to persuade Delphine. But when she looked up, the silvery mist of the top gallery had vanished. Delphine was gone.

"No," Rebecca groaned. "We scared her away!"

"Oh, I'm not scared," said a sweet, soft voice, and Rebecca had to blink away rain to make sure she wasn't seeing things. Right there, floating rather than standing on the sidewalk, was Delphine, her face as pale as the moon.

"OK — I'm cold and shivery, and I think I see a girl in a nightgown," said Phil. "Either I've caught pneumonia and I'm hallucinating, or I'm looking at one of your ghosts."

"Everyone," said Rebecca, quaking with excitement. "This is Delphine. She's going to help us."

"For Frank," Delphine said, looking worried. "Should we not hurry? I have to walk, you know. I cannot haunt one of these new . . . carriages."

She pointed at Anton's car.

"Ling, you know the house," said Anton, staring dumbfounded at Delphine. He'd never seen a ghost before, Rebecca realized. "You and Phil walk — run! — with Delphine. Rebecca and I'll go on ahead in the car. Maybe what's-his-name, Frank, is up there."

"Nothing like this ever happened to me at home," said Phil. "I love this town!"

"Go, go, go!" shouted Anton. Rebecca raced back into the car, watching Phil, Ling, and Delphine dart across Rampart Street. Someone was going to get their hands on Frank's locket tonight, for better or worse. Rebecca hoped they weren't too late.

CHAPTER TWENTY-TWO

B Y NOW IT WAS DARK. A SLIVER OF MOON APPEARED and then disappeared behind moody clouds. Rebecca had never driven into Tremé after dark. There weren't many people out on the streets now, not in such persistent rain. Light shone through the shutters of many of the houses along St. Philip Street, but the group of three derelict houses, half consumed by vines, looked like three shadowy hillocks.

She told Anton to park by a vacant lot much farther down the block, just in case Toby wasn't exactly sure which house he was looking for.

"We could park outside Lisette's house," Anton suggested, but Rebecca was worried Toby might be intent on burning something down. If they parked outside a house, he might not try to break in and search for a locket: He might just douse it with gas and light a match. Rebecca didn't want Lisette's house, or any of the houses in Tremé, going up in flames tonight.

Anton was just worried about his car, she suspected, looking anxiously around as he pulled the flashlight out of the trunk.

Thunder rumbled and a dog started barking, startling them both, but at least the rain had eased. Rebecca shivered, chilled beneath her wet clothes, even though the evening was warm.

The front door swung open at Raf's grandmother's house, and Raf emerged, letting the door slam behind him. He was still carrying his trumpet, hurrying down the stairs. When Anton beeped the car locked, Raf looked along the street toward them. For a moment he hesitated, then walked toward them in loping strides.

"You trying to get rid of that car?" he asked Anton, shaking his head. "It might not be there when you come back for it."

"We don't want to leave it outside anyone's house," Rebecca explained. "Remember the guy who almost ran my dad over yesterday? He also likes to burn down houses. Really, he's a dangerous kid. Violent and unstable. This is what he did to me today."

She pulled aside her hoodie so Raf could see the chain burn on her neck. Raf grimaced.

"What's his deal?" he asked. "Why's he hate you so much?"

"Long story," said Anton, touching Rebecca's arm. "We should go — you know."

"He's looking for the same thing we're looking for," Rebecca told Raf. "Under the floorboards of that house. It's a locket."

"You guys should keep out of that place." Raf shook his head again. "You don't know *what* is inside."

"We have to go," Rebecca said. Anton was pulling at her now, eager to be gone. "My cousin might be in there. We don't have a choice."

"Good luck," Raf said, backing away across the street. "Don't say I didn't warn you."

Rebecca felt even more unnerved now. Raf was probably right, but what else could they do? Hopefully the others would arrive soon, so they'd have strength in numbers — even if one of that number was a ghost who hadn't left her gallery for one hundred fifty years.

Anton whispered that they should get off the street, so they cut up the back of the three tumbledown houses, sneaking along the fence line with the flashlight turned off. A light rain pattered onto the long grass, and Rebecca hunched down, trying to make herself inconspicuous — not that anyone would be able to see much in the dark. She had to let her eyes adjust to the gloom, pausing when they approached the house on the end to take in the busted-in back door.

Some of the boards had been prized off, leaving a gap large enough to step through. The house sat in darkness, completely quiet. Still, Rebecca hesitated, and when Anton made a move forward she tugged his hand; they both dropped to a crouch.

"Rebecca," a voice whispered, and it was all Rebecca could do to stifle a scream.

"What is it?" hissed Anton. "Did you see something?"

"Rebecca?" said the voice again. It was Frank, she realized, but he sounded different — tired, almost — and she couldn't see him at all.

"Frank," she whispered. "Where are you?"

A shaking hand appeared, almost disembodied. Rebecca clutched at Anton to stop herself tumbling headfirst into the grass. Slowly she could see more of Frank: He was struggling to sit up, struggling to open his eyes. He was grimacing with pain.

"What happened?" she asked him, trying to keep her voice low.

"Fighting," Frank gasped. His face looked drawn, sunken-in. "Fighting with . . . him."

"He's been fighting the other ghost," she murmured to Anton, who was staring into the grass, unable to see — or hear — Frank at all. "Gideon Mason."

"How can ghosts fight?" he whispered back. "They can't kill each other. They're already dead."

Rebecca had no idea, but there wasn't time now for Ghost World 101.

"The girl," wheezed Frank. "He had the girl with him. Aurelia?"

Rebecca nodded, her whole body tensing.

"What happened?" Her mind was racing with possibilities. Where were they now?

"While we were fighting," said Frank, "she climbed inside the house. She's still in there now. So . . . so is he. He followed her in."

Frank sank back into the grass. The thunder was growing closer now, erupting into a roar.

"Aurelia," Rebecca told Anton, her heart pounding. She leaned forward, wedging her knees into the damp ground. "Aurelia's inside. With Gideon Mason."

"If he's holding her hand, we won't be able to see her, right?" Anton whispered. "What do we do? Wait for Delphine?"

"Frank," Rebecca hissed. She didn't want to lose any more time. "Can you stand up? We need you to come in with us. We need to *see* Aurelia."

"Just give me . . . give me a few minutes." Frank sounded spent. Whatever the other ghost had done to him, it must have been bad.

"Didn't you say," Anton asked, so close his face brushed her ear, "that ghosts can only hurt each other?"

Rebecca nodded. Anton was right. Maybe she could just talk Aurelia out of the house. What could the mean ghost do to them? There were no precipices to fall off of here. She crawled on all fours to the rickety back steps, and peered into the black interior of the house.

"Aurelia!" she called. "Aurelia, can you hear me?

There was silence, and then something that sounded like a

squeak. *Not a rat*, Rebecca prayed. *Please, not a rat!* But perhaps the squeak was Aurelia? She might be terrified of Gideon Mason, Rebecca thought, especially after seeing him fight Frank.

"You know the ghost can't hurt you," she said, trying to sound as calm and reassuring as possible. "He might tell you he can, but there's nothing he can do to harm you. You don't have to be afraid of him. You can come out!"

Rebecca strained to hear the slightest sound. Another squeak, and then something like a whimper. And then — Aurelia.

"I'm not afraid of him," she called back, her voice quavering.

"He's not holding you?"

"No."

"Then come out, OK?"

Some rustling, and another whimper.

"I can't," Aurelia said, her voice breaking into a sob. "My — my — my foot is stuck. These floorboards . . . they're all rotten."

Rebecca exhaled with relief. Everything was going to be OK. She'd get Aurelia out of there, and they could go home. Her father would know what to do next.

"Hang on," she told Aurelia, gesturing to Anton for the flashlight. "I'm coming in to get you."

"Are you — are you by yourself?" Aurelia bleated.

Rebecca froze. She didn't like the sound of that question at all. She had no idea why Aurelia was even asking her that. Was the ghost planning something? Was he whispering in her ear? Was he planning to make her disappear as soon as Rebecca crossed the threshold?

"I'm with Frank," she lied. Frank was still lying prone in the grass, but nobody else needed to know that. She wanted Gideon Mason to think that invisibility wasn't an option. If Frank entered the house holding her hand, she'd be able to see anything that cruel ghost was up to.

Now Rebecca could hear mumbling, as though Aurelia and the ghost were having a conversation.

"Ghosts can't hurt you!" Rebecca called in through the hole in the door. She leaned closer, trying to see anything, but it was too dark. The smell of damp and mold was overpowering. "Remember that, Relia! They can only hurt each other!"

Aurelia whimpered again.

"I'm going in," Rebecca mouthed to Anton. "Wait."

He frowned at her, shaking his head. She understood: He didn't want her to go into the dark house alone. But something nagged at her; something wasn't quite right. Better to have Anton out here — a secret, a surprise — just in case. Rebecca held up her hand to him, stopping him from following her up the stairs, and Anton stepped back onto the grass. She held a finger to her lips, and he nodded.

The flashlight wasn't much use in a house that was falling down. Rebecca shone it through the hole in the door, illuminating bare posts, dangling vines, a broken upturned chair. The place looked like it had been ransacked and smelled as though it had been left to rot in a swamp. She had to bend down to climb through the gap, tapping with one foot to make sure the floor was secure enough to take her weight. A giant rust-colored roach scuttled across the floor and ran straight over her foot. Rebecca shuddered in disgust.

She was all the way in now and upright, brushing a spider's web off her face. .

"Aurelia!" Rebecca called, her voice echoing. She wished Anton was in here with her, because this strange messed-up place, consumed by darkness, was scary. Her legs were shaking. No wonder poor Aurelia was terrified. But Rebecca had to be brave, and not stand here cowering in what must have once been a kitchen.

She took a few more tentative steps forward, through an opening where the door had been kicked in. It lay flat on the ground, laced with vines. Before her lay the main room of the house, a jumble of stripped walls and exposed posts. The remains of a brick fireplace stood stranded in the middle of the room. In front of it lay a ripped mattress, spewing stuffing and sprinkled with dusty broken glass. It didn't look as though anyone had slept on *that* for a long time.

Rebecca beamed a ray of light into the far corner, willing herself to keep her hand steady. When she saw Gideon Mason slumped there, she almost dropped the flashlight. But he made no move at all. He just lay there, his back to the wall, clutching the old wound in his chest. His face was twisted with pain. *Frank must have fought him hard and long*, Rebecca thought. And even though the sight of this awful man made her jumpy, at least he wasn't holding onto Aurelia.

"Aurelia?" she said, circling the ray of light around the room. Why couldn't she find her? Rebecca took another step in, then another.

"I'm stuck," Aurelia whimpered, but Rebecca still couldn't see her. She glared at Gideon Mason, slumped in the corner.

"What were you thinking?" she asked him.

"I wanted her to crawl under the house," he croaked, struggling to sit up.

"What, in the dark?"

"No matter — your English boy turned up and tried to act the big man, fighting me. Shame he didn't do that when he was alive. . . ."

"Whatever," she said. Rebecca took a few more tentative steps toward the chimney breast, careful of where she was placing her feet. She didn't want to end up stuck herself. "It's OK, Relia. The ghost can't hurt you. I'm here."

"Oh, yes, you are," said a male voice, and a light flickered on: It was an electric lantern, sitting on the mantel. Rebecca blinked, trying to adjust her eyes.

Toby Sutton stepped out of the shadows, dragging Aurelia with him. A crowbar dangled from one hand. The other hand was around Aurelia's neck.

"Toby!" Rebecca shouted. Rage surged through her — rage and fear. And the louder she shouted, the more Anton was likely to hear. They needed a Plan B in a hurry. Thank God he hadn't come in with her.

"Who were you talking to just then? 'Frank'?" Toby demanded. He couldn't see Gideon Mason, Rebecca realized. Gideon had made himself visible to Toby before; why wasn't he doing it now? Maybe he knew he had more power over Toby if Toby thought he was real. He'd "arrive" later, once Toby had the locket in his hand.

"And let me guess," Toby continued. "Frank is your little ghost friend. That's what your stupid cousin just told me. Which means you've either brainwashed her or she's as dumb as she looks."

Toby gripped poor Aurelia as though she were a rag doll. She gazed up at Rebecca, eyes smudged with tears, clearly terrified out of her wits.

"Let her go!" Rebecca ordered Toby in her most imperious voice. "She doesn't know where the locket's hidden! She's of no use to you!"

"I don't know about that," he sneered. "She led me here, didn't she? And now *you're* here, so it's all working out pretty well. Aw, what happened to your poor little neck? Did a bad man hurt you?"

Rebecca clenched the flashlight. If she was standing any closer, she could lunge forward and clunk Toby over the head with it. But he was too far away, and if she made the slightest move forward he'd hurt Aurelia. She knew he would. Toby would hurt Aurelia just as he'd hurt Rebecca today — not because it would help him find the locket, but just to show he could. What Rebecca had to do right now was play for time and hope that Anton — and the others, if they ever arrived — could get her and Aurelia out of this mess.

"Where's your boyfriend?" Toby sneered. "Got bored looking for you at Jazz Fest? Or is he out buying you more jewelry? Tell him to get something with a stronger chain next time. That one broke way too easily."

"Leave Anton out of this," Rebecca shouted. "He took me home after Jazz Fest. He doesn't know anything about this place. He's never been to Tremé in his life."

"Why would he?" Toby looked around the collapsing house with contempt. "They should burn this whole neighborhood down. Move everyone into projects. Better still, move them all to Texas. Or straight to prison, 'cause that's where most of them'll end up anyway."

"You'll be able to hang out with them there, won't you?" Everything Toby said enraged Rebecca. "Because unless you let Aurelia go, that's where you're . . ."

Rebecca was too startled to finish her sentence. Frank had just walked in, straight through the front wall of the house. He stood gazing at her, his blue eyes bright as the sky.

CHAPTER TWENTY-THREE

REBECCA HAD NEVER BEEN SO HAPPY TO SEE Frank. He'd take her hand, so Toby couldn't see her, and then she could bash Toby with her flashlight. She could knock him out, she was sure.

But before Frank could reach her, Gideon Mason grabbed his legs and pulled him down hard onto the floor. Now they were fighting again, rolling on the floor, and through the wall and back, punching each other and groaning in agony when the other got a jab in at a wound.

Aurelia gasped, and Toby shook her.

"Shut up!" he bellowed. "What are you two staring at?"

Rebecca tried to think clearly. She could make a break for it, running over to Frank and grabbing his hand, but that would put her out of range with Toby: There was no point in being invisible over there in the corner. And by the time she dragged Frank away from the other ghost, Toby could have struck Aurelia with the crowbar.

"Stop staring over there!" Toby roared. He pushed Aurelia forward a few steps and peered toward the dark corner where the ghosts were fighting. All he could see, Rebecca guessed, were floors and walls and what looked like a tree branch. "You're not gonna fool me with some stupid trick! I'm tired of your games!"

"Toby, just let Aurelia go," Rebecca pleaded. Maybe Toby would listen to reason. "She really doesn't know where the locket is."

"We *both* know. It's under the floorboards. Why'd you think I brought this with me?" Toby waggled the crowbar.

Rebecca tried to hide her fear. "So what — you're going to pull up every floorboard in this house, and hang onto Aurelia at the same time? How long will that take? Sure, Aurelia knows it's under the floorboards. I know that, too. But *where* exactly? The man who brought Aurelia here today — even he doesn't know exactly where it is."

"Who are you talking about?" Toby looked at her with contempt. "There wasn't any *man* bringing her here. She came by herself. I was following her!"

"The man was Gideon Mason!" Rebecca spat back. "You couldn't see him today because he's a ghost!"

"Yeah, right," scoffed Toby. He tapped on the floor with the claw of the crowbar. "You're still trying this?" he said. "You think just because you had some ghost pal last year, who helped you to *murder* my friend, that you can come up with another pathetic little ghost story this year — and what? Scare me? I've met Gideon Mason. He's no friend of yours, and he's no ghost."

"He *is* a ghost," bleated Aurelia. Toby silenced her with a glare, tightening his grip around her neck.

"Leave her alone!" Rebecca shrieked. She couldn't stand this. "Frank! Help us!"

"Stop it!" demanded Toby. He whacked the crowbar against the floor to get her attention. "Stop pretending there are all these ghosts! Now listen to me. I'm gonna burn down this house and all of us in it unless you start listening and doing what I say."

There was a scuffle and a creak, and now someone else was in the room with them. Ling!

"What the —" Toby roared, and Rebecca kind of agreed with him. What was going on? Where was Delphine? Why didn't Ling hold Delphine's hand and sneak in through the back door, so she'd be invisible to Toby? What were they *thinking* out there? That Rebecca and Ling could overpower Toby by themselves? That Ling could break up the ghost fight?

Ling was clearly on some kind of mission, because she'd run straight to the corner where Frank and the other ghost were still fighting.

"You! Stop right there!" Toby shouted. "Or I'll . . ."

He held up the crowbar and gestured at Aurelia. Ling was already standing still, breathing heavily, and shooting anxious looks at Rebecca.

"And you!" Toby gestured at Rebecca. "Roll me that flashlight. Now! Then get over there."

She rolled the flashlight along the floor toward him, then backed away toward the corner where Ling was standing very still. Even if she had the flashlight, Rebecca knew she'd be out of range all the way over here. Where were the boys? Where was Delphine? Ghosts could walk through walls, but Anton and Phil were going to have to come through the hole in the door.

If they were thinking of rushing Toby, it wasn't going to work. He was the one with the weapons. Even if Delphine smuggled them in and they tried pouncing on Toby, Aurelia could end up badly hurt. Toby was strong, and he was cunning, and he was violent. It was just too risky.

"So now I got three stupid girls," he was saying. "And that means I can get rid of three stupid girls at once."

He tapped something with his foot, something Rebecca hadn't noticed before. It was a gasoline can. Her stomach churned. She should have known. Where Toby Sutton went, arson always followed.

"Anyone tries to jump me, this whole place is going down."

Out of the corner of one eye, Rebecca could see Frank struggling to push away from Gideon. They were both exhausted now, twitching on the floor; maybe Frank had a slight advantage, maybe not.

A chill breeze blew through the thin walls, ruffling Rebecca's hair. Delphine! She floated in, beaming at Frank. If only they were standing closer to Toby!

Frank had managed to roll himself almost free and Delphine wafted toward him. Rebecca wouldn't have believed it was possible if she hadn't seen it herself, but the sweet Delphine, the girl who'd spent more than a century languishing on the gallery of an old Creole town house, leaned over and walloped Gideon Mason right in his wound. He doubled up in agony, and Delphine's face puckered, as though she'd just eaten something sour. Frank was up on his knees now, gripping his own wound, but Mason lay curled up and groaning. And then Delphine was gone, sucked back through the wall. Rebecca looked at Ling. What was going on? Were the ghosts ever going to stop with the revenge fantasies and get on with helping the living?

"I told you before," growled Toby. "Stop looking in that corner!"

"Please, Toby," said Ling. "Let's work something out. Let us look for the locket, and if we find it we do a trade. We give you the locket. You give us Aurelia."

"Shut up!" he snapped. "Like you're going to give *me* the locket. You were rude to my sister. I know who you are."

"We give you the locket," Ling repeated. "You give us Aurelia. That's a fair trade."

Was Ling serious? Was this the plan? Ling sounded impressively cool, given the situation.

"I'm worried about you, Toby," Ling was saying. "I'm worried that you're in a bad dream. I'm worried that you may be seeing things that aren't real. But it's just a bad dream — isn't it, Toby? It's just a bad dream. . . ."

"Stop talking!" Toby's eyes were wild. What was Ling up to? Rebecca had no clue. Frank was right behind them now; she could sense him rather than see him. Rebecca glanced over her shoulder, as quick as she dared. He'd shuffled up on his knees. He was close enough to touch.

"But what if you *are* seeing things, Toby?" Ling's voice was hypnotic. "How about if, on the count of three, we just disappeared?"

"One," said Frank. "Two. Three."

Rebecca felt his hand on hers. She grasped it.

Ling must have done the same, because Aurelia was still gazing at them, wide-eyed, and Toby was roaring with rage. And Delphine was back now as well, floating from the back door. This time she ignored Gideon Mason, slowly making for the center of the room. She positioned herself right in front of Rebecca and Ling, then raised her hands. Suddenly Anton, and a dazed-looking Phil, materialized on either side of Delphine.

She must have been holding their hands, Rebecca realized, with a thrill of triumph. Aurelia gasped, and Toby jerked his head. The boys said nothing. They just stared at Toby.

"Get out of here!" he shouted. He looked more scared than angry now.

"One, two, three," counted Delphine, grasping Anton and Phil's hands. The boys disappeared at the exact moment that Frank let Ling and Rebecca go. Aurelia didn't seem so freaked out now: She knew about ghosts and their disappearing acts, and must have figured out what was going on. But Toby stared, openmouthed. All he could see were the girls.

"It's a bad, bad dream," Ling said again in that monotonous, whispery voice. Frank counted again, and they dropped his hands. Now they were invisible, and the boys materialized again.

Toby stood perfectly still, watching Phil and Anton appear and then disappear, replaced — so it must have seemed — by Ling and Rebecca. The look on his face was that of a cornered animal, frozen in the spotlight. Rebecca would have felt sorry for him, if he hadn't been such a vicious brute.

Nobody spoke now, not even Ling, though the house was creaking and complaining in the wind, floorboards squeaking. Rain pattered onto the roof. The thunder growled like a wild animal moving in for the kill.

"Stop!" Toby's voice was a strangled scream, still clutching Aurelia. "Or I'll smash her head in, I swear!"

"Let her go." A deep voice boomed out of the shadows, startling Rebecca so much she almost let go of Frank's hand. Just visible in the half-light, looming behind Toby, was Raf. *He must have crept in*, Rebecca thought, *while everyone else distracted Toby with their disappearing act.*

"Let her go," he said again, in a hard voice Rebecca had never heard him use before. "Or I'll shoot."

Toby drew his hand away from Aurelia's neck and she scrambled to safety, circling around the boys and throwing herself at Rebecca. Rebecca drew her trembling cousin close, patting her back.

"This is OUR house," growled Raf. Toby buckled forward, as though Raf was jabbing him in the back. Did he really have a gun? "What you doin' in OUR house, white boy? Drop it!"

The crowbar crashed to the ground: Toby was beaten.

Rebecca realized she'd been holding her breath. She hung onto Aurelia with her free hand, fighting back tears.

Anton let go of Delphine's hand and walked forward.

"This is a bad dream," he said in a cold voice, and he punched Toby hard in the face. Aurelia flinched, turning quickly toward Rebecca.

Toby clunked onto the ground and Anton stepped back, rubbing his knuckles. Rebecca couldn't speak. She wanted to walk right over to him and hug him, but that could wait. They had time.

"Man, I never got to use my judo," complained Phil.

"I got to use my glue gun," said Raf, his voice normal again, holding up his "weapon." "If he hadn't dropped the crowbar, I was all out of moves. Maybe I could have glued him to the floor."

"Thank God you came back," Rebecca said to Raf. Her heart was still thundering.

"I figured you could use some help." Raf grinned. "Do I get to see these ghosts now? Whoa!"

Delphine had clearly obliged right away. Then she spun around and curtseyed to a wide-eyed Aurelia. Rebecca had forgotten that Aurelia had never seen Delphine before.

"I know," Phil said to Raf. "An actual ghost. This is much better than Jazz Fest."

"Thanks so much, Delphine," Ling said to her. "I wish I could hug you, but I don't know how that works with ghosts. We couldn't have done this without you."

"Really?" Delphine said shyly.

"Thank you, Delphine," Frank said, and the two of them looked at each other as though no one else was in the room.

Gideon Mason groaned and tried to roll over, but he clearly wasn't going anywhere. Toby was stirring as well, but Anton and Phil were taking care of that situation, binding his ankles and wrists with twine supplied by Raf, and removing the lighter from his pocket. Phil carried the gas can out the back door, just in case.

"Frank! The locket!" Rebecca remembered why they were here. "Where is it? You have to point it out."

"We better hurry," said Raf. "If my grandmother sees the light in here, she'll call every Indian in the neighborhood. And the police probably already towed your car."

Anton picked up the flashlight, shining it onto the floor so they could see.

"Here?" Raf jimmied at a floorboard with Toby's crowbar, tearing back the rotting wood.

"It fell onto some kind of cross-plank, running underneath," Rebecca explained. They were all trying to help now, tugging at boards, positioning the electric lantern so Raf had more light.

"A chain!" Aurelia exclaimed. "See it? It's all black."

She pointed to what looked like a thin, snaking line of dirt, and Raf reached in. Gently, he plucked the chain from its resting place.

Rebecca's breath caught. *There it was.*

The chain was long and very delicate, black with age and filth. At the end dangled a locket, so tarnished it was almost black as well.

Frank had staggered over, but at the sight of the locket he fell to his knees again.

"Can we open it?" Ling whispered. Raf passed it to her.

"My hands are too big," he said.

"Give it to Rebecca," suggested Ling.

Rebecca took a deep breath. Then she ran her thumbnail down the locket's joint, feeling for the clasp. It didn't want to give at first; it had been closed since that day in March 1873, when Edgar Degas had handed the locket to Frank on the New Orleans dock. She pushed on the clasp, not wanting to damage it. The catch popped, and the locket opened like a little book.

Inside there was just one picture, an oval miniature that looked like oil, dotted with damp spots. But despite the damage, Rebecca could still see that it was a portrait of a woman with dark hair, a ribbon around her neck.

"It looks like you," said Anton, peering down at it.

"It looks like a Degas," said Ling. She was crying, Rebecca realized. In all the years they'd been friends, she'd never seen Ling cry before.

"We got it, Frank," Rebecca told him. The ghost gazed at her but said nothing. He'd been waiting so long for this moment, she thought. "Tomorrow we'll make sure it's handed to one of the Musson descendants. And then everything'll be over. Your promise won't be broken anymore."

Rain hammered down onto the roof, washing the crumbling house clean, and drowning out the sound of a distant siren. Gideon gave another anguished groan, and Rebecca shivered in spite of herself. He couldn't hurt her, or the locket, or Frank anymore. But she wished he would take his groaning some-where else.

"This was the locket that was lost?" Delphine asked Frank. He nodded. "And now it's found." She smiled around at them all, and then her smile began to fade. *Delphine* began to fade. Rebecca knew what was happening. She'd seen it once before, the day the curse on the Bowman family ended and Lisette left the ghost world forever. Because she had helped them, Delphine was free.

"Good-bye, Delphine!" Rebecca, called, but the girl was already gone.

"Where did she go?" Aurelia wanted to know. "Who is she?"

"She haunts a house on Rampart Street," said Ling.

"Not anymore," said Frank, and he sounded wistful. He was lying on the floor again, rubbing the wound on his stomach. Rebecca looked into his deep blue eyes. They shone with tears.

CHAPTER TWENTY-FOUR

TWO MONTHS LATER, ON A HOT JUNE NIGHT STEAM-
ing with rain, Rebecca and Ling found themselves back in
New Orleans.

They were just there for the weekend, with a full comple-
ment of parents in tow, not to mention both of Ling's sisters.
Their new high-heeled shoes clattered across the marble-
floored lobby of the art museum. It felt like a cool cave after the
lush humidity of the evening.

Anton was easy to spot in his black St. Simeon's blazer. He
was standing with two adults who were clearly his parents. Mrs.
Grey, in a pale pink Chanel jacket, was blonde and petite, but
Mr. Grey was tall and dark-haired, an older version of Anton.
Rebecca felt shy about approaching, shy about meeting his parents at last, but her posse — led by the indomitable Ling — swept
straight toward them, and the awkwardness of the moment was
lost in the flurry of handshakes and hugs.

"Nice to see you," Mrs. Grey purred to Rebecca through a

perfect, frozen smile, as though they were old friends. "I know Anton is *so* looking forward to his trip to New York."

She turned to Rebecca's dad, who was waiting to introduce Ling's parents to the Greys and to Phil's parents. Anton flashed Rebecca a tense grin and squeezed her hand.

"That wasn't so bad, huh?" he murmured in her ear. Rebecca was relieved he hadn't kissed her hello in front of everyone, though Phil seemed much more at ease, as ever. He grasped Rebecca by the shoulders and kissed her on both cheeks.

"What, are you European now?" Ling asked, rolling her eyes.

"West Coast all the way, baby," Phil said, with his usual goofy smile. He slung an arm around Ling and squeezed her so tight she cried out in mock agony.

"You're so weird," she complained.

"Hey, I'm just in a good mood," he said. "The Four Musketeers, back together again — right?"

Rebecca started laughing. Phil was right: It was good to be back together again. And it was good to have someone like Phil there, laughing loudly and kissing Ling's startled sisters and making everyone feel at ease.

"Hey Raf!" he shouted, and Rebecca looked over to the staircase: There was Raf's familiar face, and his father and grandmother and cousins. Miss Viola was wearing a dramatic yellow hat, and appeared to be lecturing the mayor.

"I know he's a total doofus," Ling whispered to Rebecca, nodding her head toward Phil. "But you have to admit he looks hot in that blazer."

"Hot and itchy, probably," Rebecca muttered back. She and Anton made their way over to Raf's group, squeezing through the crowd. The clinking wineglasses sounded icicle-sharp over the blurry hum of talk and laughter, and a clarinet playing "Eh, La Bas."

"They could have hired *us* to play this," Junior was complaining when they walked up. Both Raf and Junior were dressed in what looked like new suits, and Junior in particular, looked almost unrecognizably handsome. "Those old dudes don't need the money!"

"Man, how come you get to wear your own clothes when we're stuck in our school uniforms?" Anton asked.

Raf grinned.

"Dispensation from Mr. Boyd," he said. "He said we needed to look sharp for the photos."

"You look really good," Rebecca told Raf, suppressing another laugh when Anton immediately grasped her hand again, as though he was staking his claim to her.

In the center of the room, pinned against black velvet and protected by a cube of glass, a silver locket hung open. A crowd of young people Rebecca remembered as the work party at Basin Street High clustered around, peering at the small, smudged picture of a dark-haired young woman.

"No fingers on the glass!" roared a familiar voice. Mr. Boyd was there, of course, in charge of his workforce. Ling squealed at the sight of him and dragged Rebecca over to say hello.

"Look who we have here," he said, one eyebrow raised. "My best worker and . . ." He looked at Rebecca. "Miss Sherlock Holmes. If you come by the school on Monday, I can find you more mysteries to investigate. Or at least more trash to pick up."

"We have to go back to New York tomorrow," Ling told him, and Rebecca couldn't believe the look of genuine disappointment on her face. "But next time, maybe?"

They made their way back to their parents, stepping over a rope of power cords as they skirted a TV crew. A woman in a red suit — pencil thin and very elegant — had flown over from Paris to authenticate the painting as a Degas. Yes, she was telling the interviewer, the young woman in the miniature was probably his cousin, Desirée Musson. No, she didn't know if Degas was ever in love with her.

"I know about art, not love," she sniffed.

"I only know about love," Phil joked, sidling up to Ling.

"You are hilarious," she said, with a melodramatic sigh. "How I've *longed* for your sophisticated sense of humor."

Anton was by Rebecca's side again, steering her through the crowd. A man in a dinner jacket had climbed up the sweeping staircase, and everyone was turning to hear his speech.

He was the director of the museum, and he wanted to thank the Musson family, he said, for their generous donation to the museum.

"There's also a number of teenagers here we have to thank, for rescuing this fascinating piece of art history — and New Orleans history — from what would have turned out to be its tomb," the museum director said, and Rebecca's eyes prickled with tears of pride and relief. "We still can't believe that for almost a hundred and fifty years, this priceless locket lay under the floorboards of a tiny house in Tremé. It just goes to show you how this great city of ours continues to offer up treasures, how it never ceases to amaze us."

Anton nudged Rebecca's shoulder, and she smiled. The man was right, she thought. It *was* amazing that something so precious had survived all these years, and that the painting within it had survived. That the locket's delicate chain, light as a feather, remained unbroken.

Rebecca blinked her tears away, hoping no one had noticed. Being back in New Orleans was always an emotional experience for her, and tonight was particularly intense, of course. She was with Anton again, and Raf. She had new friends here now, as well as old ones. It was an ever-widening circle, drawing in other people from outside as well, like Ling and Phil. Strange to think that once upon a time in this city Rebecca had felt like a complete outsider.

But when they'd driven along Rampart Street that evening, crammed into Aunt Claudia's car, Rebecca couldn't help but think of what she'd lost as well as what she'd gained. The town house on the corner of Orleans Avenue was obscured by scaffolding, dangling UNDER RENOVATION signs. The gallery where Delphine had wafted, surrounded by her eerie cloud of silvery light, would be cleaned, or replaced. Before too long, Rebecca imagined, it would be dripping with flowers, or clustered with languid ferns. Mardi Gras beads would hang from the railings, and the new inhabitants would lean out, drinks in hand, to watch the world go by. But Delphine herself was gone, free forever from the imprisonment of the ghost world. Rebecca wouldn't see her sweet smile again.

And tonight, Rebecca thought, Frank would disappear as well. The ceremonial handing over of the locket to the Musson family was scheduled for eight P.M., just a few moments away. Raf would hand Mr. Musson the locket, and Frank's promise would be complete: The locket would be restored to the family. Then the assembled media would take their pictures, and Mr. Musson would hand the locket to the museum, as a gift to the City of New Orleans. It would be placed on display for all the world to see.

Earlier tonight, driving along Rampart Street, Rebecca had looked for Frank, of course. She wanted to see him one last time. And he hadn't disappointed her, standing all the way out on the neutral ground, so she couldn't possibly miss him. It was light now in the evenings, and Rebecca had no problem making out the familiar chiseled angles of his face, the supernatural blue of his eyes. She smiled at him, and he smiled, too — though she wasn't sure if he'd really seen her, or if he just smiled all the time now. His limbo as a ghost was almost over. Tonight he'd be free of this place, this world. He'd vanish to the other side, where sweet Delphine was waiting for him.

The clock struck eight, and Rebecca let out a breath. There were more speeches, and handshakes, then a storm of camera flashes. Raf stood looking nervous, but proud. He held the black velvet cushion on which the locket lay, posing for what felt, to an impatient Rebecca, like forever. Then Mr. Musson, who was wearing a tie as blue as Frank's eyes, took the cushion and its precious cargo into his hands. Applause erupted, echoing through the marble hall of the lobby, and some boys — Junior? Brando? Phil? — started whooping. Rebecca was clapping, too, but she couldn't watch anymore. She was blinking back tears, thinking of Frank. This was the moment he'd been waiting for. This was the moment he'd be free.

Later, when they drove back along Rampart Street, Frank wouldn't be there. She knew that, and she was happy for him. But part of her was sad, too. Last year Lisette left her. This year, Frank. She wouldn't see either of them again — not in this lifetime, at least.

Anton slipped his hand into hers and squeezed. Rebecca didn't trust herself to look at him, but she was happy to know he was there. Tomorrow she and her father, and Ling and her family, had to leave New Orleans and get back to New York. But she knew she and Anton would talk almost every day, as they had ever since she returned from New Orleans in April. There were no more awkward pauses between them now; everything was out in the open. Anton was coming to visit her in New York in a few weeks, and joining Rebecca and her dad and Ling for a vacation on Cape Cod.

Rebecca wasn't sure when she'd be back in New Orleans. But at least now she knew for certain, in her heart, that she *would* return. A piece of her would always be a part of this city. A piece of her would always belong here, and never want to leave.

On St. Philip Street in Tremé, no physical traces remained of the row of three derelict houses. Rain fell onto the muddy earth, pounded into waves and plateaus by a giant bull-dozer. In a few days construction would begin on the schoolyard extension and a new auditorium.

A solitary ghost wandered the site, his footsteps making no impression on the soft earth. He scowled at the ground, dark eyes scanning the ridges of dirt, as though he was looking for something that might be buried there in the mud. The gloom of his expression, however, suggested that he knew the truth.

Other ghosts, passing by on their way toward Rampart Street and the river, or to the cemetery and up to the bayou, knew what he was looking for. They shook their heads, and made sure they walked on the other side of the street. They knew that the ghost sifting through the dirt on St. Philip Street would never find what he was looking for, because it was gone forever — just like the boy with blue eyes, who nobody had seen for months, or the girl on her gallery on Rampart Street, no longer illuminating the night with her silvery swirl of moonlight.

That was the way it was in New Orleans, and in every old haunted city across the world. Ghosts vanished, and new ghosts arrived to take their place. Things changed. Things stayed the same.

POSTSCRIPT

The locket in this novel is fictional, but much of its historical context is not. The Impressionist painter Edgar Degas left Paris in October 1872 to spend the winter in New Orleans, where he had close family connections.

Degas' mother, Marie Célestine Musson, was born in New Orleans. In 1873 her brother, Michel Musson, was living there with his three adult daughters: Estelle, Desirée, and Mathilde. Degas had already met Estelle and Desirée in France. Estelle, a Civil War widow, married one of his younger brothers, René.

Times were difficult after the Civil War, and Michel Musson had to sell his home and move the whole family to a rented house on Esplanade Avenue. René — who spelled his last name De Gas — had joined the family firm, though he wasn't a good businessman and ran up huge debts. He was soon joined in New Orleans by the third brother, Achille. New Orleans was the hub of the huge international cotton trade, and they were both hoping to make a lot of money.

In 1872, during a trip back to Paris, René persuaded Edgar Degas to return with him to New Orleans. They made the ten-day voyage from Liverpool to New York, and then the four-day train journey to New Orleans.

By this time Degas was already establishing a name for himself as a painter. He was also experiencing severe problems with his eyesight, so he found the bright New Orleans light painful. These were difficult and violent days in Louisiana — corrupt state elections, coup attempts, economic uncertainty, rampant crime, a return of the dreaded Yellow Fever. Degas missed Paris, and spent much of his time that winter in the house on Esplanade Avenue, drawing and painting his cousins and their children. Estelle, who was going blind, was one of his favorite models. Degas was also very fond of his cousin Desirée, who — like Degas — never married.

He painted one major work while he was there, *A Cotton Office in New Orleans*, featuring portraits of his uncle and two brothers. Degas stayed longer than he intended, until March 1873, so he could finish the painting. By then his uncle's cotton office was out of business.

Five years after Edgar Degas left New Orleans, his brother René caused a huge family scandal. He abandoned Estelle and their children, and eloped with the married woman who lived next door, making his way back to France and starting a second family. Edgar was furious with his brother and refused to speak to him for years.

His uncle, Michel Musson, legally adopted Estelle's children, changing their name from De Gas to Musson. When

René died in 1921, the two surviving children had to file a lawsuit in France to claim their share of his estate. His children in France had no idea that this New Orleans family even existed.

While he was in New Orleans, Degas seemed entranced by what he called the "black world." In a letter he declared that "I have not the time to explore it" — but he wouldn't have had to look too far. Although Degas' uncle Michel and brother René were both members of the White League, bitter opponents of Reconstruction and black suffrage, their family had an Afro-Creole side. The internationally renowned inventor Norbert Rillieux was the son of Degas' great-uncle and a free woman of color. Descendants of the Musson/Degas and the Rillieux families still live in New Orleans today; both have family tombs in St. Louis Cemetery One. Edgar Degas and Norbert Rillieux are buried in Paris.

After the scandal of René's abandonment of Estelle, Degas stopped all communication with the New Orleans branch of the family. He would never see or write to Estelle, Desirée, or Mathilde again. But when he died in 1917, many of the pictures from his five-month stay in New Orleans — including pictures of his beloved cousins — were found in his studio.

ACKNOWLEDGMENTS

Many thanks to my insightful and patient editor, Aimee Friedman, the team at Point/Scholastic, and Richard Abate at 3Arts. Tom Moody, as ever, served as sounding board, research support, and first reader.

Thanks also to our New Orleans insiders — especially Rebecca Lewis, Russell Desmond, Sarah Doerries and Jay Holland, Nicola Wolf, and Trina Beck and Chris Noyes — and the Marksville/Jazz Fest crew: Paige and Rodney Rabalais, and Tiffany and John Ed Laborde.

I'm indebted to the New Orleans African American Museum (www.noaam.org) in Tremé, and I learned so much from the excellent and informative tour led by Milton Carr. And I would have known much less about the finer points of high school dances without the expert advice of Sara Tobin, and Ashland Hines and her class at Sacred Heart.

While all the restaurants mentioned in the novel are real (and highly recommended), the three schools — Basin Street High, St. Simeon's, and Temple Mead Academy — are all fictional.

Readers keen to learn more about New Orleans should explore the wonderful books in the Neighborhood Story Project (www.neighborhoodstoryproject.org). For insights into Degas' time in the city, see *Degas and New Orleans: A French Impressionist in America*, edited by Gail Feigenbaum, and *Degas in New Orleans: Encounters in the World of Kate Chopin and George Washington Cable* by Christopher Benfey.